The Velvet Fix

A Small Town Brother's Best Friend Romance

Rachel Kaye

Book & Brew Creative LLC

To anyone who has ever been made to feel less-than by someone who was supposed to love them.
F*ck them. The shame belongs to them, not you.

And to Tom. You won't read this book, but thanks for washing all those dishes and being the best tech-support person I could ask for. I love you always.

Content Note

The Velvet Fix is the second book in *The Greyport Series,* a series of interconnected stand-alone romance novels set in the fictional small town of Greyport. This book is an open-door romance featuring on-page sexual content.

Though *The Velvet Fix* is a light-hearted read, there may be some topics that lead to discomfort. Please treat yourself kindly.

Verbal/emotional abuse by an intimate partner. Depicted in flashbacks.

Brief discussion of parental abandonment. Not depicted on page.

Brief discussion of death of a parent. Not depicted on page.

On-page depiction of recreational alcohol and marijuana use.

Intense sipping...you've been warned.

Chapter One

Jill

THE RAVEN-HAIRED MAN ACROSS the table droned on about the latest logo he'd designed for a local law firm. Colors and layering and ratios. I'd asked him to tell me about his work, but I hadn't expected him to take it so literally.

He was attractive and nice enough. Too bad I was bored to death.

"Are you alright?" he asked.

"Peachy," I said as I pulled back a sip of tepid water.

I was avoiding alcohol, despite the fact that we were in a dimly lit dive bar halfway between Greyport and Merlin Heights. I wanted a clear head for this date. The one I'd been on last week—featuring special appearances by Jack and Tito—had been a disaster.

The woman I'd met on the dating app, My Cup O' Joe, had been beautiful and held a decent conversation. Things had been going well, right until I'd overindulged on liquid courage and puked all over her killer combat boots when she'd leaned in for a kiss.

My attempts at finding a *friend with benefits* had so far been a disaster.

A server in bedazzled denim shorts strutted up to the table, sparing me from more logo talk.

"Hi, I'm Mel. What can I get for you?"

"Hello, Mel. I'm John."

I was appreciative he'd shared, as I'd already forgotten his name.

"Good for you, John." If she'd been chewing gum, now would have been the appropriate time to pop it. "Now, can I get your order?"

I cut in, handing her my grease-stained menu. "I'll take a steak bomber."

John ordered the same thing, and we both followed Mel with our eyes as she walked away, hips swinging.

"I must note," he said after a beat, "that you eat meat."

"Um, okay?"

He hadn't been this abrupt when we were chatting on the app, but I reminded myself I wasn't looking for a soul-deep connection.

Sex. Benefits.

Experience.

That's what I was after.

"The last woman I dated was a vegetarian. It did not end well."

"I'm sorry to hear that. But hey, uh, different strokes for different folks, right? It's good to meet people of all different views, and backgrounds, and...diet preferences. See who best suits you."

"We're hardly 'stroking' anywhere. We're sitting in a bar."

"Yeah, right...it's just a saying."

I reached toward my purse hooked on the back of my chair. My phone was inside. I could message Emma or Kristi, ask them to extricate me from...whatever this was.

But then they might ask questions I wasn't sure I was ready to answer. Questions like, *Jill, why are you meeting strangers at shady bars in the middle of the night? Or how the fuck are you striking out this bad?*

I would have to pull on my big-girl panties and end this date myself.

"It's a strange saying. You are quite different from the last woman I kissed. Her name was Fern." His voice got all breathy. "I haven't used the My Cup app since. It just reminds me of...her."

Oh no, now he looked demoralized. He wasn't going to be my FWB, but he seemed like a decent guy. I opened my mouth to offer a comforting word but was once again saved by Mel with a conveniently timed tray of food.

"Here you go, lovebirds. Enjoy."

I would eat as quickly as possible before making a polite excuse to leave.

Maybe this search for a *friend with benefits* was a distraction I couldn't afford. As much as I needed the experience, my time would be better served preparing Velvet for its opening in a few months.

I'd purchased the space months ago. It had been a rash decision, one made in a fit of pride. I envisioned Velvet as a sex toy boutique-slash-speakeasy, a space to host bachelor and bachelorette parties, maybe even a BDSM workshop or two. Sex toys had helped me regain my confidence when I'd needed it most, and now I wanted to share that with others.

Right now, it was a shack.

I was ripping off a bite of my steak sub when a woman walking into the bar caught my eye—a statuesque blonde in a cute, fluttery, purple sundress.

The food caught in my throat when I got a full look at the man behind her.

Light hair clipped close to his skull, ice-blue eyes, a firm jaw. A dark fitted shirt that showed off the bulk of his shoulders and the corded forearms engraved with sleeves of Sailor Jerry tattoos. Strong thighs clad in worn-in Levi's jeans that powered the movement in his trim hips.

The woman in the cute dress said something, and the man laughed, his white teeth and that one slightly crooked incisor flashing.

Ben Till. The person I'd once thought believed in me. The good-guy son of the mayor. And my older brother's best friend.

James hadn't mentioned Ben having a girlfriend. Right now, he looked awfully cozy with his date as they got settled at a table, making lovey-dovey eyes at each other.

As if he felt the force of my stare on the back of his sun-reddened neck, Ben turned and looked straight at me.

He winked.

Oh, hell no.

"John!" I said brightly, turning back to the man across the table.

"Yes, Jillian?"

My name wasn't Jillian. I was just Jill. I introduced myself as Jill, and My Cup listed me as Jill. But I thought of Ben and his obnoxious wink, rolled my shoulders back, and ignored my annoyance with John.

"How is your meal?" I batted my eyelashes, leaning forward to place a hand on my date's forearm. The angle showed off my modest cleavage, and his gaze dipped down for a moment before he dragged his attention back up to my face.

Ben's date giggled on the other side of the room.

"I think you have a bit of mayo...right there." I pointed to the corner of John's lip. "Let me get that for you."

I stood over the table, hovering on half bent legs, and swiped the bit of stray mayonnaise from his mouth.

I stole a peek at Ben. He and his date had their heads bent close together as they examined the menu.

How precious.

There were five items on the menu. It didn't take that long to read it over.

I sucked the white glob from my thumb in a failed attempt to be sexy.

I gagged. I hated mayo, but I hated the thought of Ben Till witnessing my humiliation even more.

As I moved to sit back down, the table wobbled, sending my water and John's Bloody Mary careening across it.

"Oh, shit!" A mix of square ice cubes and tomato juice soaked John's lap. I rounded the table, searching frantically for anything to help get him cleaned up. "I'm so, so sorry."

All I found was a stack of tissue-thin cocktail napkins, only good for absorbing rings of condensation.

Note to self: make sure Velvet has real napkins.

I shoved the entire stack in John's lap, dabbing at the mess while I crouched near his feet.

"Jillian, I can take care of it." His voice was clipped, as if he was in pain.

"It's my fault," I said, feeling guilty. "Why don't I run to the bathroom and see if I can find some paper towels. I'm sure they have something."

"No. I've got it." He rose in one stiff movement, ice and celery spilling onto the floor near my shoes, and walked robotically toward the back hallway.

A snicker drew my attention, and I pivoted, still kneeling at the base of the table.

Ben Till and his...friend...were looking straight at me.

Laughing at me. *Judging* me.

They could take that judgment and shove it.

I was a business owner now, an entrepreneur. Ben was...well, also those things, but that was beside the point.

The point was, I was doing it on my own. I didn't need the opinions of Ben, or my brother, or any crappy ex to get me down. After years of working dead-end jobs and floundering my way through life, I finally had a purpose, and I wasn't letting it go.

I lifted my chin high and rose from my crouch in one smooth move. Pinching my shoulder blades together, I stepped in my heels along the sticky plank flooring and back to my seat to wait for John's return.

Chapter Two

Ben

WHAT THE HELL WAS Jill Klein doing in a no-name biker bar with a guy who looked more like he drove a minivan than a motorcycle?

"Do you know them?" Casey asked.

"Huh?"

My date flicked her gray eyes up to the ceiling. It was subtle—Casey wasn't a rude person—but I still clocked it. "The couple over there. With the spilled drink. You keep looking at them."

She wasn't wrong, and now I was the one being rude.

"Sorry, uh, that's James' little sister. I don't know the guy she's with."

"Oh," Casey said, smoothing a hand down her long curtain of hair. "I didn't realize James had a sister. We should go over and say hi."

That sounded like a terrible idea. Jill had been icing me out for over a year now, ever since we'd had a formal sit-down chat to talk about her business plans. And no matter how often I told myself that her avoidance was a good thing, I hated it.

Because my emotions for Jill were inappropriate, and inconvenient, and so far from hatred that it wasn't even funny.

"Maybe later," I said as I focused back in on my date. "We're here to get to know each other, not talk to my best friend's sister."

This was my third date with Casey. The first two had been fine, if not a little boring—dinners at upscale restaurants in Rockberry Park and Merlin Heights. I avoided dates in Greyport at all costs—too many people to report back to my parents, like I wasn't a grown, thirty-five-year-old man. Public attention made me break out in hives.

My mother had set me up with Casey, but I refused to give her a play-by-play of my dating life. I knew she wanted me to be happy, to have a love like her and Dad, but the woman needed to relax. I would find The One, like my parents had in each other. I just needed to get past my silly infatuation with Jill first.

Asking Casey here to this dive bar in the middle of nowhere was my attempt to shake things up, to get away from all the trappings and fancy shit, to see if that underlying boredom went away.

She had pulled a face at the worn clapboard building and scowled when my pickup bounced over every pothole in the lot.

The truck had been another point of contention. On our first two dates, I'd driven the red two-seater I reserved for special occasions. It probably wasn't fair to test her, but tonight showed me that Casey and I weren't compatible. I liked the finer things as much as the next guy, but that wasn't all there was to me. I still liked to play around in the dirt sometimes.

Despite the realization that Casey wasn't for me, the night would have been fine. If only I hadn't been forced to see Jill. If I didn't see her, then I could ignore the uncomfortable pull I always felt toward her. Instead, I couldn't stop noticing the way the neon lights of the bar reflected off her golden hair and the way her brows crinkled just the tiniest bit when her date walked off.

She was oblivious. She hadn't even realized the guy she was with had run to the bathroom so he didn't pop a boner at the table. The way she was aggressively shoving those useless napkins on the guy's dick?

Yeah, she was a liability. Too flighty and all over the place. She wasn't a serious person and never had been. It was the reason—well, that and who her brother was—why I'd tried nothing with her, despite my wild attraction to her.

It was more than lust—I had figured out that much—given that it hadn't faded in the last eight years or so. I'd first felt that strange stirring around her when she'd moved back from Albany after she finished her undergrad. And while Jill was beautiful, I also *liked* her as a person, even if the feeling wasn't mutual these days. But liking her wasn't enough for me to ignore how unsuitable we were for each other.

I watched as the dark-haired man sitting across from her gave her a dopey smile.

Was he her type? I had never seen her out with anyone before, but maybe, like me, she kept her dates out of Greyport and off the radar.

"Ben."

"Yeah?" I whipped my head back to Casey as she placed a gentle hand on my wrist. Her fingernails were painted an off-white, pink color that reminded me of the azaleas I'd planted this morning on the Kendrick property.

The sound of Jill's laughter came from the other side of the bar, and I battled the urge to turn.

"You seem distracted. What do you say we finish these drinks, forget the food, and go back to your place?" Casey's teeth were blinding white. She worked as a dentist. She probably stocked up on all sorts of tooth-whitening samples. I bet her under-sink cupboards were jam-packed with the stuff.

What did it say about me that I was thinking more about what was under her sink than under her skirt?

I rubbed the back of my neck and gave what I hoped was a charming half smile. "I'm pretty wiped from work. We hauled a lot of stone today. Not sure I'd be the best company."

That shiny smile fell. "Oh. I figured you had people you paid to do that."

I *had* employees. But I owned a landscaping company, and it was the middle of summer. There was never so little work that I didn't need to get my own hands dirty.

"None that I would ask to do a job I wouldn't do myself."

Casey sipped her gin and tonic, drumming those azalea-pink nails along the glass as she placed it on the warped tabletop. "This isn't going to work, is it?"

Thank god she'd said it first. Casey and I weren't a good fit. And if tonight was anything to go by, she certainly wasn't going to be the one to help me get over whatever it was I felt toward Jill. I was starting to think nothing and no one could do that.

"Probably not. I'm really sorry, Casey."

"You seem like a great guy, Ben. On our first date, you said you were looking for a serious relationship. I hope you find that. And I hope, when you do, you put a little more effort into it."

How was I not putting in effort? I did care, but I wouldn't put up a front. I had standards, and I wouldn't deviate from them.

"I am who I am, Case."

She smiled, less toothy this time. "Well, no hard feelings, right? I'd hate for your mom to think she can't come get her teeth cleaned with me."

The last thing anyone in town wanted was to lose Mayor Olena Till's business.

"No hard feelings. It's been nice getting to know you."

She downed the rest of her G and T in one gulp. "I'm gonna take off."

"But I drove you here." I would still get her home safe, regardless of the outcome of our date.

"No, no. Sit down. I would prefer you not bring me home. Honestly, I think my pride is more bruised than I want to admit, and I need the time alone."

"At least let me pay for your ride."

"I'll accept that."

I pulled up the rideshare app on my phone, lucky to find a car only five minutes away—a surprise, considering the remote location.

I stared at my phone for the whole five minutes, watching the progress on the little cartoon car.

A notification chimed, announcing the white sedan's arrival, and we stood in unison.

"I'll walk you out," I said.

The loud sound of a chair scraping on the floor came from the direction of Jill and her date. They were leaving too.

Good.

Jill shouldn't be hanging out in shady places with strange men. I was worried about her safety, not my own jealous self-interest.

I turned my focus back to Casey as we stepped into the balmy night air. A chorus of crickets chirped from the surrounding trees.

She pulled open the car door. The driver gave me a nod.

"Goodnight, Casey. I hope you find what you're looking for."

"You too, Ben," she said as she slammed the door shut behind her.

Fat chance of that. I had to do something different, though I wasn't sure what.

The car pulled into the road, tilting wildly as it left the parking lot.

I turned toward the section of the gravel lot where I'd parked not even a half hour earlier, the taillights of my truck lighting up in rhythm as I depressed the key fob. I'd almost made it inside the vehicle when Jill and the minivan dude made their appearance.

The guy was practically salivating on Jill's shoulder.

I leaned back against the side of the pickup to watch. Was I choosing to torture myself by watching this after my flop of a date? Yes. But it wasn't like I had anything better to do.

Jill pressed a hand to the guy's chest. I wasn't sure if she was trying to push him away or drag him closer. I clenched and unclenched my fists, fighting the urge to storm the distance between us and tear him off her.

He bent his neck and pressed a kiss to her lips. It looked...sloppy, even from this distance.

One, two, three seconds ticked by before Jill pulled her face away. I couldn't hear, but I could see her mouth moving and her head shaking. I almost felt bad for the guy as he walked over to a gray four-door and hopped inside.

Jill watched him drive off, and I watched Jill as she tiptoed on spindly heels to her SUV. Her black dress, patterned with bright-yellow lemons, swished around her calves.

She brushed past me, bringing the familiar sweet scent of moonflowers with her.

"Hey," I said.

She screamed.

CHAPTER THREE

Jill

"**W**HAT THE FUCK, BEN?! You scared the shit out of me!"

He was lurking in the dark, leaning on that big white work truck of his. I didn't care if he needed it to transport dirt or mulch or whatever. No one needed a truck that large.

"Sorry."

"You don't look sorry at all." He was smiling, his stupid mouth twitching, and those freaky silver-blue eyes sparking in the moonlight. I wasn't sure what about scaring me made him *happy*, but I'd discovered over the last year or so that I didn't know Ben as well as I'd once thought.

"What happened to your date?" he asked.

"It ended." I crossed my arms, mirroring his stance. "What about yours?"

"It also ended."

I snorted. "Can I ask why you decided to stick around to spy on me like a creepy stalker?"

He shrugged. "Just looking out for you."

"That's unnecessary. You're not responsible for me, and even if you were, it wouldn't matter because I'm an adult. I don't need or want a babysitter."

"Maybe you do need a babysitter if you thought coming to a place like this was a good idea."

"Why is it okay for you and your date to come here, but not for me?"

His silence was answer enough. "That's what I thought, Benny Boy," I said with a smirk.

"I'm serious, Jill. What are you doing here? And with a guy like that?"

"John is a perfectly nice man!"

"Yeah, and you clearly weren't into him—at all."

"How would you know?"

Again, he gave me nothing. Just waited me out.

We sounded like children arguing. My heart was hammering in my ears. I hadn't been alone with Ben in...I couldn't say how long. Maybe last winter, when I'd learned what he really thought of me.

"What do you think James will say when I tell him what you were up to tonight?"

I narrowed my eyes at him. Was this what his weirdly protective act was all about? Him standing in as a surrogate for my brother? I wasn't the sixteen-year-old girl I'd been back when I first met Ben. "You wouldn't."

"Why shouldn't I?"

"Because it's not your business. *I* am not your business. You—and my brother, for that matter—can kindly fuck off."

Ben shook his head in exasperation. "Are you hanging out here just to piss him off? He's doing a lot for you, getting your building ready, and..."

My hand slashed through the air, cutting him off. "Me being here doesn't concern my brother. I have my own reasons for it." Reasons like reclaiming my confidence and sexuality. Things I was fairly positive Ben wouldn't understand. Not when he walked with what could only be described as *Big Dick Energy,* and dated gorgeous women like the one he'd been with earlier.

"What kind of reason has you meeting some boring-ass dude at a shitty bar?"

God, he was like a dog with a bone about this. "I'm desperate, okay? Are you happy to hear that, Ben?" I hissed.

He fell back against the side of the truck, his brow furrowing. "Why would I be happy to hear that?"

"Uh, maybe because we hate each other?"

His light eyes were suddenly dark in the moonlit parking lot. "I don't hate you, Jill."

"Well, if you don't hate me, you do a pretty great impression of it."

"I don't hate you," he repeated quietly.

The truth was, I didn't hate him either, no matter how much I wanted to.

"I can't do this right now." I spun on my heel, but his hand was on mine.

We hadn't touched in so long. The last time I could remember was when he'd hugged me the day I'd graduated from college. His whisper of congratulations in my ear had left me feeling like I'd won a Nobel Peace Prize, not just earned a BA in History.

I wished he still inspired that feeling in me.

"Why are you desperate, Jill?"

For some reason, I wanted to tell him. Maybe because I wasn't looking straight at him, and it was dark and private in the parking lot.

Or maybe because I knew his opinion of me couldn't get any worse. He already thought I was a fuckup who was too silly to make a go at anything.

"I'm desperate," I said, looking past Ben's ear to focus on the wall of trees surrounding the gravel lot, "because I'm about to open what amounts to a sex club, and I'm terrible at sex."

He said nothing, but he kept that warm grip on my hand, rubbing his thumb along the inside of my palm.

I tugged away before he noticed my trembling.

"Nothing to say? No smart-ass remark?"

"I, uh…" His neck and face were beet red.

I snickered because I couldn't help it. Ben of all people was embarrassed by the word sex.

"It can't be that bad. I mean, you've…done it before, right?"

"Yes, Ben, I have *done it* before," I said, throwing up air quotes.

"Well, then, just…do it some more. Practice." His mouth twisted like he was tasting something sour.

I scowled. "Why do you think I was on a date?"

"You're hardly going to have good sex with a guy you're not into. I can tell you that much."

"Isn't that the point of going on a date? To find out if there's chemistry? I'm not looking for more than that, and all I'm finding are duds."

"If all you want is chemistry, why bother with the date at all? I could name ten men in Greyport who would be down for a one-night stand with you. Just…get in your SUV and head straight to Maven's." He was strangling on the words, like it hurt to say them.

I shook my head. "I've tried the one-night-stand thing. When I'm with a stranger, I end up getting anxious, and I can't come."

"So, you want a boyfriend to help you…come?"

"Or girlfriend. And no. I don't want a relationship at all."

The very thought of commitment and connection had me ready to run for the hills. I'd tried that once. It had been an epic failure.

"If you don't want a one-night stand and you don't want a relationship, what do you want?"

"A *friend with benefits*. Someone I can be comfortable with but who won't get too attached."

He rubbed his thick palm along the back of his neck, a move I was slowly recognizing as his nervous tell.

"I should get home," I said, turning to go.

"Jill, wait!"

I sighed. "What is it, Ben?"

"Why don't you use me?"

"What?"

"Your *friend with benefits*. The sex practice. Use me."

My stomach dropped out, like I was riding the crest of a rollercoaster. What was he playing at? Practically all of Greyport knew Ben wanted to find The One. He had to be screwing with me, returning the favor, because otherwise, his offer made no sense. He wanted a relationship, and I wanted a *friend with benefits*. The upstanding son of Mrs. Mayor would never get down and dirty with me.

"Do you think it's funny to say something like that?" I spit out, recovering from my initial shock.

His pale eyes went wide. "I— It wasn't a joke. I'm being serious."

"Didn't we establish that I hate you? I don't buy into the myth of hate sex being hot."

"You don't hate me. It's mild dislike at best."

"Mild-dislike sex sounds thrilling. No thanks, Benny Boy. If I was looking for mediocre, I would have let John keep slobbering on me."

Ben stepped up, invading my space. An owl hooted low in the distance as I stared up into his eyes.

"You think it would be bad between us?" His voice was soft, almost hypnotic.

My mouth moved, but no words came out. What was happening right now, and why couldn't I look away?

His lips quirked up, and that crooked incisor came out to play.

He took one rough, dirt-stained fingertip and brushed it along the scalloped edge of my cap sleeve. The red-and-black anchor tattooed above his wrist flexed with the tendons as he traced the delicate fabric.

"Think about it, Blossom. You'd never get attached to me. I'd be the ideal guy. You let me know if you change your mind. I don't mind being used."

Who was this man, and where had mild-mannered Ben gone?

And *Blossom*? The nickname came out of nowhere, and I wasn't sure how to feel about it.

"I—"

"I'll see you around, Jill," he said, leaving me in a wake of dust as he hopped up into his truck and drove off into the night.

❦ ❧ ❦ ❧ ❦ ❧ ❦ ❧ ❦

I STOMPED UP THE stairs to my studio apartment, still reeling at the way I'd let Ben get in my head.

Use me, he'd said. Like he was my personal sex toy.

He didn't mean it. He would never risk my brother getting mad at him. Besides, Ben dated *serious* women. I was the opposite of serious. It made no sense.

I stripped out of my sundress and tossed the slinky number in the general direction of the hanging laundry bag hooked to the bathroom door, leaving me in just my black lace balconet bra and matching cheeky panties. When I had put them on, I'd felt powerful and sexy, like the type of woman who owned an establishment like Velvet. Not one who balked at the idea of sleeping with a partner because of years-old hang-ups left by a shitty ex.

I flopped backward onto the daybed that doubled as my couch, the mass of plush pillows caving in around me.

Tracing my fingertips along the edges of my bra, I enjoyed the contrast between the lace and my smooth skin. It reminded me of the way Ben had dragged his finger along my biceps.

My breath quickened. Was I getting turned on thinking about Ben touching my arm?

Use me.

No one had to know what I was about to do.

I sat up, fumbling my way out of my pillow fort and stretching toward the storage chest hidden under my bed. My torso tilted off the edge of the mattress as I blindly rooted around until my fingertips hit the jackpot. Gripping the hard edges, I dragged the sticker-covered treasure chest out into the light.

The stickers, most acquired during college, were faded and peeling. Some people collected knick-knacks or custom artwork, but my collection was of a more...adult variety.

I flipped the metal latches, revealing the varied, colorful sex toys within. Vibrators and lingerie were my two indulgences.

Fittingly, they were things I didn't need anyone else to enjoy.

I jumped up to cut the lights and set a match to a candle. Might as well make it a proper date. One where no one wound up disappointed.

And the power was solely in my hands.

I bounded back to the chest and grabbed the clear-blue silicone vibrator on top.

I lay back again, setting the vibrations to the medium setting. Easing into it, I first dragged the vibe across my nipple and over the top of my bra. My tip hardened, and I sighed.

There was nothing better than self-seduction.

I brought my other hand up to tug on my opposite nipple as I dragged the wand down. Gently, teasingly, I played for another minute on top of my panties until my hips were rocking, and I couldn't hold back.

I paused long enough to strip the black scrap of fabric down over my ass and legs, kicking them off at the ankle.

I traced the vibrator over my center until it was wet with my arousal then slowly inserted it into my opening. There was relief, a sense of filling an emptiness, but it wasn't enough.

My body stretched to accommodate the toy, the silicone slipping and sliding with ease. I turned my head into the throw pillows, biting into the puffy down-filled fabric. It was noisy and wet, and I had not an ounce of self-consciousness.

My legs twitched as I approached climax, moving the stiff shaft in and out in a thrusting motion.

This was exactly what I needed. No attachments. No dates. No cloying reminders of things I couldn't get out of my head. I could enjoy my company and my body while remaining firmly in charge of my own pleasure.

The words whispered across my frontal lobe.

Use me.

I came hard at the familiar voice, the force of the orgasm hitting me like a freight train.

Ben Till had ruined masturbation for me.

Chapter Four

Ben

D ANY, TILL LAWN AND Landscape's longest-standing employee, loped into the small room off my garage that doubled as both my in-home office and laundry room. I didn't always enjoy staring at dirty clothes while working on invoices, but there was a door separating the room from the rest of the house, and some days, I needed the distance between my work and home lives.

I would have loved to add an addition to the house, but the cookie-cutter ranch needed a new roof before I could make any other investments.

"Morning," Dany greeted.

"Morning, Danylo."

"Did you sleep well?" he asked.

I hadn't. I'd been up half the night, staring at my ceiling fan, wondering why I'd chosen last night as the moment to give in to my attraction to Jill. Offering myself as her *friend with benefits* had been a spur-of-the-moment thing...at least at first. But the second I'd offered, I realized how much it made sense. Avoiding Jill, trying to ignore how I felt about her, hadn't been working. Maybe I could get her out of my system this way. Her brother being my best friend was an added complication, but James didn't need to know everything. I'd kept my feelings for Jill from him this long without him noticing.

"I slept fine," I lied. "How about you?"

"Like a baby. How'd your date with the dentist go?" The shorter man waggled his thick eyebrows.

"How do you know I had a date last night?" I said with a groan. So much for meeting in an out-of-the-way location.

Dany posted a hip on the side of my wobbly desk. James kept offering to build me something custom, but I refused each time. I didn't need a big, hulking thing when I used the office as little as I could. Once spring hit, I was outside as much as possible.

"Your Ma mentioned it to mine. She was all giddy about it, kept flapping her hands around and making jokes about more grandkids. Said she gets the short end of the stick with your sister and her kids living so far away."

Dany's mother, Yana, and mine both liked to gossip. When the two of them got down to talking, it was hard to pull them away from each other.

"It's not going to work with me and the dentist."

Dany gave a mocking gasp, his hand covering his mouth. "What a surprise. Another one bites the dust. What'd you find wrong with this one?"

"Why assume it's my fault? I'm pretty sure Casey hated my truck, and I think she was afraid to sit down at the bar we went to."

"Let me guess, you took her to the nastiest hole-in-the wall place you could find, right?"

I nodded, and he threw up his hands.

"For a guy who claims he wants to settle down, you're not trying very hard. From what your mom said, Dr. Casey sounded like she was exactly your type. Driven, smart, successful, focused. And blonde. Can't forget about that one."

"Sure, she's a catch. For someone else, not me. And I resent that remark about blondes. I almost proposed to Stef, and she isn't blonde." Probably not, anyway. She'd changed her hair color as often as she'd changed her career path back when we dated. Her wildness had been fun...until it wasn't.

"Stef, your college girlfriend who dumped you almost ten years ago? That was so long ago it doesn't count."

"I just don't want to get burned again. But I'm still trying. I'll find the right woman eventually." Even if I had to convince Jill Klein that I was the perfect *friend with benefits* first.

"I want you to be happy, Ben. I know you have standards, and you're afraid to get hurt, but maybe you need to open up your mind."

He was right, and that was why my plan to get Jill out of my system was a good one. Dany—in his happy, long-term, monogamous relationship—couldn't possibly call me having a *friend with benefits* not *opening my mind*.

"I'm working on it, Danylo."

"Fine, fine. I'll quit bugging you. Now, you ready to get to the job?" He gestured behind him with a thumb. "We should get there before the new guys."

"Lead the way."

D ANY HOPPED OUT OF my truck when we reached the Daniels property, a large, stately house on the lake front. Mulching the flower beds alone would take almost a week. A small, potted lemon tree sat perched on the wraparound porch, brought outdoors now that the warm weather was here to stay.

Those lemons made me think about Jill and that silly dress. That dangling string that tied in a bow above her breasts, leaving only a tiny keyhole of smooth skin peeking through. Her matching braids, the strands a mixture of gold and white silk.

I could swear I still smelled that moonflower scent lingering in my periphery.

Frustrated with myself, and determined to quit ruminating, I shoved out of the vehicle and popped open the tailgate. I heaved a bag of mulch over my shoulder and walked over to Dany.

"Grab a shovel. We've got work to do."

"You know, maybe you should stop worrying so much about finding The One and find one for a night. Get laid. It might help that cranky disposition of yours."

If only he knew it was exactly the thought of getting laid—and by whom—that had me short on sleep and grumpy. I ignored him, slamming a black baseball cap over my buzzed scalp and getting to work.

CHAPTER FIVE

Jill

I WIGGLED THE RUSTY padlock until I felt the slow click of its opening, thrusting the door open with my shoulder.

Velvet.

It wasn't much, not in its current, falling-apart state. But I could envision it. The dark-stained floors polished to a shine with gold and cherry-red area rugs thrown atop. The tin ceiling and elegant hanging lights surrounded by paneled walls and red velvet chairs.

And, of course, lots of dildos and vibrators and butt plugs. Couldn't have the place looking too classy, after all.

I had already put James to work, constructing the bar and crafting an interior wall that would separate the boutique from the speakeasy. Guests would need a special password before being given a chance to pull a lever to enter the bar.

I'd purchased the building with the money Mom had left me in her will. It wasn't much, but it helped. The last several years, I'd hustled and worked three different jobs. A couple months ago, I had cut it down to two, leaving my retail job behind. My part-time position in the children's section at Greyport Public Library—a role that allowed me to work with my two best friends—and the job I had working for an online sex toy business kept me afloat for now.

If I didn't completely fuck up Velvet, maybe one day my only job would be running this place.

The old building was set into a hill with the storefront sitting on top. The back door spit out onto the other side of the slope, where the land was low and flat. It never failed to throw my equilibrium off when I first stepped out back, like I'd somehow stepped into an entirely unfamiliar landscape between the front and back doors.

The first time I had seen the place, I'd known it was the perfect setup. Still, I'd hesitated, too afraid to commit.

When James asked Ben to meet with me last year to discuss my ideas for Velvet, I had been so excited to share that I might have found the right location. Ben had seemed like the ideal person to bounce my ideas off. He had always been unfailingly kind, offering me an encouraging word when I'd needed it most, whether it was stopping in to tell me my art project with the kids at the library looked good, or that I'd been the best second clarinet player Greyport High had ever seen. We'd drifted some when I'd gone away to college, and even after I'd come home, but part of me always felt like Ben had faith in me.

Instead of leaving that meeting with a sense of confidence, I'd left with a pit in my stomach.

He still didn't know that I had heard him on the phone after I'd come back from the bathroom, telling whomever he was talking to that my plans, my dream, *I*, wouldn't amount to anything.

He'd given voice to my worst fear—the one that said I wasn't good enough to overcome the obstacles life threw my way. And worse, he'd proven, like so many others, that I wasn't worth believing in.

That evening, after I'd made polite excuses to Ben, I'd called my realtor and told her to put an offer in on the building.

I grabbed the push broom leaning against and wall and began moving some of the construction dust and debris into a pile.

I'd been sweeping for a few minutes, working up a layer of sweat on my back, when I noticed a change in the air. Something smelled wet, beyond the usual summer humidity.

Nothing had been amiss when I arrived, so I decided to check the rear, walking toward the heavy back door. The air grew thicker as I stepped, the sickening scent growing more and more overpowering. My stomach lurched. We'd gotten some heavy rain the last three days, but that didn't explain the odor. What the hell was going on?

I hesitated with my hand on the crash bar of the door, afraid of what I was about to find on the other side. Inhaling, I squeezed my eyes shut as I forced myself to push it open. I took one step, then another, still not brave enough to look. My toes dampened as my sandals made a terrible, squelching noise.

This was bad. Really, really bad.

I opened my eyes to find the wide range of grass that made up the backyard flooded with a slimy layer of foul-smelling, stagnant water.

Fuck my life.

"**W**HAT DO YOU MEAN you can't get over here? Did you hear what I just said?" I was practically shouting down the line at James.

"I heard you, Jill, and I'm sorry. Emma and I are two hours away, and we're in the middle of something."

"What are you doing two hours away?" It was difficult to adjust to the fact that my brother had his own life and commitments apart from me and our cousin. That he actually had fun now.

I was happy for him, but there was an underlying sadness to it, too. James had always been the one I could count on when I got into my inevitable messes. He grumped about it, and gave me crap, but he was *there*. Now, he was someone else's person, and I was on my own.

"A wedding cake tasting. Emma saw a picture on social media and wanted to try this bakery. We made a day trip out of it."

"You drove two hours away to taste cake?"

I heard his smile over the phone. "Fuck, yeah. If you had seen the look on Emma's face when she walked in, you would understand. They had a cake shaped like a stack of books. She looked like she died and went to heaven."

"You're deliriously loved-up, and it's absolutely disgusting, Jimbo."

I *was* happy for him. I was. No one deserved it more than my brother.

"You'll understand when you find somebody, Jilly Bean."

I snorted. He might say that, but I was certain he would commiserate with anyone I dated about what a lousy partner I made. Not that I wanted a relationship, anyway. Been there, done that.

"I'm too busy to date," I lied, thinking back to my latest My Cup disaster.

"Busy with what?"

"I don't know, my jobs, my business, and the *flood in my backyard?*" A heavy pressure was building behind my eyes.

"Like I said, I'd be there if I could. But I'm currently watching Emma stuff her face with a piece of red velvet cake. You really think I'm about to rip that happiness away from the love of my life? Think again."

"Jimbo, Emma is just as obsessed with you as you are with her. She would understand. I'll explain it all to her, I promise." Emma was my friend too, and I knew she would gladly help in my time of need.

"Jill, I won't even be able to get there anytime soon. Besides, what makes you think I know how to handle a flooded yard in the first place? I'm a woodworker. It's not my area of expertise. The answer is no."

I pouted, thankful there was no one around to witness it. "You're getting better at setting boundaries. I like it for you, but I hate it for me."

He chuckled. "It's a work in progress. Therapy helps."

"Do you think Harry will know what to do about this flooding?" I asked, hoping our cousin was around.

He let loose a full-bodied laugh. "That's funny. For one, he's at work. And two, no, Harry would not know what to do. He'd probably turn the lawn into a swimming pool and invite his friends over to race him. Remember that year he was convinced he could be the next Michael Phelps? Besides, this is your project. Own it. What would I do if I were there?"

"Find a really big Shop-Vac and suck all the water up?"

"Not quite. C'mon, who would I call?"

Ugh. I *knew* this was where he was going. "Maybe 911?"

"Seriously, Jill?"

"I know, okay, I know! You would call Ben. But I don't *want* to call Ben."

Especially not after the way we had left things last weekend. I was half convinced he had offered to sex me up as a cruel joke. It didn't fit his character, but then again, neither did trash-talking a person's dreams, and he'd definitely done that.

"Ben would bend over backward to help someone in need. I still don't understand what your issue is with him, and frankly, I'm tired of asking. You used to get along fine. Just accept his professional help and get over it."

"Aren't there other landscaping companies in the area?" I whined. "I can look them up."

"There are. But how many do you think you can get on the phone immediately? And if you do reach someone, how many would come out right away?"

I pursed my lips. There was no good rebuttal, and I wasn't proud of the way I was handling this conversation either. I was doing what I always did: making excuses and chickening out.

"Call Ben," James continued. "Stop wasting your own time. You know he'll show up for you."

Chapter Six

Ben

Jɪʟʟ Kʟᴇɪɴ ɴᴇᴠᴇʀ ᴄᴀʟʟᴇᴅ me on the phone. If she was calling, it meant something was wrong. Was she okay? I ripped off my thick gloves as I powered down the weedwhacker. Wiping a shaky palm down the back of my jeans, I swiped to answer.

"Are you alright?" I asked.

My stomach dipped when at her brief pause. "Um, hi, Ben. It's Jill. How are you?"

She didn't *sound* distressed. So then why was she calling me? "I know it's you, Jill. I have caller ID. What's wrong?"

"Nothing is wrong. Well, okay, maybe something is a little, *tiny* bit wrong. Do you think you could swing by Velvet? When you get a chance. Don't go out of your way if you're busy or anything. I know you're a busy, busy guy."

I pulled the phone back from my ear. She sounded...different. Gone was the acerbic, cutting Jill from the other night. She'd been replaced by a breathless, uncertain version of herself.

I pressed the device back between my ear and shoulder blade. "Tell me what's going on."

"Um. A flood?"

That I could manage. "I'll be there in ten minutes."

"Do you know where to find me?"

I knew exactly where she was. "Like I said, give me ten minutes."

❧ ❧ ❧ ❧ ❧ ❧ ❧ ❧

I MADE IT TO her in five.

She met me at the front of the building, dressed in a floaty skirt the deep green of American Pillar Arborvitae, a clingy white shirt, and gold sandals that were so thin she might as well be barefoot.

It was an asinine thing to wear during an active renovation. If she stepped on something, it would go straight into her foot. A rusty nail, a chipped tile, *anything*.

"I hope you're up to date on your tetanus shot," I said.

Her forehead creased. "I am. Are you?"

"Yes. I would be an idiot not to be in my line of work."

"Good, good," she said, chewing her lip. "Ben, why are you asking me about tetanus shots?"

I tipped my head down. "Your shoes."

She lifted one foot and looked down, as if only now recalling her choice in footwear. "Oh yeah, these. Probably not the best call, but I came from a lunch date."

I shouldn't care. She could go on lunch dates, dinner dates, and naked dates, with whomever the hell she liked.

It was only that my chance at getting over this thing I had for her was contingent on *me* being her *friend with benefits*, not some other person.

I cleared my throat. "Did you have a nice time?"

"Have a nice time doing what?"

"Having lunch."

She smiled like she held a secret trapped between those pretty pink lips. "It *was* nice. Fun."

I swiped at a smear of dirt on the side of my jeans, suddenly feeling filthy and underdressed. "Great. Fun is a good thing to have."

Her eyes twinkled. "Are you sure about that, Benny Boy? Because you don't sound very convincing."

I felt my cheeks growing hot. "You and your quest to find a hook-up buddy is none of my business." I needed to play it cool for now.

She made a *humph* noise and placed a hand atop each hip. I diverted my eyes from her breasts and the way they jutted out with the move. "I see you've changed your tune since threatening to tattle on me to my brother."

Didn't she realize there were people who worried about her? She couldn't go about living her life all wild and crazy, pretending she didn't have anyone who would be upset if she got hurt—or worse.

It wasn't like the worry came from nowhere either. There had been the time she'd landed herself in the hospital overnight because of dehydration and sleep deprivation. She'd been doing online tutoring for kids learning English in China and staying up to work all hours due to the time difference. Remembering to eat and drink water had been low on her priority list.

Or the other time she'd spent the last of her rent money buying recording equipment to start a podcast where she reviewed local coffee shops. James had to make sure she didn't get evicted once she realized My Cup o' Joe already had a podcast and blog centered on the same topic.

"I just think the *friends with benefits* thing you're doing, meeting up with strangers in shady places, is a bad idea."

"Well, I'll have you know, I met a really great guy for lunch today. I think my search for the perfect *friend with benefits* may be over."

Was I out of time already? Maybe I needed to drop the play-it-cool act. "What's his name?" I asked, like some sort of masochist.

"Pat. He's an investment banker. He *loves* to eat out. Oh, and get this: his favorite band is Huey Lewis and the News. Talk about a throwback."

I gave her a blank look, consciously holding in a barking laugh. In the year she'd been avoiding me, I'd nearly forgotten how funny Jill could be. "Are you describing Patrick Bateman from *American Psycho*?"

Her smile was blinding, a flash of light on an overcast day, ripping a hole straight through my center.

"Got it in one, Benny Boy." She dragged the toe of her flat sandal along the ground, and I followed the path as she drew a heart shape in the dirt. "You make it too easy to mess with you. No murderous businessmen were harmed today. I met my friend Glenn at Greyport Grinds. We had coffee and talked about the birthday gift he's buying his boyfriend."

She kept on tracing that heart as she spoke. I dragged my gaze up over the fine bones of her ankles and the toned calves that peeked out from under her skirt. I paused on her hands as she unclenched them from their spot on her hips, shaking her trembling fingers loose.

"Are you nervous?" I asked.

She fixed me with a withering stare, her dark irises sparking. "No. I'm pissed off about the flood, and I'm doing my best to contain it. Why are we still talking in the parking lot?" She was all brisk efficiency again, that hint of vulnerability now vanished.

"I'm just following your lead." And getting whiplash while doing it.

"Well, come on. The problem is in the backyard."

I followed the swaying of that dark-green skirt through the building. Dust flew up as we walked, illuminated by the shafts of light filtering in from the old windows. Jill's improvements to Velvet were evident. And despite my family's complicated relationship with the place, I had to admit that the building was looking distinctly less dump-like.

"It's looking good," I admitted.

She cast me a skeptical glance. "Thanks. I appreciate that."

"I mean it."

"I— Okay. Thank you. Take a look." She threw open a metal door and gestured to the rear lawn.

"Oh, damn." The whole yard was a swamp.

"It's bad, isn't it?"

I turned toward her, finding her shoulders turned in, all traces of that sparking attitude gone, drowning along with the grass and shrubs.

Jill wasn't supposed to look like that. "It's bad, but I'm going to fix it. I've got you." It was going to eat into my already back-breaking schedule, but I would do it if only to wipe that look off her face.

There was a tremor in her voice when she spoke. "I don't know what I'm doing, Ben."

"That's okay, because I do." I stepped back, squinting at the yard. It was poorly graded, the way the lawn sloped and the building sat in the lowest spot. I was willing to bet the soil was compacted, too, underneath all the water. It needed to be re-graded, but in the lawn's current state, my heavy equipment would sink.

A drainage swale it was. It wouldn't be huge in the narrow space—basically a wide hole that we'd fill with river rocks and plant features to prevent it from eroding too quickly—but it would be a good start.

I looked at Jill, wanting to hug her so badly. I'd once been free with hugs for her, until she'd moved back home after college, and I'd started noticing her more than I should have.

She looked back at me, her face open and vulnerable. Maybe this was my chance. I took a step forward.

Her phone rang, and the moment was over.

"Yeah?" she said as I tried not to listen. "Yes, I called him. He's here right now. He said he's going to help. I *know*, Jimbo. I don't need a lecture. Go back to your cake tasting and your fiancée. I'll talk to you later."

She glanced at me as she ended the call.

"Your brother?" I asked.

"Yep. What gave you that impression?"

I just shook my head. "I'll get started tomorrow morning. Will you be here?"

"Do I need to be?"

"Not necessarily. Only if you want to be."

"How much will I owe you?"

"Nothing." I wouldn't take a dime from her. This wasn't transactional for me.

She was shaking her head before I even got the word all the way out. "Absolutely not. You are not doing this for free."

"I'm planning to do all the labor myself between my other jobs. I can choose to spend my free time however I like."

"Well, then, if you won't let me pay you, then I'll help you with the work."

"It's not going to be easy. And you can't wear what you're wearing now." I looked pointedly at those silly sandals.

"Believe it or not, I *do* have other clothes."

"Fine. I'm starting at six."

"In the *morning*?"

I held her gaze, an unspoken challenge. "Still wanna help?"

She picked up the gauntlet. "I'll see you at six, Benny Boy."

CHAPTER SEVEN

Jill

I MENTALLY ADDED SEVERAL strikes to the anti-Ben list as I pulled up next to his work truck the following morning. First, he made me wake up earlier than I had in years. Unless I was boarding an international flight and rushing through airport security, waking up at five a.m. was not okay. I'd learned the hard way that me and lack of sleep were a lethal combination.

I also hated the clothes—namely the jeans. I didn't care who claimed denim was having a moment, hard pants were uncomfortable. I'd found an old pair in the back of my wardrobe that still fit. If they got ruined, so be it. My ratty t-shirt from Greyport High School's production of *Grease*—pit orchestra clarinet player number two, at your service—was only marginally less offensive.

"Nice shirt," Ben said as I hopped down from the seat of my SUV. "I remember that show."

"Thanks. I forgot you were there."

I hadn't forgotten. It had been the year Mom died. My brother—just shy of twenty-one and floundering under the weight of raising a fifteen-year-old girl—had shown up at every performance, although I was barely visible in front of the stage.

Ben had joined him each time, quietly confident, even at twenty.

"You ready to get started?" he asked, breaking the thread of my reminiscence.

"Lead the way."

He wordlessly grabbed two large shovels from the back of the truck and held one out.

I stared at it. "What's this?"

"A shovel."

"I know it's a shovel. What am I going to do with it?"

"Dig."

"Aren't you usually better at talking than this? Your mom is great with people. What happened to you?"

Mayor Olena Till was an inspiration to all of Greyport. Even before starting her career in local politics, she'd served on multiple community organizations and spearheaded town events. If I was on shift at the library when she stopped in, the entire building felt energized.

Ben shot me a dark look. "Guess I got my talking skills from my dad."

"Your dad is personable too!" Robbie was a regular library patron, and everyone raved about him.

Ben wiggled that shovel in my face. "Just take the damn thing, Jill. And for the record, you're the only person who's ever said I'm not good with people. Maybe I'm not the problem here."

I snatched the offending tool from his hands, and he rolled his eyes. I stomped ahead of him toward the back lawn.

It was difficult to sashay while dressed in grungy clothes and clunky rain boots, but I made a valiant effort.

Forty minutes later, regret over agreeing to help Ben weighed me down. I should have accepted his offer to do the work for free and swallowed my pride.

We were digging a giant hole. There was no other way to describe it, though Ben seemed to have a plan in mind. On the bright side, the water had receded overnight and was only up to my ankles.

"Remind me again why we have to do this by hand?" I asked, my hands chafed and my shoulders screaming.

He looked up from his side of the hole—far deeper than mine—and sighed. There wasn't a hint of sweat on him. The three-masted sailing ship tattooed on his forearm flexed as he choked and then relaxed his hold on the shaft of his shovel. It was positively obscene how hot he was.

"We're doing it by hand because my equipment is too heavy. It'll get bogged down in the wet ground, and then we'll be stuck."

"So, this giant hole is going to solve all my problems?"

"*All* of your problems? No. But your landscaping ones? It should help. This giant hole will be what's called a drainage swale. Once it's deep enough, we'll fill most of it with coarse stone. The top layer will be river rock, and then we can do whatever kind of design feature you want on top. If we incorporate some flowers and other vegetation into it, that should help with erosion. It'll give the water someplace to drain the next time we get heavy rain."

Ben knew what he was talking about, and his competence was strangely appealing.

"What about the rules about digging and calling to make sure we don't hit gas lines or whatever?"

He swiped a hand down his chin. "Jill, if you want to get out of this, just say that. I'm not forcing you to do this. I told you I would do it for free, and I meant it."

"I'm not trying to get out of it, I swear!" Okay, maybe I was, but only a little. I was also strangely annoyed that, instead of pushing me, Ben was giving me an out. Like I wasn't worth the time it would take to convince me to help. "I'm genuinely concerned we might blow up the town."

"This is my job," he said, his endless patience wearing thin. "You think I don't know the rules related to digging?"

"It's not that. I was only thinking that I didn't call anyone to get the go-ahead. This whole thing is a little overwhelming."

The tight lines around his mouth relaxed a fraction. "Don't worry about it. I took care of it after I left yesterday."

"That fast?"

"My job, remember?" he said dryly.

I almost laughed but held it in.

"I appreciate you doing this," I said. "In case I didn't make that clear before."

"You're welcome. Now, are you ready to get back to work?"

My whole body hurt, and I still had to work a shift later for Fantasy Dongs.

"Can I run inside to use the bathroom first?"

I didn't actually have to go, but I needed some separation. It hadn't even been an hour, and I was already finding myself dangerously close to enjoying Ben's company the way I used to.

This whole thing would be so much easier if I actually hated him. He was being kind, and supportive, and so much like the Ben I'd thought he was before I'd heard him bashing me on that phone call, that my head was spinning.

He shrugged and scooped up another chunk of heavy, wet dirt with his shovel. "You don't need my permission."

I stuck my tongue out at his bent neck—ever the picture of ma-turity—and took a slow step on the wet ground. My left boot heel caught against something under the thin layer of water, causing it to drag. The other heel kept moving, the sole of the cheap rain boots I'd bought online offering little resistance in the slick mud. Worse, I could feel the seams of those fucking jeans slowly beginning to split. Ripping my jeans in front of Ben sounded like my worst nightmare. I scrambled to balance myself, arms flailing wildly, but it did little more than make me look like a drunk baby deer.

I went down with a splat into the brackish water. It didn't quite cover my legs, but my entire ass and the back of my pants were completely soaked. I could already feel the moisture seeping into my underwear. A splatter of mud left a gritty taste on my lips.

Ben was there in a flash, crouching at my side, graceful as he gingerly avoided the water's surface.

I batted his offered hand away, humiliated and dejected. "I'm fine."

I put my weight on my hands, careful not to think about all the grime collecting under my fingernails as I shifted my feet underneath me. He reached for me again as I rose on shaky legs. "Ben, I said I'm fine."

He lifted his hands up in a defensive gesture. "Sorry. Just trying to help."

"I don't need your help."

"You're so stubborn sometimes—"

He hadn't even finished the sentence before I was going down again. This time, I reached for him. I grabbed at his arm, hoping to prevent a further soaking, but he was unprepared and off balance.

We fell together in a heap, Ben on all fours above me while I lay in the mud. A clump of wet hair stuck to my cheek.

Ben burst into a deep belly laugh, his head dropping low and the brim of his baseball cap coming close to my collarbone.

"I hate you so much right now," I said with a choking gasp.

"What?!" he said between bouts of laughter. "How is it my fault that you fell?" Another chortle. "Twice?! And I wasn't touching you either time. If anything, *I* should be mad at *you*." His body vibrated above me as he worked to get himself under control. "It's just mud, Blossom. It'll wash."

"Yeah, but you have hardly any hair. I wasn't planning on washing mine tonight, and now I have no choice."

He huffed out an exhale, his gaze falling on the slab of blonde stuck to the skin below my eye. He took a finger—the same one he'd trailed across my arm the other night—and lifted the wet lock away from my face.

"It's not so bad," he said, his voice quiet. "I like you like this."

I inhaled slowly, not wanting to break whatever it was that was happening.

Those ice-blue eyes hit my deep-brown ones. His mouth dropped open. I waited with bated breath to hear what he was about to say.

"Doesn't look like you two have gotten much done," said my brother, his voice booming from across the lawn.

CHAPTER EIGHT

Ben

I PRACTICALLY LEVITATED OFF Jill at the sound of James' voice.

"Uh, hey James. Jill fell, then I fell, and we were about to get up," I said, heaving myself to my feet. James would attribute my breathlessness to the exertion, I hoped.

I extended a muddy hand to the woman in question, pulling her up. We stayed upright this time as I avoided looking at James, lest he read the wild thoughts that were running through my head about his sister.

"What are you doing here, Jimbo?" she asked. She didn't seem remotely affected by our proximity—not the way I was. It was...humbling, to say the least.

I had been careful not to bring up the hook-up topic this morning. It hadn't seemed like the time, not with the stress she was under with the flood. But when we were pressed together, covered in dirt and mud, I couldn't help but think about it.

"I'm here to help. What else would I be here for?" James asked, reminding me of his presence.

Stop thinking about screwing your best friend's sister when he's right there.

"I only brought two shovels," I said. It didn't seem right that James was here. This was supposed to be my thing with Jill.

"That's fine. Just give me the one Jill was using." He flicked two fingers toward himself.

"What am I supposed to use, then?" Jill chimed in.

Oh, great. I recognized this pattern. Another Klein sibling fight was about to go down. When I watched Jill and James, I was grateful my own sister lived across the country.

"Don't you want to head home and change out of your wet clothes?" James ask.

"I'm here to work, not stand around and look pretty."

"I'm pretty sure Ben and I can handle things, right?"

James turned toward me, but I was staring right at Jill. She looked a little like a drowned rat. An angry one, with her lips pursed and eyes narrowed. It was cute.

James cleared his throat, waiting for my response.

Stop being so damn obvious, dude.

"No, no, no," I said. "The two of you are not pulling me into this. Why don't I show you what Jill and I have gotten done so far." I looked at her, but she'd gone quiet, avoiding eye contact.

Maybe I was reading her wrong, and she did want to go home to change. She looked uncomfortable, but she'd looked that way before falling in the puddle too.

"Are you good, Jill?" I asked.

She was tugging her wet shirt away from where it clung to her back. I waited until she was done. She looked up at me and nodded.

I picked up both fallen shovels, passing one to James. I stole a glance at Jill while I did it, watching for a reaction. She stayed silent.

"We started the digging today," I finally said to James. "Once we fill it, we'll turn it into a landscape feature."

James nodded. "Filling it with coarse stone and some of that nice river rock?" James wasn't a landscaping expert, but he knew enough from having worked on his own yard.

"Yep."

"Could do a bench out here, a couple of planters. That would look nice."

I hadn't planned on landscaping the entire property, but now that he mentioned it, my wheels were turning. "There's a good wholesale deal on at Garden Spot. I could pick up a couple flats of perennials."

"You planning on anything else out here once the drainage is done?"

"Probably could level the lawn a little more, work on that slope a bit. A French drain might be good, but we'll have to let this dry some before I can get my excavator back here."

"Um, hello?"

James and I flipped our heads away from the expanse of the lawn and back to Jill, who had shifted from disengaged to spitting mad.

"What's up, Jilly Bean?" James asked cluelessly.

She stalked up to her brother and poked a finger in his chest. The delicate silver ring on her pinky caught my eye. There were four shiny letters resting atop her finger. I could barely make them out, but I was pretty sure they spelled 'Fuck.'

Pretty, yet subversive, sort of like its wearer.

"Don't you *Jilly Bean* me, Jimbo."

"What the hell did I do? I'm here to help, like you wanted."

"You're not helping by just..." She waved her hands around nebulously. "Showing up and taking over!"

"Jill, that is exactly what you wanted me to do when you called me yesterday. I basically had to force you to call this guy."

James pointed to me, the shovel in his fist swinging like a pendulum.

I threw up both hands and backed away slowly. When they got going like this, it was important to get out of the crossfire. I'd witnessed it enough times over the last decade and a half.

"Oh no you don't, Benny Boy. I'm not happy with you either." Jill's eyes flashed at me.

I couldn't hold in my snort, even knowing it was only going to set this simmering situation on fire. "Me? I didn't invite James."

"No, but you encouraged him! Showing him the hole, talking about the hole, making plans for the hole. And now something about drains, and excavators, and even landscaping the entire property! If you have plans, *I* should be the one you go over them with, not my interfering ass of a brother."

She was right, but how interested was she, really? I'd tried to get her to take part in the conversation, and she'd totally blanked.

"I didn't mean to—"

James bulldozed in. "Jill, give him a break. You know Ben meant well."

She gave a splashing stomp of her foot in reply. "Nope. You two can continue this cozy chit-chat without me. I'm going home. You know, since I'm such a delicate flower who can't handle a little mud on my clothes."

She waltzed off, those oversized rain boots slapping in the sloppy grass.

"Fuck," I said, turning toward my best friend.

"Fuck is right."

CHAPTER NINE

Jill

I WHIPPED THE HEADSET off when I heard the knock at my door. I glanced down at the small clock icon in the computer's lower corner. There were only a few more minutes left of my shift.

Shoving up from my daybed, I set my overheated laptop on the coffee table. Another knock sounded, louder this time, as I reached the door.

"Hang on, please." Even if it was a salesperson or someone with religious pamphlets, I wouldn't be rude, no matter how irritating I found the excessive knocking.

I cracked the door slowly, peering through the narrow opening.

Ben stood on the other side. "Oh. It's you," I said, opening the door fully. His blue eyes flicked down, taking in my attire. I'd swapped my wet jeans and t-shirt for a calf-length, flowing dress made up of vary-ing shades of orange, yellow, and red.

He cleared his throat. "You changed."

"I did."

He stood there, hat in hand, and rubbed a palm over the back of his buzzed scalp. "You look really pretty."

I knew he wasn't here to compliment my dress. But what *was* he doing here? "What do you want, Ben?"

"I came to apologize. And talk to *you*—not your brother—about what we could do at Velvet once we get the flood under control. Am I interrupting something?"

"I'm working."

"Oh, okay. I'm sorry. I can come back another time if you want." He lifted one foot to take a step back.

"It's fine. My shift ends in"—I stole a peek at the time on the microwave clock—"two minutes. You can come in, but you'll have to wait if I get a call."

He met my eyes for a fraction of a second before slipping inside. I swanned back to my daybed, putting as much space between us as possible in the small room.

I doubted I would get any calls in the next minute or two, but making him wait was fun. I sat crisscross on the bed, pretending to type an email, painstakingly tapping each key with my pointer fingers.

Ben and James are annoying jerks. Ben and James are annoying jerks.

I snickered. It was immature, but I didn't care.

I heard Ben shift where he stood like a statue just inside the thresh-old of the door.

The clock flipped, and I logged off, snapping the laptop lid shut. Overtime was *strictly not allowed* at Fantasy Dongs dot net.

I looked toward the tall man hovering in the closed doorway. "So, Benny Boy, how can I help you?" I said brightly.

The hat was back off, and he was switching it from one hand to the other, squeezing the brim tight.

"Like I said, I'm here to apologize. I got carried away with James. We shouldn't have been talking about you like you weren't there."

"No, you should not have been."

"Would you be willing to talk about the plans, then? Now? To-gether?"

"Sure."

I scooted over on the bed. He glanced down at his dirty boots, then at my off-white throw rug and baby-pink comforter, before leaning down to untie and remove the heavy footwear.

He walked slowly toward me, the hum of the window air condi-tioner filling the silence.

"Here?" he said, tipping his chin down toward my bed.

"Where else?"

I didn't have one of those fancy studio apartments where every-thing folded up into the wall and stylistic choices made one room feel like seven. There wasn't even room for a chair.

"It's just that I'm a little dirty still. From work. Do you really want me on your...bed?" His voice trailed up at the end of the sentence.

"Don't think of it as a bed, Benny Boy. It's also my couch. Relax."

He tugged up the knees of his loose jeans before lowering himself to the mattress. He was stiff and uncomfortable, and I *loved* it.

"So, tell me what you're thinking," I said.

"Alright. So, you and I had talked about adding some greenery and flowers in the swale once we're finished."

"Right. You alluded to James that you had other plans too." Ones Ben had conveniently not mentioned to me, as if I wasn't important or adult enough to be involved.

"I have *ideas*, not plans. They can't be plans unless you're involved too."

I lolled my head at him. "It didn't quite feel that way earlier."

"Yeah, I know. Again, I'm sorry. Your brother and I have been best friends since we were seventeen. Sometimes we get talking, and we don't think. For the record, I wouldn't have actually made any decisions without your involvement. That's not how I do business."

"I'm willing to hear you out," I said, grabbing a sip of the now-lukewarm coffee I'd poured earlier. I needed something to steady myself because I was strangely bothered at the thought that Ben considered this business. We'd once been almost friends. The rift I'd put between us this past year was still hard to reconcile.

"If you're interested, I thought I might landscape the rest of the property for you. Nothing intense, unless you want that. I brought a catalog with some pictures of what's available through the wholesaler I use."

"That's the place you mentioned had a sale on flowers?"

He nodded. "Yeah, but don't feel pressured to pick something because it's cheap. If you fall in love with something, I can negotiate a good price."

I glanced up as he shifted, making space to slide his hand toward his back pocket and pull out a wrinkled pamphlet. The move brought him a fraction closer to me, and I could smell him. He smelled like...dirt? But somehow good dirt, mixed with fresh, minty soap. It made zero sense. Maybe it was a mix of my hormones and desperation. After all, I hadn't had a single date since meeting up with John the other night. I'd spent hours mindlessly swiping through profiles on the My Cup app but hadn't made a match, hadn't found a single person I was even interested in having a conversation with.

As if on cue, my phone sounded with a My Cup match alert—that signature coffee pour trickling into a porcelain mug. So satisfying, yet so deadly when one needed to pee.

I met Ben's eyes as he held out the flyer to me, and a wave of panic hit. I could tell he recognized that sound. Did Ben use the app too? And why did that make my stomach go all topsy-turvy?

I snatched the glossy paper out of his hand and lunged for my phone in one swift movement.

"Um, sorry, let me just silence my notifications." I depressed the volume button on the phone's edge. "There. All done. Now we won't have any interruptions."

He propped his forearms on his knees and leaned forward, hands steepled at his lips. He turned to face me, spearing me with his gaze.

"Are you still going on those dates?" he asked quietly.

His blue eyes were burning me up. That clean, dirt scent scorched my nostrils.

Distance. That would help.

I stood, banging my shin on the edge of the narrow coffee table that doubled as my nightstand. Holding in a cry, I hopped on one leg to the fridge to pull out a bottled water. I pressed the cold plastic to my neck to cool my overheating body.

The phone vibrated again, calling my attention back to the source of Ben's question. If I continued to ignore it, it would be even weirder.

"No new dates," I said. "But I am looking."

"Why?"

"Why what?"

"Why are you still looking for a fuck buddy? It's a bad idea."

"Why do you even care, Ben?" I asked, setting the water bottle on the counter with a patience I didn't feel.

His mouth gaped like a fish.

"Don't worry, I'll wait." I crossed my arms and leaned back against the edge of the wheeled kitchen island.

He took a second, his jaw flexing, before he settled on a response. "It's just not smart. Your family would worry."

I laughed bitterly. "Since when does my family, as a collective, get a say about what or who goes in and around my vagina? And again, you didn't answer the actual question. Why. Do. *You*. Care?"

He stood up, prowling toward me on socked feet. His chest rose and fell as he stepped into my space. Close, but not touching.

"Remember my offer?" He'd now taken on the same tone he'd used the night of my date with John.

Of course I remembered the offer—the one where I *used* him—but I didn't want to give him the satisfaction of knowing I'd been thinking about it.

And getting off to it. Repeatedly.

"What offer was that?" I said, popping a hip to the side. The breathy words lent little to the attitude I was trying to project.

He saw through me. "You know exactly what I'm talking about."

I did, but part of me still felt like he couldn't possibly be serious. Ben could be with anyone, so why me? I couldn't lie to myself and say his offer wasn't appealing on a visceral level, but if I failed at sex with a guy like Ben, I'd probably never recover. Then again...could someone as hot as Ben—someone as different from the person who'd destroyed my confidence as one could get—be the key to accomplishing this part of my sexual journey?

He took one big step back without breaking eye contact. "Flyer is on the table. Let me know what you decide."

As he walked out the door, I realized I didn't know if he wanted me to make a choice about the flowers or him.

Chapter Ten

Jill

I STARED A HOLE roughly the size of the one growing in Velvet's lawn at the side of my brother's head. I was about to commit fratricide, and he was clueless, chattering away on the phone.

He'd invited me for dinner, but didn't realize I was in the house yet, spying on him from the hallway that led to the kitchen.

"Ben, all I'm saying is you have to let her lead the way. You can't run in, guns blazing, ready to fix the problem for her. I used to jump in and do everything, but now I'm learning. I mean, remember when she started that dog-walking business and then quit after a month because she realized it completely conflicted with her class schedule? The schedule she had made only three weeks before and never thought to cross-reference, mind you."

Muffled words came through the phone, and the distant sound of Ben's voice sent a trail of goosebumps down my arms. I wondered if he was agreeing with James' assessment of the situation. I'd been eighteen and a freshman in college, away from anything familiar for the very first time. The dorms had been lonely, making friends was slow going, and being around dogs had sounded fun. I'd called James one night on the phone to tell him about the dog-walking idea. He'd sounded skeptical, but Ben—who was there listening in on speakerphone—had been encouraging. Kind. Like he had always been.

Too bad I couldn't count on that encouragement from him any longer. That quiet faith I'd once had that Ben believed in me was gone. It still rankled.

I'd avoided him this morning. He'd been back at Velvet, working on the yard, but I'd come up with an excuse, asking James to meet him instead.

I couldn't put Ben off forever, though. Not when his stupid flower pamphlet was burning a hole in my pocket. Plus, I'd made a promise to help him, and I was sticking to it. Velvet was my responsibility, no one else's.

I could also see that Ben wasn't letting go of his offer to be my *friend with benefits*. He'd been serious, though I couldn't be sure of his motivation. If he only wanted sex, surely he could do what he'd suggested I do—walk into Maven's and find a woman interested in one night only.

But he wanted *me*. And despite his hurting me and my having spent the last year and a half trying to hate him, I was wildly attracted to Ben. Maybe that level of insane attraction was exactly what I needed to get me over the hump in bed.

The door leading in from James' backyard opened, and my friend and future sister-in-law, Emma Hartwell, walked in carrying a paper bag of groceries.

"Hey, Jill! I'm so glad you decided to come over for dinner," she said, ruining my chance to further eavesdrop. Brother-murder would have to wait.

I returned Emma's warm smile as James said his goodbyes and hung up the phone. He stepped close to his fiancée, pressing a soft kiss to her smiling lips. Annoyingly, he didn't look the tiniest bit ashamed at my catching him gossiping about me with Ben.

"You ready to eat?" James asked us.

"Yep. I can't wait. I'm starving." I rubbed my hands together. I had skipped lunch today in order to meet with the plumber at Velvet this afternoon.

"Well, you won't have to wait long. We prepped most of it this morning. James, did you pop the dish in the oven to heat?"

"Soon as I got home. It should be ready now."

"What time is Harry getting here?"

"Supposed to be here already, but you know how things go with him."

"What about Ben? Is he able to join us?"

I froze.

"No," James answered. "He said he had dinner plans."

Was Ben on a date? With that blonde in the purple dress again? Or someone else? Was my window of opportunity to accept his offer to use him gone already?

"Is he seeing someone?" Emma asked. Bless her and her little nosey heart.

James shrugged. "No clue. He didn't go into detail. Just said he was in the mood for some good food."

"I'll pretend not to be offended that he doesn't consider our food good," Emma said with a laugh. "If it is a date, I hope it goes well. He's such a good guy. He deserves to be happy."

The front door flew open, and my cousin, Harry, burst inside like a whirlwind.

"Jay and Ems! And Jill! Sorry I'm late. I ran into Corey, and he invited me for karaoke. Did you know there's a new karaoke bar up near the college?" Greyport State, or G-State to the locals, made up its own section of town, filled with businesses that catered to the student population.

"Karaoke?" James asked. "Since when do you sing?"

"Since never. But I tried it out, and Jay, I was *so* fucking good. Like, I'm pretty sure people were crying I was so good."

"Are you sure that's why they were crying?" I asked. "And not because they were in pain?"

"*No.* I'm telling you, I have a gift. Maybe I picked the wrong career path."

"No, no, no. You're not up and changing jobs because of one evening of karaoke, Harry," James said as he pulled a casserole dish from the oven.

Harry groaned. "Relax, Jay. I'm just messing around. I'm the best mechanic in town. Greyport would fall apart without me."

He wasn't wrong. Harry had been picking up more and more responsibility at the local garage, Canalside Auto, and seemed primed to take over the business when his boss retired.

Even Harry—the town screw-up—had his shit together before I did.

"Well, in that case, let's eat." James gestured at the steaming dish on the counter, a stack of porcelain plates sitting next to it.

"How are things going at Velvet, Jill? James said you're dealing with some flooding in the yard," Emma asked as we walked to the table, plates piled high.

I nodded slowly. "It's...going. Ben is helping with the lawn issue."

"I heard. And that's why I wondered how it was *really* going." Emma had witnessed the aftermath of that first business meeting I'd had with Ben, though she still didn't know the full story. I hadn't shared it with anyone, not even my best friend, Kristi.

I kept my face carefully neutral as we slid into our chairs. "He's good at his job."

Lately, I couldn't help but wonder if he was good at other things, too.

"That's good to hear. Because the two of you will both be in the wedding party, and I would hate for you to be uncomfortable. Maybe the flood thing was meant to happen so the two of you could work things out."

I swirled my fork around the plate. "I don't know that I'll ever see the flooded lawn as a good thing."

"Maybe not now. But you'll look back and smile when Velvet is a booming business, and you're making bank, selling booze and butt plugs."

"Did somebody say butt plugs at the dinner table?" Harry said around a mouthful of food.

"I did, Harrison. And close your mouth. No one wants to see your dinner after you chew it."

Harry shook his head at Emma. "You're perfect for this dude," he said with a gesture toward James. "I take full credit for this relationship and engagement, by the way. That's why I'm making my case to be best man."

James groaned. "Harry, for the last time, I haven't decided between you and Ben. And whoever I choose, it's not personal."

Harry slammed his silverware down. "It is the *definition* of personal, James. There is no greater calling than to be best man. But don't fear, your decision will soon be easy. I'm prepping a virtual slide show presentation on why I'm the best candidate for the job. I am going to make your wedding the best wedding ever. You won't feel an ounce of stress or jitters, because *I'll* take care of *you* for a change."

"I'm not really stressed, though. I'm excited." My brother slid his hand over top of Emma's, and they shared matching smiles.

"Then I'll just bump up the excitement even more. I want this to be great for the two of you." Harry's face was serious and determined. "Jill, how are you feeling about being maid of honor?"

"I'm maid of honor?"

I looked at Emma, who was massaging her temples. "I *was* going to ask in a cute way. Propose to you, kind of, with a big bottle of wine. But now that's blown. Thanks for that, Harrison." She turned toward me. "So, what do you say?"

I jumped up from the table, pulled her out of her chair, and hugged her with a squeal. "Absolutely, one hundred percent yes, I will be your maid of honor."

"I was hoping that would be your answer. And I'm also selfishly hoping we can use Velvet for the bachelorette party...in say, three months?"

"Three months?" I would have to spend every spare minute at the building to have it ready that fast.

I looked from Emma's beaming face to my brother's more subdued one. Even Harry was staring at me in expectation. "Sure, I can do three months."

Even if I had to break my back—and quit avoiding Ben Till—to do it.

CHAPTER ELEVEN

Ben

I WAS A MOTHERFUCKING idiot.

I scared Jill off. That was the only reasonable explanation I could come up with for why she kept ducking out of helping with the digging at Velvet. I'd opened my mouth and pressed the *friend with benefits* decision, and now she was ignoring me.

I'd always intended to bring it up again, because it was important, but maybe it had been too much too soon. My hands shook around my shovel as I scooped another mound of dirt out of the hole. She hadn't said no. I had to remember that. If she said no, I would respect it, but it had to mean something that she hadn't outright rejected me—yet.

The force of my fascination with Jill was only growing stronger with each moment we spent together, and I had to find some way to get her out of my head. This could all blow up in my face, but at this point, I was desperate enough to overlook her relation to my best friend and all the potential complications that came with that.

I was willing to bet that Jill didn't even need help in the sex department. There was no way she was *bad* at it. She was a good listener and communicator. As far as I was concerned, those were the top skills someone needed to be good at sex. Everything else was just smoke and mirrors. Real life wasn't the same as a performance on YourEyesOnly.

What Jill needed was confidence. And I wanted to be the one to give her that. I found it hard to believe no one ever told her how much they loved those soft, shiny lips of hers. That no one had spent hours wondering how they felt pressing kisses to their neck, trailing down their stomach, wrapping around their cock...

There I went again. This was a problem—and not a new one. These stray thoughts of Jill had been cropping up like flies since she had moved back to town, but the frequency had increased exponentially after we'd met up alone to talk about her business plans last winter.

That was the first time I could remember being alone with her, ever. And it had ended poorly.

I jabbed the metal shovel into the damp earth, the sound of the sharp edge cutting through wet grass tickling my ears. My t-shirt was already damp with sweat.

Deciding to take a break, I stalked over to the cooler where I kept my lunch and several chilled bottles of water. I grabbed a plastic bottle, unscrewed the cap, and dumped the contents over my head. I was clearing the water from my eyes with the hem of my shirt when Jill's SUV rolled into the lot.

"Hi, Ben," she said through the open window. She had braided her hair again and tied it off with a pale-blue ribbon. The color, combined with her golden strands, reminded me of the carpet of bluets that framed the walkway leading up to my house.

"Um, hey," I said, letting my shirt drop. "I didn't expect to see you this morning."

Her focus darted up guiltily from the general direction of my belt buckle. Had she been checking me out? If she had been, that would be...gratifying. And a good sign on the *friends with benefits* front.

I wished for another dose of cold water—a fifty-five-gallon drum might be enough—when she hopped out of her vehicle in the tiniest shorts I had ever seen. They looked like what volleyball players wore, stretchy and tight and covering very little. Jill's were hot pink, a perfect match for her vibrant fingernails. That delicate ring that spelled out *Fuck* was sitting pretty on her pinky again.

I swiped my hand down my face, closing my gaping jaw on the upward swipe. "Are you here to work, or just stopping by to check on things?" I asked once I regained the power of speech. It felt like I'd been staring at those long legs for an eternity, though it was probably only mere seconds.

"To work. This is my place of business. Why else would I be here?"

I raised my palms. "No need to get your back up. I haven't seen you much recently, so I wasn't sure. And you're not exactly dressed for the occasion."

She looked down at her outfit. I finally noticed the shoes—a beat up pair of black Chuck Taylors. An improvement over flimsy sandals and stiff rain boots.

"What's wrong with what I'm wearing?"

I lifted my shoulders, projecting a casual air I didn't feel. "It's a lot of skin."

Her eyes narrowed. What did I say wrong this time?

"Are you implying that I look too slutty to help you or something? Do the Till Lawn and Landscape employees have a dress code? You *do* know what type of products I plan to sell in there, don't you, Benny Boy?" She tipped her head toward the building.

I could not get my foot out of my mouth with her—and just when it seemed we were getting somewhere. "Whoa, okay, that is *not* what I meant. I don't care if you dress slutty—not that I think that's how you're dressed. Your clothes are your own business. I don't have a problem with them."

She tapped the white rubber toe of her sneaker in the gravel as she waited for me to take a breath.

"What I meant is that your legs might get beat up," I continued. "It helps to have a barrier between the dirt and rocks and naked skin. It wasn't a comment on your body or your sex life."

She snorted. "What sex life? It's pretty much nonexistent at this point."

"No, uh...forward movement on the *friends with benefits* thing, then?"

Please say no, please say no. Or just put me out of my misery.

"Nope. Not unless you count furious masturbation as sex."

I choked on my spit. "What the fuck, Jill?"

She let out a laugh—a genuine one this time. "I'm screwing with you. You make it way too easy. Now, shall we get digging? I'll be extra careful not to scrape up my legs."

I shook my head as I passed over her designated shovel. "Why do you always do that?"

"Do what?"

"Deflect with a joke or some outrageous statement when you're uncomfortable. Do you do that with everyone, or am I a special case?"

Her eyes widened before she lowered them to the ground. "I don't do that. I just like messing with you. It doesn't have to have a deeper meaning."

"If you insist," I said, internally smirking. She wasn't believable in the slightest.

"I don't like your tone."

"I don't have a tone. I'm not a moody preteen."

"Ben, you absolutely have a tone. Attitude isn't reserved for people of a certain age group. If it were, how would you explain my entire personality?"

I bit down on a sharp laugh. "That's an excellent question. I doubt I'll ever find the answer."

She smiled at me, all white teeth and pink lips. I had the urge to run back up to my truck and jump inside the cooler. I didn't care if my lunch got flattened. I needed to calm down.

Deciding that would be raise too many questions, I settled for backbreaking work to ward off the tingles running down my spine. I shut up and got to shoveling.

Jill got started on the other side of the hole. Once she got into a rhythm, she kept up her own steady pace. It was impressive. When she'd been here the other day, we'd made little headway, but she was clearly determined this morning. I shouldn't have been surprised, given the improvements she'd made so far to Velvet.

We talked little after that, working in companionable silence until the sun rose high in the sky, and the heat grew unbearable. I had to get out to the lake to meet Dany for another job. I'd be running payroll into the wee hours of the night.

"I've gotta take off," I said.

Jill's head shot up. Her blonde braids were hanging on by a thread, the pretty blue ribbon drooping. "Already? But it's still morning."

"Yep. Which means I have to get to my other job site before it gets too hot to do anything."

Her face was set in a determined line. "Oh, okay, then. If you're cool with me hanging onto this shovel, I'll just keep digging for a while. It's weirdly calming."

"I'd rather you didn't." I wasn't certain she would know when to stop—not in the mood she was in right now. I'd seen her drive herself to exhaustion before, and I didn't want that on my conscience.

"I can manage digging a hole, Ben."

"I know you can. But I'm asking you to wait until I get back. It's not as simple as it seems. Besides, working outdoors, alone, on a day like today isn't a great idea. If you end up overheating, you'll want someone else around."

Her eyes shuttered. I frowned.

"Is everything okay?"

"It's fine," she snapped. "I just really need to get this done."

"It will get done."

"Can it happen in three months?"

"What, the hole? I sure hope so."

"I don't just mean the hole. I mean all of it. Velvet. Can I do this?" Her voice was small and soft.

"Jill," I said, jamming my shovel back into the earth, "things have been weird between us for a while, but I know you can do anything you put your mind to." I was convinced that half her problem was she hadn't settled on anything she wanted bad enough until now. Maybe all those half-baked plans and chaotic ideas of her past hadn't called to her enough.

She smiled wanly. "Maybe. Maybe not. But three months isn't a lot of time."

"Where did that deadline come from? I wasn't aware you had a hard time-frame for the grand opening."

She sighed. "Emma wants to have her bachelorette party here. And truthfully, it's a great idea. Hosting a small event with friends and family *would* be an awesome way to dip my toes in before opening to the public. But it's the pressure, you know? If I screw this up, Emma will be disappointed, which means James will be disappointed too."

"Your brother loves you, Jill. He would do anything for you."

"That's the problem, though, Ben! I need to do this on my own. I'm a thirty-year-old woman, and I should be able to do some of this myself."

I stepped up to her, my dirty boots coming toe to toe with her black Converse. I gently pried the metal shovel from her pale fingers.

"Okay, so tell me what I can do for you. What are *you* thinking? I'll help, but you're the one in charge."

She smoothed a hand over her hair, squinting up at me. "Would you be willing to meet me here tonight? When the sun goes down?"

My face must have shown my confusion, because she quickly cut in.

"That sounded shady, and it wasn't meant to. I want to get this done as soon as possible, and if I can't dig without you, I'm hoping you'd consider doubling up on our dig time after dark." Her cheeks were tinged a curious shade of pink.

I grinned. "Still sounds shady."

"Oh, shut up, Benny. Will you, or won't you?" The joke had been stupid, but she was smiling, so mission accomplished.

"Sun goes down around nine thirty. I'll be here." I'd get up extra early tomorrow to work on the payroll.

"Shake on it?" She held her hand out.

"Sure."

Her pale hand, adorned with those neon-pink fingernails, was soft in my grip. Her skin was hot from where she'd been handling the shovel, but not sweaty. I wanted so badly to tug her closer and wrap her in my arms. To use my hold on her hand to press her palm flat to my abdomen—the spot I knew she'd been eyeing earlier—and drag it down toward my dick.

Fuck.

"Gotta run," I said, practically ripping her shoulder out of its socket in my haste to pull away.

"Bye, Ben!" she shouted as I threw open the door to my truck and ran off like the coward I was.

CHAPTER TWELVE

Jill

R AIN CAME DOWN IN a steady drizzle as I stood in the open door of Velvet, looking out across the empty lot. Headlights illuminated the building's rust-colored siding as a car whipped by in the dark.

Despite the weather, I was waiting for Ben. He hadn't called or messaged me to cancel our late-night digging session, but I hadn't reached out to him either.

When he'd left this morning, and I'd switched gears to paint the interior of Velvet, the place had felt oddly lonely.

Talking with him had been...nice. I could be vulnerable with Ben in ways I couldn't with anyone else.

It was a foreign feeling. I usually *liked* being alone.

When his white truck came around the corner, the muscles in my lower back loosened.

"Sorry, I got caught up with a client and didn't notice the time," he said, rushing past me to get out of the rain. He swiped off his black ball cap and ran a hand over his damp neck.

"I wasn't sure you were still coming."

He furrowed his brow.

"Because of the rain," I said in response. It definitely wasn't at all related to my own anxious overthinking.

"I'd have told you if I was canceling. I figured you could still use my help with something in the building, even if we can't get much done outside."

"Yeah. Okay. That sounds good."

"Why don't you show me where to start."

"I'm painting some of walls now." We walked over to where I had arranged a large tan dropcloth and two matching paint trays in a small alcove. Ben didn't skip a beat, immediately grabbing a roller and getting started.

"What's this area going to be?" he asked as we applied burgundy paint to the fresh drywall.

"It'll be the place where people go to enter the speakeasy part of Velvet." I side-stepped over to the secret-door bookshelf James had installed and pulled the thin metal lever. "See?" I said as the door slid open.

"Damn. That's really cool. This is really shaping up. You're doing an amazing job, Jill."

I blushed and looked away, squirming under the praise. Did he mean it? "Thanks. James is the one who did most of it. I'm just here to polish it and make it look pretty."

"Somehow, I doubt that. This is your brainchild, right?"

"Well, yes, but...I'm not exactly doing the manual labor. That's all." If we could leave the topic of my glaring insecurities, that would be great.

"How'd you settle on the idea for a sex toy speakeasy, anyway? I don't think we got that far last winter."

"Did I never tell you?" I knew very well I hadn't. But if I played dumb, acted like I didn't replay that meeting in my head on a never-ending loop, then maybe I could avoid answering uncomfortable questions.

"Nope." He dipped his roller back into the paint tray.

"Well, I guess it goes back to when I was nineteen. I was away at school in Albany." I'd seen little of Ben, or James, or anyone else from Greyport during that stretch of time. I had been a new Jill, discovering a new world back then. "The first year of college was great. I got involved in the Gay Straight Alliance, finally felt comfortable coming out, and everything about sex was fun and free and casual. Toward the end of that year, I met someone, and we dated for a while. It didn't end well." I paused, flicking a glance at Ben from the corner of my eye. He was carefully painting the wall and avoiding eye contact, but I had the sense he was listening intently. "Please don't share this with James, okay?"

He nodded stiffly. "Did this person...hurt you?" His voice was measured, like he was worried I would fly off if he said the wrong thing.

"Not in the way you're thinking. He was just...ugh. I really hate talking about this." Bringing up Oliver always felt like giving him more power over my life than he deserved.

"If it helps, I proposed to a woman in my early twenties, and she dumped me immediately after. Probably not exactly the same as your experience, but no one is without at least one shitty ex."

Ben had almost married someone? And how had I not known this? Although, looking back, if he'd been in his mid-twenties, it would have been around the time I was caught up in the Oliver cycle, the good and the bad of it. "That makes me feel marginally better, actually."

"I'm glad I could do you that small favor. It all worked out in the end. Stef and I weren't compatible in the long run. If we'd gotten married, I'd probably be divorced already."

I chuckled lightly. "It sounds like you've recovered for the most part. I wish I could say the same. This guy basically killed my confidence, especially in bed." I still heard his voice in my head on bad days.

"So where did the sex toys come in?"

"One of my friends dragged me to an adult boutique one day after the breakup. A place near the airport. It was super seedy from the outside, but the clerk was really kind and patient. I found products I liked, and then eventually, I was going to more stores, and finding online spaces, and having fun with sex again, even if it was sex by myself. I want to bring that joy and confidence and freedom to other people." I took a breath. I was getting carried away, and maybe Ben didn't want to hear me droning on, even though he'd been the one to ask.

Only, he was smiling, just a little, under the shadow of his hat brim. "I think that's pretty amazing."

Did he really think so? I couldn't be sure, but he sounded sincere. "I—well, thank you. I hope the rest of Greyport agrees." For the sake of both my mental and financial well-being.

"They will. I have no doubt."

There he went, sounding genuine again. Like the way he'd talked on that call about my dog-walking business, and at my college graduation, and when he'd told me I'd played the best second-chair clarinet part he'd ever heard.

"Do you want to see how I plan to hide the lever?" I said, abruptly changing the subject. It was cowardly, but I was desperate to move onto lighter topics.

If Ben found my diversion suspicious, he gave no indication. He set his roller in the tray, dusting his hands off on his jeans. "I definitely want to see."

I grinned madly. This was my favorite part of the setup. It was a little wacky and one hundred percent me.

"It just arrived today, and I've been dying to show someone."

I hurried over to the large rectangular shipping box resting on a chair. I opened it up and pulled the item out with a flourish, brandishing it like a sword.

"Ta-da!"

Ben's jaw dropped, and his cheeks reddened. "Is that, uh...a, uh..."

"It is a large gold dildo, yes." I gave it a shake, the silicone wobbling like an over-sized sausage.

"And what does that have to do with the bookshelf lever?"

"It's hollow inside." I turned the object so he could see. "Custom-made just for this."

"And?"

"Patience, Benny Boy. All will be explained in a moment." The idea had popped into my head weeks ago, and I couldn't let it go.

I gripped the golden shaft in both hands, thrusting it firmly onto the oblong lever. It took some wiggling and waggling, but I finally achieved the proper position, the lever completely covered.

"How does it look?" I turned back toward Ben.

His mouth stood open, his eyes fixed intently on my hands.

"Ben?"

He came out of his stupor, dragging a hand over his mouth before he replied. "It...looks like a dildo sticking out of a wall."

"I know that. But would you guess there's a lever there if you didn't already know?"

"I'm not sure. I can't un-know what I already know, you know?"

I snickered, watching as he bit down on an emerging grin. This was the stupidest conversation I'd ever had, and I was having the time of my life.

I flapped my hands in a shooing motion toward the exit. "Here, walk out the door really quick. I want to try something."

"Huh?"

I came up behind Ben and nudged him toward the entryway. "Go outside for a second and pretend you're coming in for the first time."

"Jill, it's raining." He looked over his shoulder at me beseechingly as I continued to budge him along.

"It's just for a moment. Long enough to turn around and come right back in. I need you to act like you're seeing the dildo-lever for the very first time so you can tell me if it's a convincing disguise or not."

"Fine." He gave me one last long look before jogging toward the propped door. I watched as he exited then quickly spun in his boots to make his way back inside.

I took him in as he walked—no, stalked—toward me, all prowling, lion-like grace. Those silver eyes looked dark in Velvet's dim lighting. A shiver went down my back at the thought of them fixed on me.

I was out of breath when he closed in, though he had been the one exerting himself. We stared at each other for a beat, the air around us growing heavy. I cleared my throat and took a step back, grabbing back up the paint roller. "So, what do you think?"

"I'm convinced," he said, his tone flat.

"Really?" I stole a look at him. "Or are you just saying that to appease me?"

"This plan is inherently flawed, Jill. It's impossible for me to give you a truly unbiased opinion on the lever when I watched you shove a gold dick onto it."

I sighed. I'd gotten ahead of myself in my excitement to have another person's opinion. "Yeah, you're right. I'll take a picture and send it to my friend Glenn. He hasn't been out to see the place yet."

"Would you be willing to say that again for me? I want to take a video."

I shot him a bewildered look as we painted side by side. "Say what again?"

"The whole 'you're right' thing."

"You're the *worst.*" It would have been more believable if I'd been able to hide my giggle.

"So, have you had a chance to take a look at that flyer I gave you? If you want me to landscape the full property, that is."

"A little, and I do." It was a simple choice. I wanted Velvet to succeed, and making it look presentable was part of that. And Ben was the best at what he did. "I don't have the flyer with me."

"That's okay. I have another one in the truck."

"There's nowhere for us to sit." I gestured around the empty room.

Ben tipped his chin down to the dropcloth where our paint trays still rested. "I can manage sitting on a floor for a few minutes. Can you?" he challenged.

I narrowed my eyes, knowing I was taking his bait. "Fine. Go get your silly flyer."

I tried valiantly not to stare at his firm ass as he walked away.

CHAPTER THIRTEEN

Ben

"THESE ONES ARE PRETTY low-maintenance and hardy. You won't have to water them much if we don't get rain. And they're affordable too."

"How many different colors do they come in? Am I saying that right? It's not like someone's in a factory, mixing up dye to make different colored flowers." Jill looked up at me as we sat with bent heads over the pamphlet of flower variants. Her brown eyes held genuine curiosity as we made eye contact over the scant space between us on the dropcloth.

"You're not completely off base. There's an entire field of study related to plant genetics. And farmers have been cross-breeding plants and crops for ages. But no, it's not exactly the same as custom ordering a product in an exact shade. These bloom in white, pink, purple, or blue."

"I like it. Let's go with the pink." She drummed her hot-pink fingernails on the shiny paper. I wondered what that subtle point might feel like running down my spine and felt my cock leap at the thought.

I ripped the flyer from under Jill's tapping fingers, earning a startled look, and folded it into a tiny square.

"Ben?"

I focused on her open face, just for a moment, before looking away and clearing my throat. I had to get myself under control. I wasn't sure yet that Jill was willing to go in the *friends with benefits* direction with me, and I couldn't risk overwhelming her with the force of my...thing...for her.

"Yeah?" I finally responded, flicking the soft edges of the pamphlet with the thumb.

"Are you...okay?"

"Fine. Why?"

"You seem tense. Up here," she said, reaching a hand tentatively toward the spot where my neck and shoulder met.

I watched, transfixed, as her delicate hand inched closer and closer. I felt, at once, like predator and prey—so tempted to reach out and grab hold like a Venus Fly Trap, to feel all that smooth skin on mine, while at the same time ready and willing to let her have her way with me.

I stood abruptly and her fingertips hit open air.

What was wrong with me? I wanted nothing more than for her to touch me, so why wasn't I letting it happen? Was I chickening out at the precise moment the woman I hadn't been able to get out of my head for years was giving me a semblance of a shot?

"What is wrong with you?" she asked, echoing my inner thoughts. She rose to her feet, brushing a few stray flecks of dried paint chips from her bare knees.

"Nothing is wrong," I said, stepping back as she moved an inch nearer. "I just remembered that I have a…thing…to go do."

"A *thing*?" Her light-colored brows rose skeptically. "Ben, seriously, did I say something that—"

"No! It's not you, it's—holy fuck!" I shouted as the backs of my calves struck something behind me on the floor. Surely that hadn't been there a minute ago? My feet shot straight out from under me. There was nothing but air beneath me for a split second and braced for impact.

Instead of hitting the floor, I found myself sitting directly inside a taped-together cardboard box.

"Oh my god, are you okay?" Jill rushed to my side. She offered her hand, and this time, I couldn't shy away from the contact. I needed the help because my ass was *stuck*. There was no dignity to be found here.

"Thank you," I said, releasing my grip on her fingers as I steadied myself.

The box fell off my ass, thudding on the hardwood floor. Jill snickered. I glared.

"I'm sorry! I don't mean to laugh, but come on. That was funny."

I felt a reluctant smile growing under the surface. "Yeah, well, I just hope there wasn't anything breakable in that package. Because I'm pretty sure I crushed everything inside."

"No worries," she said with a hand wave. "Your ass might be thick, but this bad boy is built to take the weight of a human body. Here, I'll show you."

I blushed, watching as she peeled off what little tape remained on the box and pulled the stiff flaps apart. Jill was showing me a lot tonight, both around the building and about herself. I was beginning to understand that she was near to bursting with ideas for Velvet. I couldn't stand the fact that some asshole had hurt her, but the way she'd turned that hurt into something positive was pretty remarkable.

Maybe I could stand to learn a thing or two from that.

"Okay, this is it." Her voice strained with effort as she hoisted two large, black-fabric-covered cushions into the air. Both cushions were wedge-shaped, one slightly smaller than the other. Several straps with dangling buckles were attached to each.

I looked at her blankly.

"You have no idea what I'm holding, do you?" she asked.

"Nope."

Shuffling over, she offered me the larger cushion. It was surprisingly sturdy, but the fabric was soft under my fingertips.

"It's for sex," she explained. "It's to help partners get into the appropriate positions. The two wedges can stack on top of each other. It's supposed to be easier on the joints."

A clear picture hit me of Jill laid out on the black material, her ass tilted up at just the right angle for me to tug those hot-pink shorts down her long legs.

The cushion in my hand fell to the floor in a loud clatter, metal buckles clanging. Jill giggled as I frantically collected it from the scratched hardwood.

"What are all these straps for?" I asked.

"Bondage."

I choked. "I see."

And I did see. Now that I was looking, there were obvious connecting points for cuffs or other restraints.

"Have you, uh...ever used this before?"

She huffed a breath through her nostrils. "No. It's not really the sort of thing you can use alone, is it?"

"I suppose not." I rubbed the back of my neck. "How is your search going? For someone to...help you practice?" I needed to indulge my morbid curiosity, to see if I still had a shot. I thought I might, but her mixed signals didn't give me much to go on.

"Not well. I have to get this place ready in three months, but I'm so busy I can hardly make time to meet people." I couldn't help but notice the way she carefully avoided my eyes, fiddling with the metal fasteners on the wedge she was holding.

"Have you talked to Emma about the timeframe?" Jill was obviously working herself to the bone to get Velvet up and running in time for the bachelorette party. I could see the exhaustion in her eyes.

"No, and I don't plan on mentioning it, so you'd better not say anything to James either. They would rearrange everything if I asked them to, which is exactly why I won't be asking. I need to do this on my own. I don't want anything to delay the wedding plans."

"They are moving awfully fast, aren't they?" Most of my buddies who'd gotten engaged over the years complained about weddings that took a year or more to come to fruition. I didn't think I would mind that so much, so long as the woman I married was having fun with it.

"If you asked my brother, he'd say the planning wasn't moving fast enough."

"That's a lot of pressure on you, Blossom." The endearment fell past my lips. Thankfully, she didn't notice.

"It is. But I can withstand it. This is what I want. Velvet is my dream. It will be worth it in the end."

My hands clenched with the urge to tug her close. She would fit perfectly under my chin. I could rest my cheek in her hair and inhale that moonflower scent like I was taking a hit of something illicit. "Let me know if you need anything."

Her lips twitched. "Thanks, Ben."

We stood awkwardly until an alert went up from Jill's phone—the sound of coffee dripping into porcelain—and broke the thick silence.

It was that stupid My Cup notification—and my cue to leave. "I'd better head out. It's getting late."

She glanced down at her phone screen before shuttering it again. "Hey, Ben?"

I stopped at the threshold of the door, letting the cool night breeze brush over my skin. "Yeah?"

"Your offer? The one to...use you... Does that still stand?"

Chapter Fourteen

Ben

"How are things going with Dr. Casey?" Ma asked. She sat at one end of the table while my father bookended her at the other. They'd been sitting in those same chairs since we moved into the house when I was ten and Galyna was fourteen.

Similarly, I kept the spot I always used when I came for dinner. Galyna's sat empty, as if she would randomly appear from California just in time for stuffed cabbage and fresh garlic rolls.

We had dinner together once a month, even though I saw my parents more than that. Small towns. It was unavoidable.

Ma was adamant about dedicated time together, probably because she'd ceased to have much to do with her own parents once she hit adulthood.

"You don't have to use her title, Ma. It's just Casey. She wasn't cleaning my teeth when we went out."

Ma ruffled her narrow shoulders. "She earned that title, Benjamin. And I don't think dentists are usually the ones cleaning the teeth. But anyway, you didn't answer the question."

"Don't hound him, Len," my dad said.

"I'm only curious, my love. Dr. Casey is a lovely woman. She's...settled. A good match for our Ben."

If Ma had been a cattier person, I'd have guessed she was taking a dig at some of my past girlfriends, namely Stef, who she'd always worried was too flighty and noncommittal for me. She hadn't been wrong.

"It didn't work out. Dr. Casey and I were not meant to be."

Ma's face fell the barest amount. She'd really had her hopes up for this one. I had too.

Instead, I was stuck thinking about my best friend's sister on a constant loop in my head. When Jill had dropped the bomb that she was considering my offer to be her *friend with benefits*, I'd been struck dumb. Like an idiot, I'd stared at her, stammered out some lame excuse to leave, and run away like a coward. To make matters worse, I'd asked James to help me with the shoveling at Velvet this morning to act as a buffer.

I hadn't missed the fire-and-brimstone look Jill shot my way when she'd arrived to see me and her brother already hard at work. Still, she'd grabbed her own shovel and gotten right to it alongside us. James had remained blessedly unaware of the strange tension between me and his sister.

"I'm sorry to hear that, bud," Dad said. "You'll find the right one soon."

That was easy for him to say when he'd found the right one over forty years ago. I was worried it might never happen for me, especially when I couldn't stop thinking about a certain willowy blonde.

I smiled, but my heart wasn't in it. "It's a little hard in a town the size of Greyport when you already know most of the available women."

"Have you tried one of those apps, honey?" Ma asked.

"A handful of times. But none of the matches panned out," I replied, thinking of Jill and her string of disastrous My Cup dates.

And that stupid coffee-drip notification sound.

"You are looking tired, though. Are you taking care of yourself?" Ma asked. Dad coughed into his hand, and Ma scoffed at the mere suggestion that her statement might be rude. "Robbie, I can tell my own son he looks tired. I'm his mother. Now, what's keeping you so busy if not spending time with Dr. Casey?"

I shrugged, the motion sending an almost painful stretch down the length of my shoulders and back. "I've been helping James' sister, Jill, with an issue in the backyard of the building she bought. It's got me up a little earlier than usual."

"How is James?" Dad asked. "We've missed him at dinner lately. Did he and Emma set a date yet?"

I nodded as I sipped my glass of milk. "Yep. It's pretty soon too. Just over three months out. He said to expect your invitation in the mail in the next couple weeks."

"That is fast, but you know what they say: when you know, you know." Ma gave Dad an eye-crinkling smile. They had met the day they graduated high school—Ma from Greyport High and Dad from Rockberry Park. Ma had worked the summer before that with Dad's sister, Aunt Lily, at a local amusement park. To hear Aunt Lily tell the tale, she had wanted to set Ma up with her brother the entirety of senior year, but Dad had avoided it at all costs, wanting to enjoy his last year before college as a single guy. Aunt Lily had convinced him to attend Ma's graduation party with her, and he'd been a goner from minute one. Two years in, they were engaged, and married just months after finishing college.

I had asked Dad once about how he'd known Ma was it for him. He had shrugged and told me it was just a feeling.

I swallowed down a bite of stuffed cabbage, washing it back with a gulp of milk. "Jill said the same thing about the speed of the wedding planning. I'm happy for them."

"Has Jill been doing well? I've only seen her in passing at the library lately. What a sweet girl she is. She's really come into her own. I was so worried for her when their mother died. For James, too, of course. But to be a young woman, still in high school, and facing the loss of a parent? It must have been so difficult."

Given her own complicated family relationships, Ma could relate.

Things had been tough for Jill back then, but James had stepped up after Callie Klein passed away. I'd been away, earning my degree in landscape architecture, but I'd gone with him to a handful of Jill's school events.

Dad cleared his throat somberly.

"Well, that's a lot of not-so-fun talk for what's supposed to be a happy family dinner," Ma said, slapping her hands lightly on the table. "Jill bought a building, then, huh?"

Velvet was just beyond the village limits, outside of Ma's purview as Greyport's mayor. She wouldn't know the particulars, and I'd been avoiding this particular topic for months.

"She did. She ended up buying the old Crow's Nest building on County Line Road."

Ma's face drooped. Dad's silverware made a jarring scrape on his porcelain dinner plate. This was exactly what I had been worried about.

"Isn't that—"

"Yes, Robbie, it is." Ma took a slow sip of herbal tea. "Have you talked to Jill about the location at all?"

I shook my head. "No. It wasn't my story to share."

"No, it wouldn't be."

We sat quietly for a minute, chewing our food.

"Do you want me to tell her so it's not weird for you?"

Ma laughed. "Oh, honey, don't worry about me so much. I'll be fine."

🫘 🫘 🫘 🫘 🫘 🫘 🫘 🫘

I STRATEGICALLY POSITIONED THE plastic container of cabbage in the refrigerator, nestling it between the pre-portioned meals I'd made the past weekend. Ma's cooking would make for a better lunch tomorrow than anything I had cooked. Despite living alone for over ten years and being a homeowner for seven of those, I struggled in the kitchen. I could throw together decent meals for groups at parties—hell, I hosted a killer barbecue for my employees every summer—but I hadn't quite mastered the logistics of cooking for one.

I paused to water the plants along my windowsill before shedding my sweaty clothes to shower the day away. The sun was just dipping low, but I was exhausted, deep down into my bones. Still, I doubted I would get much sleep. Rest had been hard to come by since I'd seen Jill out at that nameless bar in the middle of nowhere.

But had I really been able to sleep at all the last eight years without feeling that uncomfortable pang in my chest when I thought of her?

And now she was seriously considering using me as her *friend with benefits*. There was no other explanation for her having brought it up. I couldn't dodge her or use James as a buffer forever. Not when this might be my one real chance at resolving my feelings for her.

A notification chimed from the cell phone resting on the sink counter.

Eyeing the device like it was about to pounce, I ignored it, instead pulling out my clippers to clean up my scalp and face. I eased over the skin on top of my head, taking my time to buzz the hair to my preferred length. Satisfied with the job, I swiped the excess hair off with a fresh hand towel that I tossed into my wicker hamper. Ma would have scolded me for not reusing it if she'd seen me do it, but there were some perks to living alone. I answered to no one.

Sometimes, though, I wanted to yell across the space of my soulless ranch and hear something besides the rustling of plant leaves.

Taking a deep breath, I woke up the screen of my now-quiet phone.

It was James.

I swallowed back the feeling of disappointment that ran straight up my gut. I shouldn't be disappointed that my best friend messaged me. I shouldn't have wanted his little sister to be the one doing the messaging instead.

> **James:** Want to get breakfast at Greyport Family Diner tomorrow? I'm having a craving, and I need to get it out of my system. Gotta quit eating like shit so I can fit in my tux.

I snorted. The man exercised constantly when he wasn't working or spending time with Emma. He wouldn't have any problem fitting into a tuxedo.

> **Me:** Sure. How about nine?

> **James:** That works. See you then.

Instead of putting the phone away and heading to bed, I stood in front of the mirror. I could do this. I *needed* to do this so I could move on for good.

I pulled up the message thread just below the one with James and started tapping.

Me: My offer still stands.

Her reply was instantaneous.

Jill: Good, I was worried I scared you off. When do you want to meet?

That was funny. Here, I'd been so worried I'd been the one to scare her off.

I drummed my fingers along the rim of the counter, considering my schedule. The sooner the better.

Me: Tomorrow night. My place.

Jill: I'll be there.

CHAPTER FIFTEEN

Jill

"I BROUGHT WINE," I said as I pushed open the door to Kristi's townhouse, not bothering to knock. I had sent her a message twenty minutes before, warning her I was coming over for an emergency chat. She'd responded with a silly photo of a man winking, like she already knew I was on the way.

She likely did already know. Kristi had never confirmed that she was mildly psychic, but she also never denied it.

"What'd you bring me?" Kristi said, popping up from her cozy, forest-green velvet couch. Her long, deep-purple hair slipped from a claw clip as she plodded across the slate tile floor in royal-blue pajama pants and black cat slippers. Her calico cat, Colleen, streamed between her ankles as she walked.

I had serious home-envy when it came to Kristi's space. The two-bedroom townhouse wasn't huge, but there were three levels, giving the illusion that it was larger than it actually was. She'd decorated with rich jewel tones, and the effect was singularly *Kristi*. A little quirky, a lot colorful, and uniquely lovely.

"It was on sale at the liquor store," I said, holding the wine bottle aloft. "It's sweet."

"Yuck." She made a gagging face.

"You'll be fine. Don't act like you don't have something else in the cupboard."

She grinned, almost maniacally. "Even better. I got some weed gummies from the dispensary in Merlin Heights last week."

"Did you already take one? I have something to talk to you about, and I was kind of hoping you'd have a clear enough head to talk me out of it."

"Relax, girl. I took one right after you messaged me, and it won't kick in right away. Besides, I find I'm more in touch with my emotions and gut feelings while *under the influence*." She waved her fingers around in a vaguely witchy circle.

I snickered. "You sure you don't want some?" I tipped my chin down to the wine I was pouring into a large glass.

"Very positive. Now come sit down and tell me why you called this emergency meeting."

I sighed as I sank into the plush cushions of the couch, mindful not to spill the sweet red on the skirt of my light-blue sundress as I sipped. Kristi settled in beside me, tucking her pajama-pant-covered legs under her. Colleen hopped up on the arm of the sofa, stretching her long body out behind us, her fluffy tail whipping softly against my cheek.

"Okay. So, I told you how Ben Till is helping me with the flood and landscaping issues at Velvet, right?"

"You did, yes."

"What I failed to mention was that Ben may have seen me out with someone recently."

Kristi's brows rose a fraction. "You're dating?" I could hear the tamped-down excitement in her voice, like she was wary of asking too much, lest I go back into hiding again.

I took a sip of wine, smothering the itchy sensation in my throat. "Well, dating isn't quite the term I would use. More like...seeking new skills."

"I'm intuitive, and even I don't know what that means."

I set the wine glass down with a clink on her glass end table. Colleen sent me a bitchy look from a cocked amber eye.

"Sorry, Col," I said, running a hand along the cat's smooth back. "It's a little weird for me to talk about this."

"I'm sure it is. I mean, you've talked more about wanting to use a sperm donor to have kids than you ever have a partner. I can count the number of times you've brought up your love life to me on one hand, and we've been friends for years."

I took another pull of wine. "It's not personal, me not talking to you about it. You know that, right? I don't talk with anyone about it."

"Of course I know that, Jill. So you've got some hangups about love and dating. We all do in our own way. Hell, I was divorced before I hit twenty-five, so believe me, I can relate. But you're opening up tonight, and that's a good first step."

"Okay. I might as well say it, then." I took a bracing inhale. "I'm trying to find a *friend with benefits* because I'm terrible at sex."

I peeked up at Kristi to find her mouth agape and debated smashing her in the face with one of the many floor pillows littered around the room. "No need to look so shocked as I bare my deepest insecurity, Kris."

"I'm sorry," she said finally. "I've gotta be honest, I don't see how you could possibly be bad at sex."

"Believe me, it's very possible."

"But it's you. *Jill.* My sex-positive, comfortable-in-her-womanhood, open-about-self-pleasure, building-a-sex-toy-boutique best friend. How can you be all of those things and think you're no good at sex?"

Kristi wasn't wrong. I *was* all of those things. But sex with a partner was the one lingering, sour-tasting leftover from my relationship with Oliver that I couldn't quite swallow.

I took a gulping sip of wine, fiddling with the crystal charm that dangled from the stem of the glass. It was strange how talking about this with Ben had been so much easier than talking about it with my best friend.

"Do you remember that guy, Oliver, I used to date?"

"You mean your ex from when you were in college? All I remember you saying is that he sucked." I hadn't met Kristi until she'd moved to town about a year after I'd finished school and returned to Greyport.

"Yeah. He really, really did suck. Or still does. I'm pretty sure he's not dead—not unless someone finally got so sick of his shit they murdered him." I'd certainly entertained myself with plenty of revenge-related scenarios over the years. Maybe someone had given him his comeuppance, even if it wasn't me.

"So, he's at the heart of this, I take it?"

"I hate to give him that much power, but yes. I'd never had a relationship before him, and he seemed so...fun, and free, and down to try anything. But it was like nothing I did ever measured up. Someone else always did it better, or was prettier, or more enthusiastic in bed than I was. Sometimes I was too quiet, or my face looked strange when I orgasmed. But if I tried to be more vocal, or do what he said he liked, then I was too performative. Eventually, I figured out he was hooking up with other people, but even then, he convinced me to stay with him for a while after. I had to accept that he wasn't '*built for monogamy,*' but I was never allowed to see other people."

Kristi stood abruptly from the couch, nearly knocking into the lamp beside her. I looked at her, brows raised.

"Sorry, I need to do something with this angry energy," she said, starting a slow pace around the room. "You've really been downplaying things. This guy is the *worst*. Where does he live now? No, no, don't tell me, because then I'll be too tempted to go tell him off. Or put a curse on him."

I shrugged. "Last I heard from an old mutual friend, he worked at some coffee shop in Merlin Heights. And trust me, he isn't worth your time."

"Please tell me you dumped him in epic fashion, Jill," Kristi said as she came back to settle on the sofa. Her movements had slowed, and I gathered the edible she ate was taking effect.

I winced. "Unfortunately, I did not. He ended it with me to move in with someone else. It was hard at the time, but it needed to happen. You won't catch me thanking him for it, though."

"Absolutely not. I support you in holding this grudge. I am all about the grudge."

"Thank you." I tipped my wine glass in her direction as she did a mock salute.

"Surely you've been with other people since him?"

"Ugh, yes. I've tried one-night stands with men and women since him, and it never ends well for me."

"I think that says more about the skill of your partners than it does you."

I shook my head, my hair frizzing against the soft fabric of the sofa. "It doesn't, though. Because I had it on good authority that at least several of these people were very, very good at sex. It was one hundred percent me."

"What makes you so certain?"

"Because I get so caught up in my head, in imagining what the other person is thinking, that I can't come. It's a vicious cycle." It happened without fail every. Single. Time.

I sat up and quickly guzzled down my remaining wine before hopping up to make another generous pour.

When I sat back down, I noticed Kristi's eyes taking on a glassy effect. "You good?" I asked. She gave me a dopey smile in return.

"I'm just a little sleepy."

"Well, listen closely. I don't want to explain this more than once. Have you ever watched a video on YourEyesOnly and just thought, *wow, that person is not into this at all*? Like, you could immediately tell?"

"I guess so. Videos aren't really my thing, though. I'm more of an erotic audio gal. But I can see what you mean."

"Well, I'm the person everyone knows isn't into it. I try so hard when I'm with a partner, and I just...can't get there. At some point, all my insecurities hit, and it's like I'm only going through the motions."

"But that doesn't happen when you masturbate, does it? Otherwise, I doubt you would be so enthusiastic about sex toys."

"No problems there at all. Sex toys helped me regain so much confidence after Oliver. I'm free and abandoned and unselfconscious about self-pleasure. And frankly, it pisses me off that I can't find that with a partner."

"It pisses me off too, damn it. Alright, let's think. What do the people you've hooked up with have in common?"

I cast my mind back. "Not much on the surface. I asked myself the same question a few months ago and realized I've only been with people I don't know that well. One-night stands or friends of friends who I'd only met a handful of times. I don't want a relationship, but maybe having some connection would help, which is why I came up with the idea to have a *friend with benefits*."

"It's a good idea. I think you're onto something."

"Seriously?"

"Yes, seriously. Don't sound so shocked. It makes sense."

"Oh. Okay. I'm glad you think so." I'd thought this conversation would be much harder to have, that I would have to justify and defend myself and my plan.

"I'm not letting you off the hook yet."

"Oh, come on!"

Kristi adjusted her hair, twirling the purple mass back up to secure in its clip. "You came here for a reason."

I worried my bottom lip between my teeth. "I don't know how to start."

"You want to fuck Ben, don't you?"

The wine I was sipping sprayed out of my lips, leaving a misty pattern along the arm of the couch. Colleen leaped away, butt twitching as she walked into Kristi's kitchen. "How the hell do you know that?!" Had Ben said something to her? Was there already talk around town about the two of us spending time together?

"Do you really have to ask how *I* know?" Kristi tapped her left temple, that goofy grin back on her face.

Alright, not the gossip mill, just your average, run-of-the-mill psychic best friend.

"Sometimes I hate that you know everything."

She laughed. "I didn't need to be psychic for that one. You mentioned Ben before you got into the *friend-with-benefits* topic. It wasn't that hard to put two and two together."

I sighed. "I'm *considering* fucking Ben. He brought it up when I bumped into him on that date, and I haven't been able to get it out of my head since. But it's a terrible idea, don't you think?" Maybe she would be able to talking me out of meeting him at his place tomorrow night. That message I'd sent him had been impulsive and silly.

"Not necessarily. You know Ben. He's attractive. You're gorgeous. I'd normally say not to go there, what with him being a relationship type of guy, but if it was his idea, then he's obviously cool with it."

I couldn't help but to ask the thing that had been on my mind ever since Ben had made his suggestion. "Why do you think he would offer himself up to me? It still doesn't make sense."

Kristi hesitated, glancing at me then looking down at her black-painted nails.

"Spit it out," I prompted.

"Well, I've always wondered if Ben might...like you. In a romantic sense." She winced, like she was girding herself for my reaction to the statement.

I scoffed. There was no way. "Yeah. Right."

"I'm serious! I have a feeling about it."

She hadn't heard Ben on that phone call, though. People didn't talk that way about a person they liked. "Well, maybe your gut feeling is wrong for a change." I wrapped my arms around my stomach.

"If you're not receptive to that line of thinking, then maybe he's just attracted to you and wants to bang," Kristi said, shrugging. "You could always ask him."

"I guess." I wouldn't be doing that. It wasn't wise to ask questions when you weren't prepared for the answer.

Kristi rolled her shining eyes. "I mean, what has *you* thinking about saying yes to him?"

That I had come harder with that vibrator and Ben's words in my head than I could ever remember coming before. "Honestly? This might sound shallow, but Ben is hot. And he's the polar opposite of Oliver." If I let him, maybe he could eviscerate every ugly sex-related memory I had.

"Describe Oliver."

"Um, average height. Long hair. Kind of grungy but he also liked fancy stuff and to act like he was better than everyone." Really, he'd been painfully average in almost every way. I ground my teeth at the thought that I was letting such a mediocre asshole impact so much of my life years later.

Kristi nodded sagely. "Whereas Ben is so far above average it hurts. The buzzed hair, the down-to-earth attitude...I can see the differences. Not to mention that Ben seems like the ultimate one-woman guy, so you wouldn't need to worry about him stepping outside the boundaries of your arrangement. I have a feeling he'd eat a guy like Oliver for lunch."

She had a point. "Now that I think of it, Ben is all about being outside. The only outdoorsy thing I can picture Oliver doing is, I don't know, jerking off in the woods."

"See! Ben is a brilliant choice for you."

"What about the fact that he's James' best friend?"

"So?"

"Won't my brother be mad?"

"Does your brother get to make decisions about your sex life? Or Ben's sex life?"

"No, obviously not. But it could get complicated if things don't work out. James doesn't have that many friends, and I would hate to ruin that for him."

"If it's casual—just sex—I don't see how it would."

"How do I make sure it stays casual? I've only been with near-strangers in the first place because I don't want a relationship. How do I navigate feeling a connection while also staying distant?"

"I've got to be honest; I have no idea. I'm a catch-feelings kind of girl. But I've heard of people setting up ground rules. Boundaries. Like not spending the night or no cuddling. That sort of thing."

I rubbed a sweaty palm across my skirt. "Okay. I can do this. Right?" I asked, turning to Kristi.

The other woman had nodded off, sleeping upright on the sofa. Colleen hopped up with a chirp, settling in her owner's lap. I chuckled, covering them both with a plush throw blanket and making my way upstairs to the spare bedroom.

CHAPTER SIXTEEN

Jill

I SHIFTED THE CLUTCH into *park* as I pulled to a stop in Ben's driveway. The door to the attached garage stood open, and I could see his work truck on one side and a shiny red car on the other. In all the years I'd known him, I'd never actually been to his house before. I remembered James telling me when Ben bought the place—a modest one-story in an older development—a few years ago.

The houses surrounding Ben's were all slightly similar but not so alike that it was creepy. Most of the other homes on the street had yard signs advertising Till Lawn and Landscape, like some business version of a trail of breadcrumbs.

Follow the signs to your very own sexy landscaper!

Ben's place was a plain, tan ranch. The structure itself had little to set it apart, but the front lawn was overflowing with character. Tall grasses and flowering plants waved in the evening breeze, giving the yard the appearance of a meadow in the middle of the forest. A trio of bumblebees hovered above a group of purple flowers. It looked like no other lawn in town and must have taken significant time and dedication to get to this point.

I fiddled with the strap of my seatbelt, twisting it in my fingers. I was stalling and not afraid to admit it. Ben and I had arranged this meeting, and I knew I was planning to set ground rules. But I didn't know what Ben was expecting. If he wanted to jump right into the sex portion of this deal, things likely wouldn't work out. And I had realized, after talking with Kristi, that if it didn't work with Ben, it probably wouldn't work out with anyone.

A door inside the garage—the one leading into the house—popped open, and I made eye contact with Ben as he stood there waiting. His faded salmon t-shirt set off his tan to perfection as he crossed his arms over his chest. Even from a distance, I could make out the way the move had the tattooed muscles in his forearms rippling.

I hopped out of my SUV and took my sweet time walking up to the garage, trailing my fingertips along a spray of tall grass.

"Did you go to the car wash today, Benny Boy?" I joked, noting his shiny white truck. "Had to make everything nice and clean for me, huh?"

"Are you done?"

I blinked. He wasn't usually so abrupt. "Done with what?"

The corner of his lip tilted up. "This act you're putting on because you're nervous. It's cute, but we need to talk and figure out how this whole deal is going to go."

I glanced up at him as we stepped through the door into his office space-slash-laundry room, wondering if this change in mood was because he was nervous too. "Lead the way."

I trailed him through the short hallway that linked the makeshift office with a galley kitchen, where he paused briefly to offer me a bottle of water from the refrigerator. I accepted, suddenly feeling a tickle in the back of my throat.

We settled in the living room, the overhead light set to dim. I was on one end of a black leather sectional, while Ben was as far away as possible on the other. It was almost comical that we were about to discuss the logistics of being as close as two people could physically be while being islands on opposite ends of the sofa.

"So," he started.

I quirked a brow and sipped from my water bottle. He stared back at me.

"That's your opening line?" I asked, breaking the silence.

"The *friend with benefits* thing was your idea. Why don't you start with what you had in mind."

Oh, he was fucking evil, putting the ball in my court like that. Sure, I liked to mess with him, liked to make him blush, but deep down I could admit to being a bit of a baby. Brassy, ballsy Jill was just the mask I wore. I couldn't take the heat.

I cleared the acid building on the back of my tongue with another sip of water. The paper wrapper crinkled as I clutched it. "I'll admit to not having thought this through very far. But the main conclusion I've come to is that I need to feel *some* sort of connection with the person I'm sleeping with. But I'm not in the market for a partner, so those feelings can't go too deep. If we're really going to do this, I need boundaries and rules."

Ben nodded. I could barely make out his eyes in the dim shadow of the room.

"I agree," he said, his voice raspy. "You need to trust me enough to let go sexually. And I need to keep myself from getting too involved. That's...important for me."

We were on the same page. No attachments. Kristi's gut feeling was wrong for once. Ben didn't like me beyond a chemical attraction. My stomach roiled, but I shoved the sensation down deep with another generous gulp from my water bottled.

"How long do we want to do this for?" Ben asked.

I coughed, swiping my lips with my inner wrist. "I'm not sure. I don't know how quickly I'll get up to speed. Maybe two or three months? Right before the bachelorette party. Is that, uh...too long for you?" Would he be sick of me and my hang-ups after the first week?

"Three months is fine. What about exclusivity, condoms, testing, and all that stuff?"

I buried a scoff. "When you say *that stuff*, do you mean our health and safety?"

Ben shifted awkwardly in his corner of the couch. "Cut me some slack here, Jill. I've never had this sort of talk before. I feel like a hostage negotiator right now. I'm afraid I'll say one wrong word and send you running."

He rose to his feet, turning back toward the kitchen.

"Ben, wait." I stood to follow him.

"I'm just getting something to drink," he said as he kept moving.

"Oh. Okay." I sat back down, shoving my hands under my thighs to stop their fidgeting.

He reentered the room, holding a bottle of craft beer in a loose fist. He didn't sit on the couch, instead standing along the wall next to his large TV. A framed photo hung on the wall—Ben in a dark blue cap and gown at his college graduation, bookended by his parents and older sister. His hair was longer than he wore it now, and he looked exactly like the Ben I had first met when he'd shown up at our house with James when I was in elementary school.

I glanced down at my twisting fingers, silver rings glinting in the dampened light. When I peeked up at Ben, I saw his eyes fixed on my hands.

"Are you scared?" he asked.

I huffed out a laugh. How dare he call me out so directly? "Of course I am."

His brow came down. "We don't have to do this, Jill. You're in the driver's seat. I won't be angry or disappointed if you decide this isn't right for you."

I looked away, hiding my face in my hair, before coming back with a tease. "Giving up on me already?"

He emitted a sound that was a cross between a sigh and a groan. "Could you give the adversarial attitude a rest for five minutes?"

If I could emit laser beams with my eyes, Ben would be incinerated. But it was better he thought I was mad than he realize I'd meant what I said.

"Look, I'm not *giving up on you*," he said. "And believe it or not, I actually find your attitude sexy most of the time. There, I said it. I'm only offering you an out—a reminder that we never have to do anything you don't want to do. If this isn't something we're both enthusiastic about, it shouldn't happen at all. I'll role play almost any-thing you want, but I've never been interested in being with someone in a non-consensual way."

I gulped at the way the phrase *role play* rolled off Ben's lips. He was once again the man who'd brushed one finger along my sleeve in that dive bar parking lot and proposed that I *use him*.

He really was the perfect fuck buddy for me. Just one phrase from his lips in the right tone was enough to overpower any trace of Oliv-er-related overthinking.

I gulped. "Could you maybe come sit back down, then? You're hovering, and it isn't helping. For the record, I do want to do this, so just...get that out of your head, okay?"

He nodded and went back to his side of the sectional.

"Circling back," I said, like some sort of corporate drone, "I got tested at my last appointment, and I haven't been with anyone since. I'm happy to share the results."

Ben took a pull from his beer. "I may have jumped the gun and gotten tested this morning in anticipation of this conversation. The results should be back soon, though I'm not overly concerned. I've always used condoms. Don't take my getting tested as a sign that I assumed we won't use them too. I would never assume that. I just...yeah."

I almost laughed. "This is weird, isn't it? Just laying all the cards on the table and talking about this so bluntly?"

"A little bit, yeah. Although, I honestly think it's the most mature approach I've ever taken toward sex. Maybe I should have tried this back in my twenties."

"Same," I said with a shy smile. "But I would be fine with no condoms, so long as our test results support that, and we're sexually exclusive. I have an IUD, and I track my cycle pretty religiously. I also, um..." I paused, tucking my hair behind my ear.

"Go on." I could hear the smirk he was failing to hide. I imagine that crooked incisor was creeping out from behind his lips.

"I may or may not have a thing for cream pies. *Not* that I've had much opportunity to try, but they definitely feature in some of my fantasies."

I braved a look across the expanse of the sofa at Ben. I could only see his profile, but his face and neck were red. A muscle in his jaw ticked. I had the impression that he was barely containing himself. That if I made the smallest shift, he would either be on top of me or halfway across the house, running away.

I brazened on. "There's this website we can look at, separately or together, where we can select our individual interests and boundaries. Things we like and don't like. It will only show us the areas where our interests match up. Would you want to do that instead of listing them now?"

"Yes, please," he said, jumping to his feet. "Separately. We'll do it separately. Send me the link, and I'll fill it out tomorrow." He snatched up his drained beer to bring into the kitchen.

"Are we done already?" I asked, following quietly behind him.

He hesitated, his back to me. "I don't know. Are we?"

"What about the emotional side of things?" The major reason I was here in the first place.

"We established that neither of us want emotions to be involved at all. I'll manage it. Will you?"

He held out his hand to take my empty water bottle, tossing it in the recycling bin. "I, uh—yes. I'll *manage*. Are you sure this is okay for you? I know you want a relationship. I don't want you to feel stuck in an arrangement that isn't meeting your needs."

"I wouldn't have offered if I didn't want to do it, Jill. I'll be fine. Besides, I want a relationship with the right person. You're not the right person, so I won't be in any danger of wanting more."

His glass beer bottle shattered in the bin where it fell.

Chapter Seventeen

Ben

I STARED AT MY laptop, the cursor blinking as I hovered over a set of multiple-choice bubbles about my sexual preferences. Questions on restraints, sex toys, positions, oral sex, and more. The list went on and on.

I'd never drilled down my own tastes like this. I liked what I liked and went with the flow. But I didn't want to mess this up for Jill—not when it was so important to her.

It was important to me too. I needed to get over this obsession with her so that I could move on, once and for all. If I got my own rocks off in the process, so be it.

When she'd been at my house last night, there was a moment I thought I'd screwed up already. When I'd assured her that my emotions wouldn't get involved, she'd looked...hurt. But after I finished picking up the shattered glass from my recycling bin, she was back to her normal self, giving me sass and teasing me about my plant collection.

Two things she made clear by the time she left were that we would not be kissing or having sleepovers as part of our arrangement. The sleepover part was a non-starter. I rarely slept an entire night with a woman anyway. I kept crazy hours during the summer, so it was better for everyone.

The no-kissing part I was less okay with. I *liked* kissing. It got me revved up. As far as I was concerned, it was up there with eating pussy as the best type of foreplay there was.

But kissing, for me, was also something I enjoyed simply for its own sake, even if it never went a step beyond. And Jill's lips had been a source of distraction for years, all pink and plumper on the bottom than the top. I would have to be content going the rest of my life never knowing their taste.

I'll have to make do with using my mouth in other ways, I thought as I checked off a *Yes* bubble labeled *Biting*. That could be fun.

I was discovering there wasn't much on the list that I *couldn't* picture doing with Jill, so long as it was just the two of us. Sharing her with someone else didn't sit right.

I wondered how much of this stuff she had tried with her dickbag of an ex. Would some of these topics trigger her memories of him? I shook my head to clear the thought. Jill was trusting me with her fantasies, and I needed to trust that she knew her own limits, even if she hadn't always shown the best judgment in the past.

If it went to hell, I would do my best to pick up the pieces.

I continued down the list after marking several *No* responses in the categories related to multiple partners. Hickeys, that was a check in the *Yes* column. I could start my trail of marks along Jill's smooth neck, just behind her ear, before moving to the curve of those plump little tits that were propped up so well in those dresses she liked to wear.

I shifted in my computer chair, navigating away from the sex questionnaire and opening up my accounting software. Something nice, dry, and boring.

If I were trying to get serious about finding a life partner, I'd be better off finding a woman who could help me balance my budget. But unless I stopped thinking about Jill, there was no point in looking.

Just before she'd left, Jill had asked me what I would do if I found The One during our three months together. I didn't have an answer. My head was determined to move on from the irreverent blonde, but my heart—and my dick—weren't so certain.

Shoving the heel of my hand down on my lap—hard enough to hurt—I willed my erection back into submission and took a bracing inhale before pulling the questionnaire back up.

Oh fuck, of course. The next question was about cream pies, and my mind was back on Jill. She'd claimed it as one of her fantasies, and I didn't hate the idea either. I'd practically ordered her out of my house when she'd said it, just to keep from jumping on her like an animal. I wanted nothing more than to let her feel my cum filling her up, leaking out before I stuffed it back inside with my fingers...

My phone rang, and I jolted out of my wheeled chair when I saw the name and photo pop up on the screen.

James.

Oh, hell.

I slowly stretched my arm toward the device, keeping the bulk of my body as far from it as possible, like I was reaching for a snake.

The real serpent in the room was me—the one having dirty, devious thoughts about my best friend's little sister.

I snatched up the ringing phone and slid my finger across the screen to answer.

"Hello, James. What's up?" I kept it calm, cool, and casual.

"Uh, hey. You okay? Your voice sounds really fucking weird right now."

"I'm fine! Totally fine."

"What are you up to tonight? I was thinking about swinging by Maven's for a burger and a beer. Emma's out with Kristi for the night, so I'm bored at home alone."

The pink screen of the questionnaire glared at me.

"I'm not doing anything at all. Just sitting here, by myself, not doing a thing."

"Okay, so do you want to meet me out, then? I know you said you're fine, but you sound like you could use a drink or two."

"Yeah, I think I do. Meet you in twenty?"

M AVEN'S WAS QUIET, THE parking lot deserted except for a few regulars. The wood-paneled walls of the bar were fading and familiar. A picture of the little league team I played on hung crookedly on the back wall. I spotted James at the bar, chatting to the long-time bartender, Ellie.

"Hey," I said as I propped my forearms on the bar top next to my friend.

"You made it," he said, clapping me on the back.

I was still getting used to the consistently happy version of James. It wasn't that he was *unhappy* before meeting Emma, but he was a lot less grumpy now. I knew he worried about Jill and their cousin, Harry, but he had someone to share his burdens with now.

"I put in an order for you. I hope you don't mind."

"Nah, it's cool. You remembered to tell the kitchen to hold the mayo, right, Ellie?" I nodded at the gray-haired bartender.

She responded with a sarcastic thumbs up. The woman was perpetually annoyed, and I loved it. I once heard her epically bitch out a G-State student's family for ordering milkshakes five minutes after they'd already placed an order for their other drinks.

"So, you're a free man tonight, huh?" I said, turning back to look at James.

"You make it sound like Emma keeps me prisoner or something. Trust me, I'd rather be home with her than out with your ugly ass."

I laughed, some of the tension I'd been holding in my shoulders releasing. I could do this—act normal with James while negotiating a relationship of sorts with Jill.

"You know I'm joking. I'd love to have what the two of you have."

"You'll find it—and when you're least expecting it. Then it'll change your life. Like, look at this," he said as he picked up his phone that was resting on the bar top. He flipped the screen to show me a picture of Emma and Kristi making goofy faces at the camera, their cheeks pressed close together. I could see the barest hint of a singer dressed in black on stage behind them. He shook his head, grinning to himself as he pulled the phone back in. "She's great. Who would have thought I'd look forward to getting a text message?"

Not me, that was for sure. The man rarely responded to me, and I was his best friend. I usually had to track him down with a phone call. "I'm happy for you. What are they up to tonight without their third partner-in-crime?" I asked, fishing for more information on Jill.

Be a little more subtle, dude.

"Seeing a band Kristi loves. I guess their songs are a little too 'dark and ominous,' according to Jill. Plus, Emma said Jill was busy tonight anyway."

"Oh." I scratched the back of my neck. "Busy with what?"

James shot me a look from the corner of his eye, his brow furrowing. "Work at Velvet, apparently. Why—"

Luckily, Ellie chose that precise moment to slide over two plates spilling over with French fries, distracting him. The delicious greasiness of the food at Maven's more than made up for its taciturn serving staff.

James seemed to have moved on as we ate, chatting about work projects and wedding planning.

"Just so you know," he said, "I'm planning to make you and Harry co-best men. Harry's not too happy about splitting the duty, but I think it's for the best."

My ears grew hot. I'd never been anyone's best man before. "Wow. Damn, dude, I'm honored. Thank you."

James reached over and wrapped one of his long arms around my shoulders, pulling me into a bracing side-hug before digging back into his burger. "Wouldn't have anyone else standing up with me. You're my best friend. I'm only sorry for setting Harry on you. I don't know what sorts of antics he has up his sleeve."

Harry was an interesting guy. He was annoyingly talented at almost everything he tried, pathologically competitive, and wildly chaotic. Any ideas he had for the wedding were guaranteed to be both creative and disastrous at the same time. Deep down, I knew he truly cared about James, Emma, and Jill.

A commercial blared from the TV above the bar, piercing through the sentimentality.

Have you been searching for love in all the wrong places? The voiceover was practically shouting at me. I couldn't help but feel targeted.

If you're looking for a chance to sail away from the single life and tie the sailor's knot with the person of your dreams, you need to audition for Nauti or Nice, *next summer's hottest cruise-ship reality show!*

Well, forget that. If there was one thing I couldn't stand, it was reality TV.

James broke in with a chuckle. "What the hell is this shit? *Nauti or Nice?* Sail away from singlehood? I always wonder about the people who audition for these shows. Someone pretty desperate for love, if I had to guess."

"I'm not sure anyone on those shows is actually looking for love. More like fame and advertising opportunities."

"Yeah, you're probably right," James said as he polished off his meal. "But getting back to the wedding topic, Jill is gonna be the maid of honor. Do you think things will be okay if you're both involved with the planning? Is Jill tolerating you?"

I swallowed a French fry wrong and reached for my beer, chugging down the remaining third of the glass. I'd nearly forgotten that Jill had somehow convinced herself and half the town that she hated me.

"Yeah. I think so," I finally managed to reply.

An alert chimed on my phone, and I pulled up the screen, surprised to see the name of the site where I had filled out the sexual compatibility survey for Jill.

That could only mean one thing—Jill had just sent me her list of sexual preferences while I was sitting directly next to her brother.

Chapter Eighteen

Jill

WHEN I'D STRUCK A sex deal with Ben Till, I hadn't considered how often I would have to see him during daytime, non-sex hours. Not that I strictly believed sex to be a nighttime activity, but when both parties were gainfully employed adults, it worked out that way. I had creature cocks to sell and rundown buildings to renovate. He had holes to dig and yards to beautify. We couldn't be devoting all hours of the day to fucking.

I'd been brave last night, being the first to send over my questionnaire answers. I had been checking my email almost every hour in search of a response from Ben that still hadn't come. Was he reading my answers, judging them, and basing his own around them? I hoped not. I wanted to know the real, raw Ben. Not the polished, gentlemanly version of him—the one he thought he was supposed to show to the world.

I wanted the dirty, *use-me* Ben, not the buttoned-up mayor's son.

As I waited for him outside Velvet to continue work in the sinking yard, I looked at my phone again, pulling up my emails.

Refresh.

Refresh.

Refresh.

Nothing. Was the cell phone reception here shit?

Or was Ben having second thoughts already? If he was, he needed to tell me—today—so I could move on, forget his silly little suggestion that he could help me get over my insecurities, and stop thinking about using him as my personal sex toy.

I heard the rumble of his white truck rounding the corner, and swore I felt an answering tingle beneath my skirt.

"Good morning," I said as he opened the truck door, then slammed it shut with barely a nod.

He shot me a blistering look as he stalked to the bed of the vehicle for our shovels. He thrust one into my hand without a word and clopped over to the dig spot.

I followed slowly behind him, wary of his mood. Was he annoyed about something I'd put on my survey? Was that the real reason he hadn't sent it back yet?

"What seems to be the problem this morning?" I asked, attempting civility, even though he was the one who should be begging for my forgiveness for not returning that damn questionnaire.

"*You* are my problem, Jill." He turned on me, spiking his shovel into the soil.

"What did I do?" I hadn't seen him since I'd left his house the other night. Right after he'd more or less suggested that if he found his dream girl in the next three months, our deal was off.

Those light eyes flashed as he gestured toward me with flailing arms. "You're just...*there!* Being fucking cute and wearing a fucking *dress* to scoop dirt all morning!"

I looked down at the fluttery Lycra skirt, fingering the fabric. There was nothing offensive about it. "It's an athletic dress. It's fine if it gets dirty. And my naked legs weren't harmed last time."

"That isn't the point," he said through gritted teeth.

"Then what is the point, Ben?"

He took the four steps it took to get to me, the tips of his muddy boots brushing the toes of my worn canvas sneakers. "The point is that you're distracting as hell. The point is that you sent me that list of all the things you want to try while I was hanging out with your brother. The point is that I can't get you out of my head. You're everywhere I go, and I can't catch a break."

He panted in the sliver of space between us. My heart thrummed wildly in my chest. I swallowed. Ben's eyes tracked the bob of my throat. I'd known he was attracted to me—his offer to sleep with me had confirmed that. But this? The teeth-gnashing, feral energy he was throwing off both frightened and turned me on.

I worked to clear my throat again. "You know, it's okay if you think about me. If we aren't physically attracted to each other, this will never work."

He rocked back on his heels, running a flat palm over the top of his scalp. "I know that, but..."

That was a dash of cold water on the simmering flame of my interest. "But you don't *want* to want me, right?" Maybe I didn't love the idea of being in a relationship, but the thought of being wanted by someone against their will? I liked that even less. He was into me, and he resented me for it. To hear him all but admit it was a punch to the gut.

This was exactly why my boundaries were important. I had to keep them front and center.

"It sounds awful when you put it like that."

"Yeah, it does, doesn't it?" And it *felt* even worse.

I shifted the shovel in my grip and sidestepped away, intending to go back to work on our hole. One day, it would be big enough that I could jump in and bury myself under a mountain of embarrassment.

"Jill, wait." His warm hand at my wrist stopped me.

I whirled on him, tugging away, my skirt flying in a circle around my thighs. "No! I'm trying to put myself out there, and it's fucking hard, Ben! If you're not serious about being my *friend with benefits*, then just leave me alone. We can dig this hole and be done with it. I'll see you at the wedding, and we'll be civil, and *nice*, and we can move on."

"I am serious about this. I mean it." Red tinged the upper slopes of his cheekbones.

"Then why haven't you sent back the questionnaire? I sent you mine. Don't you realize how fucking vulnerable that feels for me? I talk a lot of shit, but I'm not made of Teflon." My armor didn't work around Ben. He kept finding ways to poke holes in it.

He blinked. "I do realize, and I did send you back the questions."

"No, you didn't. I've been checking my emails all morning, and there's nothing from you. You don't need to lie to make me feel better."

"Yes, I did. I'm not lying, Jill. I promise. Here," he said, tugging his phone from his back pocket. He brought the screen to life and scrolled for a few seconds before angling it toward me.

Sure enough, there it was in his *sent* email folder. My face grew hot, and I cursed my fair skin.

I cleared my throat as he took his phone back. "Let me just, uh...take another peek," I said, avoiding eye contact with him as I opened up my own phone.

I stared at the email, right there at the top of my spam folder, in bold text and unopened. I was an idiot.

"Did you find it?" Ben asked. His words were measured and quiet. Patient. I wasn't sure I deserved that consideration from him. But then again, he had exploded on me too.

"Yes. It's there. It went to spam. I should probably change the settings on my email account."

"Open it."

I lifted my focus from the mountain of unread emails. "What?"

"You heard me. Open it. I want you to read my answers."

"Right here? In front of you?"

"You said I made you feel vulnerable when you thought I didn't reply. Now you get to return the favor. Watching you read my answers sounds like my worst nightmare, but I'll do it for you. Make me feel vulnerable too."

Was he nuts? "That's—that's crazy. We don't need to do this. I'll read it later."

"Open it, Blossom." He placed his hand on mine, stopping me from putting the phone away. His skin was warm and rough, the dark-green, vibrant red, and shiny black shades of his tattoos rippling in the sun. "Do you think I can't handle knowing you're taking a full inventory of all the things I'd like to do to your body? How I'd like to pull the neckline of that silly dress down so I can suck on your nipples until they're red and hard? How I'd like to slide my hand up under those little skirts you like to wear? Now, go ahead and open it. I promise I can take it."

Oh, my god. Who was this man, and what the hell had he done with the Ben Till who blushed when I said the word sex? I fought the urge to squirm under the heavy weight of his scrutiny.

"What are you waiting for?" he whispered.

That was a dare, and now I wanted to play. He released my hand and stepped back when he realized I wasn't going anywhere.

I squinted from the reflection of the blistering sun off the questionnaire's bright-pink background, gulping as the first set of questions loaded. The title was *"Things to Do with Your Mouth."* I'd already nixed the kissing, but evidently Ben wanted to do everything else on the list. Lip biting, nipple sucking, pussy licking.

I couldn't take the pressure of reading the rest while he stared at me, leaning so sexily on that shovel, smelling like mint shampoo and fresh soil. Until now, I'd never found the odor of dirt at all appealing. On Ben, it was delicious.

"Um. This looks great," I said, flicking my thumb while pretending to read the full list.

He chuckled under his breath. "I know you didn't read all of it. What are you so scared of, Blossom?"

He was still a pace away, but I was melting under his gaze. "I'm just hot and uncomfortable. It's a scorcher today, am I right?" I fanned myself with a flat palm, cringing inwardly at my awkwardness.

Ben's off-kilter incisor peeked out from behind his lip, catching the soft-looking flesh in its grip. He looked poised to say something then hesitated, as if reconsidering, before shaking his head once. "I got my test results back this morning. I'm all clear. What about you?"

"Oh." The abrupt change in topic threw me off, though I was grateful for it. "Yes. All good for me too. Want me to send you a screen shot?"

"Sure. I'll do the same." He went back to scooping out his side of the hole, moving far faster than I was.

"Okay." I shifted my weight from side to side. "What's next, then?"

"Are you all in? Because I am."

"Yes. Of course." We'd come this far already, and now that both my mind and body were aboard the Ben Train, I wasn't sure I wanted to bother trying to resist him.

"I'm, uh...sorry for exploding on you earlier," he said. "I am attracted to you—obviously—but casual sex is a new arena for me. I'm good with our arrangement, but bear with me while I get used to it, okay?"

"I...sure. Yeah. Okay." I doubted I would ever fully understand what was going on in Ben Till's head, but if he said he was willing, I would take him at his word.

"So, with the *friend with benefits* thing, we're supposed to be friends first, right?"

"Yes?"

He continued. "I think the problem you were having on those bland, boring dates was that you were going into them with the wrong approach."

"Oh, Benny Boy, my dates were not *bland and boring*. The people I was dating were simply incompatible with me. Nothing more, nothing less."

"It wasn't a personal affront. And you can keep lying to yourself about the dates, but don't forget that I witnessed one. It was like watching a stand-up comic bomb on stage—up close and in person. You cared more about what I was doing with Casey than anything that dude had to say."

I crossed my arms over my chest, still holding my shovel in one hand. It went flying, and I barely shifted in time to save my shins from a brutal whack. "It's funny that you say you didn't mean your comment to be a personal attack and then proceed to compare me to one of the most secondhand-embarrassment-inducing scenarios I could possibly imagine. Dick move, Ben. Dick move."

He was looking down at the hole we were digging, but I could see the white flash of teeth he tried to smother.

We moved more dirt in silence, though I spent more time watching the way Ben's tattooed biceps and forearms flexed around the shaft of his shovel than I did digging.

I should not be thinking about Ben and shafts at the same time—at least not until we hit the benefits portion of our friendship.

"What did you mean about my approach with my dates?"

He flicked his eyes up to mine. I caught his gaze lingering on the expanse of my legs, but he glanced back down at the ground. The hole was fairly deep now, and I imagined we would finish digging it soon. All that would be left after that was filling it with stone and soil and then planting the flowers we'd chosen.

Part of me would miss these early morning meetings with Ben—the sadistic side of me, that is. I hated getting up early, and I didn't see that changing anytime soon.

"You were starting out all wrong. You went in right off the bat with romance." He raised a hand to stop me from interrupting. "I realize romance isn't the right word. Trust me, I'm well aware you don't want a commitment. But you went in with the wrong focus. If you want a *friend with benefits*, you've got to start out being friends."

"But you and I aren't friends."

"Aren't we?"

We had been—once. Now, I wasn't so sure what we were. Friends didn't talk about friends the way I'd heard him talking about me.

"See, Blossom," he said, "the fact that you can't answer that means we have work to do. What's something you like to do with your friends? With Emma or Kristi?"

"Sit on couches and drink wine. Or sit in coffee shops and drink lattes. Or sit on park benches and chug water while we pretend to exercise, but people-watch instead."

When I broke it down like that, it was a wonder I wasn't constantly peeing. The intensity of all that sipping was astounding.

The corner of Ben's lip tipped up.

"Look, I get that all that doesn't exactly sound thrilling, but what do you and James do? Go to the gym and toss around metal plates? Complain about being your own boss and making your own sched-ule?"

He was outright laughing now, holding his stomach and every-thing.

"Are you done?" I asked, twisting my lips as he swiped away a tear.

"Hoo, boy, that was good. And honestly, you kind of nailed it. I guess I never really thought about how mundane everyday friendship can be."

"That's what makes it so great, though, I think. Finding people you can just sit and do nothing with, but still make it fun."

"Yeah. You make a good point."

He smiled, straight and true, right at me.

"There's got to be something else you do for fun? You mentioned a friend, Glenn, the other day."

I couldn't believe he remembered. "He works at the library with me. But we also both hang out at The Out Alliance which is where I really got to know him."

"That's the local LGBTQ group, right?"

"It is...how do you know about it?"

"My sister used to go sometimes before she moved to California. I think it's cool you do that."

I felt myself blushing under his attention. I wasn't ashamed of my sexuality, but it had been a sore spot for others before. "It helps me feel connected to my community. To acknowledge that I'm still bisexual, whether I'm with a woman or a man or no one at all."

"I'm glad you have that, a community of people who get you." He toyed with the handle of his shovel. "Are you free tonight?"

"I am."

He nodded slowly. "What do you say we go to Fair Street Park? We can walk the loop for our first official friend outing. I'll bring the beverages. You can show me the best spots to people-watch."

"I would love that."

CHAPTER NINETEEN

Ben

T HE PARK WAS BUSY, which was both good and bad. Good, because it prevented me from doing all the dirty things I wanted to do to Jill far too soon into our friendship, but bad in that it also meant our first friend date would have multiple witnesses. I wasn't ashamed to be friends with Jill, but every so often, I got a sticky feeling in my gut when I thought of how James would feel about me being with his sister like this.

I shook my head clear of the worry. I'd kept my complicated feelings for Jill close to the vest for this long. I could keep up the act, be her friend, and give her what she needed. It couldn't be anything more than that, so James didn't need to know.

I rubbed my thumb along the ridges of the water bottle I held in my left hand—a match to the one in my right. I drew sidelong glances from a group of teenagers carrying tennis rackets as I paced at the park's entrance. Hadn't they ever seen a man in his thirties pacing before? Just for the dirty looks, I wouldn't warn them about the cranky old man who lived in the tiny white icebox house that bordered the tennis court. He loved to chase off rowdy groups of kids.

"Hey, Ben!"

I whipped my head around at the approaching voice. The water bottles I held slipped through my fingers, dropping to the pavement with a loud smack.

It was Emma. Did that mean James was here too?

"Oops, runaway water!" Emma said with a laugh as she halted the barreling bottle with the toe of her sneaker. I reached down and grabbed the other one, which had luckily landed close to my own shoe.

"Thank you," I said, snatching back the water she held out to me.

"Out for a walk today?"

"Sure am. What about you?" I asked, hoping she would mention whether she was alone.

"I'm working a community event today, so I figured I'd get a little exercise before I'm stuck behind a table all afternoon. I'm just passing through." She coordinated events for the local library. The large brick building was a straight shot across the park on the opposite side of Main Street.

"That's cool. Good for you. Exercise is a great and healthy habit."

What was I saying? At least I'd confirmed she was on her own, though. My best friend was nowhere in sight.

"Well, you know James and his workout routines. I'm not on that level, but he inspired me. I figure the more active and mobile I stay, the better off I'll be in the future." Emma had been pretty badly hurt when she was hit by a car a couple years before she moved to town. James didn't talk about it much, but from the little he'd shared, I knew she did her best to manage the associated pain that came with her old injuries.

"Well, I'd better get going," she said. "Can't be late when I'm running the event."

"Actually, I think that's one of the few times you *can* be late."

"You make a valid point. Enjoy your walk. I hope your date has fun too." Emma gave a sly grin and tipped her chin at the two bottles I was clutching before spinning around and heading off toward the library. I almost stopped her to correct her assumption, but I stayed silent.

Did I want this to be an actual date?

No. It couldn't be. Jill was dead set against anything serious, and serious was all I wanted. It was only my obsession with her that was holding me back. I was going to get over her. Once I did that, my life would be back on track.

The woman at the center of my thoughts came meandering up the asphalt path. I watched as she searched for something in her over-sized shoulder bag, paying me—and the rest of the people in the park—no mind.

As usual, she was wearing a dress. A floaty, red one that fluttered around her knees as she walked. The neckline curved into a point in the middle of her cleavage, like the top portion of a heart. Her brown sandals made flopping noises down the pathway.

I glanced down at my own attire, suddenly feeling underdressed in my plain black t-shirt and loose gym shorts. Next to Jill, I looked like an absolute slob.

She almost walked past me, still fiddling with her bag, but I stopped her in time with a quiet greeting.

She nearly jumped out of her skin. "Sorry, I didn't see you."

"Yeah, I gathered as much."

She didn't even notice me standing next to her. Meanwhile, I had been studying her like she was my next meal. I really needed to take advantage of the benefits side of this friendship before I turned into some sort of wild beast.

I cleared my throat. "What were you looking for?"

"Huh?"

"In your bag. You seemed pretty intent on finding something in there."

"Oh, James gave me the number for some guy that can help with the front sign for Velvet. He wrote it down on a piece of paper, but now I can't find it anywhere. There's so much I still have to do, and I'm running out of time."

"I think I know who you're talking about. He helped with my yard signs, but he does larger projects too. I'll send you the number."

She dropped her grip on her bag, her shoulders slumping in relief. "Thank you so much. I've been so overwhelmed. Sometimes I wonder if I knew what I was getting myself into with this whole Velvet thing. I don't want to give up, but...well. It's hard not to get discouraged sometimes."

I took a chance and placed a hand on the smooth cap of her shoulder. A sprinkle of light freckles dusted the area, and I fought the urge to trace the constellation with my thumb.

Instead, I settled on a brief, friendly squeeze and let go. "You're doing a great job, Jill," I said, surprised at how much I meant it. Jill's past ventures had all gone the wrong way, but so far, she had her act together with Velvet. "It's always hard at the beginning. I can't tell you how many times I screwed up when I first started Till Lawn and Landscape."

"I'm sure you're right, but it's hard to see where you and James are at in your careers and not feel inadequate. Heck, even Harry is doing well at the garage, and he's the most disorganized person I know." She shook her head, her blonde locks flying in a wild frizz. "I'm tired of talking about things that are going wrong. Shall we walk and check out the locals?"

"We can do that. Those kids over there are about to get screamed at for playing tennis. Wanna watch?"

She pressed a fluttering hand to the skin bared by that infuriatingly distracting neckline. "Benny Boy, it's almost like you know me. I would *love* to watch that."

J ILL PASSED ME A small sandwich bag of buttered popcorn as we sat on an uncomfortable park bench, witnessing three teen boys getting chased off the tennis courts by a man in a half-open orange bathrobe.

"Do you think he realizes that people are supposed to play tennis on tennis courts?"

"I doubt it. I don't think he even knows we can see half his ass hanging out of that robe," I replied as I tossed a handful of popcorn in my mouth.

"This is better than a movie."

"Good thing you brought the ideal snack."

"You said you'd supply the beverages. I figured I needed to step it up for the people-watching portion of the afternoon. This did not disappoint."

"Did that guy ever chase off Baby Blossom and her friends back in the day?"

Jill snorted. "Hardly. You think I played tennis? I was a band kid. I have zero hand-eye coordination."

"Hey, I know plenty of people who were into hobbies you'd never expect. Your cousin is one of them. He's on the rec hockey team with me, but I've seen him at trivia nights and down at the bowling alley."

"Sure, and what do all those things have in common, Benny?"

I waited for her response while she scooped up another handful of popcorn.

"Competition. Harry doesn't advertise it, but he's competitive as hell. He'll try any activity as long as there's a chance to come out the victor. He'll spend years practicing until he can. I'd admire it if he wasn't so obnoxious about it."

"I guess that tracks. He does get pretty into it during our games. Most of the other people are just there to have fun."

"I always forget you play hockey. It makes sense. You do have a bit of a bubble butt."

I coughed, inhaling a chunk of dry popcorn. Jill slapped me soundly on the upper back until I cleared it out.

"I shouldn't be surprised anymore by the things you say, but somehow, I still am. And it's not like I'm some hockey star. It's just the rec league."

She shrugged nonchalantly, but I could make out the edges of a preening smile forming on her lips.

"How is the painting going at Velvet?" I asked, changing the subject to one that didn't focus on my backside.

"Oh, god, don't remind me," she groaned.

"That bad, huh?" Maybe she needed a painting partner—needed *me*—again.

"The painting itself isn't bad. But I got ahead of myself. James still has to finish the bar, and the floors aren't done either. The wall got a huge scuff mark across it. I should have waited."

"You've still got the paint cans, though, right?"

She looked at me from the corner of her eye. "I do."

"So just paint over it again. No big deal. And since you haven't finished the floors, any paint you spill won't matter. Not every mishap is a catastrophic failure. You're doing just fine, Jill."

She leaned closer to me, her bare shoulder brushing mine. I wasn't sure she even realized she was doing it, but the contact had my nerves sparking.

"Who are you, Ben Till?"

I met her gaze head on, noting the ring of darker brown around her irises. "I'm the same me I've always been. Maybe you just weren't paying attention."

Because I'd been paying attention to her, even when it didn't serve me.

She took a sip of her water. I followed the movement of her throat as she swallowed, watched her pink lips tip up into a mysterious smile.

"Maybe not. So, what's the plan from here?"

"You want to come back to my place?"

"Yes. Yes, I do."

Chapter Twenty

Jill

He let me park in the garage this time, next to the flashy red car I rarely saw him drive. The interior door slowly opened as he waited for me, holding it open like a gentleman as I stepped across the grease-stained floor.

I couldn't stop the trails of shivers up my back at the thought that he was about to treat me in the most ungentlemanly of ways. Did his put-together, perfectly suitable dates see that side of him, or would I be the first?

I ducked under his arm, our eyes meeting as I crossed the threshold into the house.

I felt his attention on me as I led the way through the kitchen and into the living room. I paused at the side of that large sectional and spun to face him.

"Should we—"

He pressed a firm finger to my open lips, halting my next words.

"I think we've talked enough, don't you?"

I could almost taste the salt of his skin on my tongue. I debated taking that index finger into my mouth and sucking it in. But Ben's face, still and serious, stopped me. I suspected if I tapped on his jaw, a piece of it might chip away.

I nodded wordlessly, and he removed his finger, robbing me of his touch.

"My bedroom is down the hall. The third door on the left. Go in there, and lie down on the bed."

"What about—"

"I'll be there in a few minutes. Now go."

I listened. Because what else was there to do when he was being all hard and commanding? I had said I would be open to that sort of thing on our questionnaire, and so far, I liked it. A lot. I wasn't sure it would be enough to slip past my hangups, but I was willing to try.

I resisted the temptation to open every closed, white-framed door as I trailed my hand along the wall. The motherload of all Ben Till's secrets was awaiting me at the end of the journey.

The door knob was cold in my palm. A shot of adrenaline rushed through me, and I was grateful to Ben for allowing me this moment of privacy so he couldn't witness the way I trembled.

It was just a bedroom. One that wasn't dirty, but not as tidy as I would have expected either. Spilled-out contents of a file folder and a pile of loose change sat atop a plain black dresser. Cords from a wall-mounted TV awkwardly stretched down the wall toward an outlet, with no effort to cleverly conceal them. A stiff armchair sat in the corner next to a large potted plant.

The bed, king-sized and covered in a midnight-blue comforter, loomed large in the center of the room. I kicked off my sandals, letting my feet sink into the thick, beige carpet as I padded over to the bed, setting one knee atop the high frame and then the other. I hadn't bothered turning on the overhead light—one of those generic boob-shaped fixtures. A ray of late-afternoon sun filtered in through the thick curtains.

Ben entered the room before I had the chance to turn fully around. I twisted at my hips and simply watched him. He didn't acknowledge my presence, just went about his business, emptying the change from his wallet onto the dresser.

Plink. Plink. Plink. Each coin fell one by one.

Somehow, his complete and total indifference was turning me on like nothing ever had before. I wanted to smash through that, ruffle his feathers, make him feral.

Scooting toward the end of the mattress, I draped my legs over the side of the bed, crossing the right leg on top of the left. I'd caught Ben eyeing my legs today when he thought I wasn't paying attention.

He finally looked away from his pile of change and stared me down. A draft of cool air from the air vent brushed over my skin, spiking the fine hairs along my arms.

"Open the nightstand," he said with a tip of his chin.

"Oh, uh, okay. But I thought we decided, since both our test results came back negative, that we didn't need to use condoms? Unless you're worried about contraception, in which case that's totally fine. I don't mind—"

"Open the nightstand, Blossom, and stop asking questions."

I started an undignified shuffle along the bedspread, moving toward the boring black nightstand wedged between the wall and the bed frame. I was surprised my brother tolerated his friend's boring, awful taste in furniture. Aside from the wealth of plants, it looked like Ben had furnished the house with things he'd assembled from a box. It was odd, given that he had lived here for years.

I glanced over my shoulder just before I reached for the drawer's handle. Ben was sitting in that armchair, the clothes folded atop it now littered on the carpeted floor.

He sat with spread legs, looking like a king surveying his kingdom of dirty laundry and wanton women—well, just the one wanton woman, really.

I hesitated again. Weren't we supposed to be touching each other? "How are we going to do this if you're all the way over there?"

He shook his head slowly from side to side. "You don't listen very well, do you?"

"It's like you've never met me before," I joked, but the words were shaky.

"You're going to open that drawer, and I'm going to stay right where I am. Because I won't be touching you—not tonight, at least."

The mental image of Ben's questionnaire answers popped into my head, crawling along the backs of my eyelids. *Do you like to watch your partner?* And the corresponding question: *Do you like to be watched?*

I gulped, reaching my trembling fingers toward the drawer. The wood groaned as I tugged it open.

Inside rested a pale-blue vibrator, one nearly identical to the one I had at home in my treasure chest of toys. I picked it up in a delicate grip and turned to face Ben.

He was rigid, his knuckles white where they grasped the arms of the chair. I could see indents in the fabric where his fingertips pressed.

He wasn't so unaffected, after all.

I sat on my knees, twirled the vibrator like a majorette, and waited for his next order.

I wasn't waiting long.

"Move the pillows and lie down."

I did as he instructed until I was flat on my back and couldn't see him anymore.

"What now?" I asked the ceiling, my breath coming faster.

"Pull your dress up."

I reached for the skirt of the dress with my free hand, dragging it up the center of my body, brushing across my clit with the side of my palm. I couldn't hold back the sigh, not when I was so keyed up. I needed more. More pressure, more touching, more *Ben.* If only he weren't so damn far away.

"Did I tell you to touch yourself?" The words were strained, like he'd said them from between gritted teeth.

"No, but it felt good." I didn't care if he got mad. I'd been wanting this for too long—since that night outside the dive bar, if I were being honest. All I needed was a little relief.

He grunted in response, and I smiled at the blades of the ceiling fan.

"You can turn the vibrator on now since you're so impatient."

I barked out a laugh. "Does it surprise you that I'm not patient?"

He chuckled in response. "It shouldn't. But somehow, I'm always surprised by you, Blossom. Now, quit stalling."

My thumb hovered over the silicone button. What if I couldn't do this? What if Ben fulfilled his end of the bargain, made all my fantasies come true, and I *still* wasn't any good at sex?

What if Oliver still won, no matter what I did?

"I'm nervous, Ben," I confessed.

"I know you are." Did I imagine his voice sounding closer to the bed? "That's why we're starting out slow," he continued. "I know you know how to get yourself off. So today, you're going to show me how to do it. For next time."

"I haven't done anything like this before. I talked a big game when we answered those questions. What if I—"

"Jill, stop."

I pinched my eyelids shut, but it did nothing to stop the sick, insidious voice in my head.

Can you stop? The faces you're making are killing the mood.

Ugh, you're too wet. It's making a mess, and I don't have enough quarters to do laundry this week.

I can't stay hard because you keep crying.

"Jill." I felt the edge of the mattress depress next to me as Ben's voice cut through the noise. "I'm gonna go," he said.

I shot up, shoving my skirt back down over my knees. "No! Don't do that. I want this, I promise." And I did. Because I refused to let some asshole continue to break me years down the road.

"It's okay." Ben ran a flat palm over the crown of his head. "I'm just going to leave the room for a minute or two. I'll...get a beer or something, let you collect yourself and get comfortable. You do what you normally like to do when you're alone. I'll come in to watch, but you won't even know I'm here. How does that sound?"

It wasn't a bad idea. But...

"Will you talk to me again? When you come back in?" If Ben was talking to me, then maybe I could ignore the nagging inner monologue.

He smirked, and I almost died.

"Just so we're clear, you want me to...talk you through it?"

"Um, yeah?"

"It's a yes or no answer."

"Yes."

"Any other requests?"

"Well, I did kinda like it when you acted all...aloof over there." I gestured toward the armchair.

"You thought I was aloof?"

"Weren't you?"

"Hardly," he said, rising from the bed and walking out the door.

Chapter Twenty-One

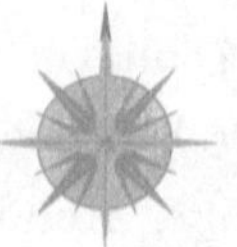

Jill

I RECLINED BACK THE instant the door closed, the soft snick of the latch a loud echo. I rucked my skirt up over my hips, not bothering with delicacy this time. There was no one here to impress. No one was judging me. I was in control. It was only me, just like when I was home alone.

I reached for my underwear, tugging the black lace down below my knees, then used my feet to shimmy them the rest of the way off. I shivered as another cool draft from the air conditioner washed over my damp skin. For a moment, I considered sinking under the thick comforter. Would it be better, more mysterious, if Ben could only guess what I was doing under the covers?

No, I decided. I wanted him to see me in all my glory. Because I was *good* at making myself come, and I was damn proud of that.

I brought my knees up, placing my feet flat on the bed as I clasped the shaft of the vibrator in a tight fist, letting the silicone warm up in my palm. I heard movement from the kitchen—the clink of a glass, the muffled seal of the refrigerator shutting. *Ben.*

A rush of wet heat pooled in my lower belly. Just knowing he was out there and might walk in at any moment had my body buzzing.

Unable to wait another second, I triggered the switch on the side of the toy and got to work, dragging it along my slick skin, running it over my clit a few times, and then dipping it inside. I pumped slowly at first, taking in the tip as my body adjusted to the intrusion.

Something dragged over the tile in the kitchen—probably the legs of a dining chair scraping—and I moaned loudly, wanting him to hear, wanting to tear apart that shield of indifference he was keeping so firmly in place tonight.

Footfalls sounded from somewhere in the house, and I worked the vibrator in and out, timing each thrust with his steps.

Soon, I was panting, fucking myself with abandon, eyes squeezed tight and head thrashing against the comforter. I was past the point of caring if I made a mess of the bed, if I made an odd face, or if Ben ever came back into this room.

"How does that toy feel inside you? I bet that greedy pussy is squeezing it so hard right now."

"Oh, fuck!" My back bowed as Ben's voice came from out of nowhere. When had he come back into the room? My eyes popped open and I started to rise, searching for him.

"No, don't open your eyes. Keep fucking yourself, Blossom, so I can see just how you like it."

If I had to guess from the nearness of his voice, he was right up close, watching me as I played. I settled back in, twisting the vibrator as I pressed it slowly in and out, letting him see the way the cool blue shaft was coated in my arousal.

"That clit of yours is just begging for attention. Do you like it rubbed hard? I bet you do."

"I do," I said, nodding frantically. God, he was really going for it with my *talk me through it* request, and it was working for me in the best way.

"Then what are you waiting for? Touch yourself so I can see."

I brought the heel of my free hand down to press against that sensitive place. My hips jogged involuntarily with the contact.

"Ahh, there you go. I bet you're so wet right now, aren't you?"

I nodded. But was that something he liked? Oliver had thought I got *too* wet.

"Good," he snarled, sending that insecurity off into the sunset. "I want to see it all over that vibrator. Soak my fucking bed, Blossom."

I bore down and rolled my hand over my clit, but the orgasm eluded me.

"Ben," I gasped. "I can't."

"Yes, you can. You're doing amazing. I want that orgasm you're working up to, and you're going to give it to me."

"I need more," I said, humping my hips in the air.

"I won't touch you tonight, Jill."

I whined, feeling no shame. "Please, I need something."

The surface of the bed depressed around my hips, and my eyes shot open. Ben could yell at me all he wanted, but I needed to see him, needed to see that he was Ben and not somebody else.

He straddled me, knee to knee, hovering over me, careful not to make contact. Bringing an inked hand to the waistband of his gym shorts, he tugged it down a fraction.

"Is this okay?" he asked.

I swallowed, trying to get some relief for my suddenly dry throat. This was about to get even more real. I was about to see Ben Till's cock. "Yes."

There was no hint of blue left in his irises as he dragged the silky fabric down to reveal himself fully.

His dick was the prototype of dicks. The one all other dicks aspired to be. It was thick and long, but not too long. A drop of pre-cum glistened at the head. The *pierced* head.

Ben Till had a pierced cock.

"Who the fuck are you?"

He smirked. "Didn't I tell you that you weren't paying attention?" He circled the pierced flesh in his fist, the silver barbell glinting in the final rays of light invading the room. "Are we going to come now, or what?"

The suggestion of his weight on top of me and the sight of his hand working his shaft were exactly what I needed. I started in again, timing the thrusts of the vibrator with his strokes, imagining it was him filling me instead of the toy.

"You're so fucking sexy," he said, his teeth gnashing. "You're going to take me so well. I bet you feel amazing."

His words, his clean dirt scent, his *everything* pushed me head first over the edge, my back bowing and hips twisting under him.

Holy shit. I did it. We did it.

A splash of wet heat hit my inner thighs as Ben's face contorted in a mix of pleasure and pain. I wanted his cum, and if he wasn't going to share it, I would take it. He stared at me, rapt, as I slid the toy out of me, gathered up a layer of ejaculate, and slowly pumped it up into me two, three times.

It was hot and slippery, making my inner muscles spasm once more at the thought of how debauched the fantasy was. Every secret, dirty part of me loved being filled with Ben.

"That's the hottest thing I've seen in my entire life." A bead of sweat dripped from his hairline and onto my chest. Our breathing faltered as his arms buckled, shaky on either side of my head. With a groan, he flopped to his side next to me.

I shifted to face him, unable to hold back my smile. He bit down on his own, grabbing his bottom lip in his teeth.

"I did it, Ben," I whispered. Beyond that momentary hiccup, I had been lost in the moment, not a thought of Oliver to be found.

"You are incredible, Blossom." He sounded like he meant it, but then why did he seem almost...sad?

"Well, when are we doing this again? Because I need all the practice I can get." I also wasn't willing to settle for mutual masturbation when I suspected that full-on sex with Ben would be mind-blowing.

A flicker of something resembling joyful surprise flickered across his face. "Oh! Whenever you're free. I can make time for you."

Maybe I'd only imagined the melancholy note in his voice. Apparently, the promise of more sex was enough to perk him up.

"Awesome," I said.

"Great," he breathed back. I felt the exhalation across my lips.

We were smiling at each other like a couple of idiots. I was tempted to shift, to burrow deeper into his side and stay there all night.

Boundaries.

I quickly sat up, giving Ben a perfunctory pat on the hip as I shimmied back into my underwear.

"I'm gonna head home to shower. That cream-pie thing is hot, but super messy, am I right?"

Now I sounded like a gross frat boy.

"Ah, okay."

"Talk tomorrow!" I said over my shoulder, practically running from the room.

The bewildered expression on Ben's face followed me all the way home.

Chapter Twenty-Two

Ben

I TIPPED THE HEAVY wheelbarrow, dumping a load of stone into the hole in Velvet's backyard. Jill wasn't around. She had an early shift at the library and couldn't get away.

I missed her like a lonely idiot. I was putting in the stone today—one of the last tasks left in taking care of Velvet's flood. When Jill had messaged me to say she couldn't make it, I was glad she couldn't see the disappointment on my face.

I was already getting the *friends with benefits* arrangement wrong. The whole point was to cure me of my feelings toward Jill. Instead, the itch under my skin—the *Jill* itch—had only grown worse.

She didn't seem so affected. After our joint masturbation session, she had taken one look at me, sprawled out and boneless beside her, cracked a joke, and hopped up from the bed like she hadn't just had the most mind-blowing sexual experience of her life.

I knew she had, though—or at least she'd come close. That look on her face afterward, the one of well-deserved pride in herself, had been unmistakable. She'd overcome something last night, something that was eating at her before I'd left the room. If I ever found the dickhead who'd put her in that headspace, my stance on violence would probably change.

But Jill had gotten past it—and in fine form. In fact, she had done so well I'd been worried that she wouldn't want to continue with our *friends with benefits* plan any longer.

Thank god she wasn't finished with me yet, because I needed more time. I wasn't even close to getting over her.

Luckily, she was willing to give me that time, slotting me in between a library shift, continued work at Velvet, and a shift selling fantasy dicks. I was impressed—and surprised—at how organized she was about it all. She hadn't been that way in the past.

We were meeting tonight at The Sticky Pig for dinner. Jill claimed that eating sloppy barbecue together would signal to everyone in town that we were platonic friends. Apparently, it was common knowledge that she wouldn't be caught dead getting *messy* if she were truly romantic with someone.

I would pretend, for her sake, that I wasn't aware of how wet and messy she could be. If checking the cream-pie fantasy off Jill's list had gone that well, I could only imagine the rest.

I looked up over my sunglasses as I heard the crunch of wheels on gravel, finding Harry Klein climbing out of a black sedan. James and Jill's cousin was alright enough, as long as you liked obnoxious, irresponsible people. But James, Emma, and Jill insisted he had a good heart underneath it all.

"Hey, Ben!" he called as he tripped down the slight decline toward me.

"Harry." I tipped my chin in greeting and got to work scraping the poured stone into some semblance of order.

"How's it going?"

"Fine." The less I responded to his questions, the fewer he asked. I'd learned that trick some time ago.

"It doesn't even look wet back here anymore. I wouldn't have guessed it was flooded recently. You and Jill have done a great job. She's really kicking ass with this place, isn't she?"

She was. He was being nice, and now I felt like an asshole for internally judging him. It wasn't Harry's fault he'd caught me in a moment of overthinking about his cousin.

"She's been working hard. I can't believe how far she's come."

"Who would have thought it of Jill, right? I mean, I know people say I'm all over the place, but I don't think she's ever stuck with anything before now."

I bristled at that. It wasn't far off from what I'd always thought of Jill myself, but now it struck me as unfair. Jill had transformed Velvet almost completely. So much so that I wondered if even my mother might manage a positive thought about the space.

"Maybe she didn't have anything worth sticking with until now."

"Oh, don't get me wrong," Harry said, clearly sensing my back was up. "I don't mean that as a dig. Jill can commit to things. She's as loyal as they come to the people she loves. She *is* serious when she decides something is important. It's just taken her longer than usual to find her passion."

"That's...shockingly astute of you."

He gave me a silly smile. "Hey, I've got hidden depths."

Maybe so, but I still didn't want him interrupting my morning. "So, what brings you by?"

"I wanted to run some ideas by you for Jemma's wedding."

"Who is Jemma, and why am I supposed to care about their wedding?"

"Jemma. Like James and…" He trailed off, rolling his hands as he waited for me to finish.

Oh. "Emma. I get it now."

"Anyway, I want to incorporate that name into their tagline somehow. Maybe a play on the word gem…" His eyes went glassy for a moment before he popped out of the trance. "I'll have to work on that one."

"Harry, I appreciate the enthusiasm, but I have a lot to get done today, and I don't even know what a tagline is. I doubt I'll be much help." It wasn't an excuse. After I finished up at Velvet, I was meeting Dany to lay mulch at another job site. Then, I had a meeting with a new client to review plans for a backyard pond and fountain. Jill would be lucky if I was awake enough to eat pulled pork tonight.

"Ben, a tagline is like…the first glimpse at the theme of the wedding. It sets the tone and gives the guests a hint about what to expect. It's *very* important, and if you're not going to take your responsibilities as co-best man seriously, I may have to bring my concerns about your fitness for duty to Jay."

Was he serious with this? "Have you actually met your cousin, Harry? I don't think he cares about taglines or guest expectations. He wants to marry Emma, and that's it."

He narrowed his eyes at me. "This attitude concerns me, Benjamin."

"What attitude? The one where I take my friend's personality into account?"

"You're crabby today. I know I'm not your favorite person—thankfully, I am many other people's favorite person, so it doesn't matter—but you're usually better at faking it. Are you feeling alright?"

I was not about to have a heart to heart with Harrison Klein. I would rank that alongside *drinking watery coffee* and *putting biodegradable autumn leaves in plastic bags* at the lowest tier of my list of preferred activities.

"I'm fine." My jaw whined from all the clenching.

"Dude, you look kinda crazy right now, I'm not gonna lie. I don't believe you."

I started walking my empty wheelbarrow back to my truck, hoping he would get the message and leave.

He didn't, instead following close at my heels.

I released the tailgate, ready to toss my equipment inside, but Harry got there first, scooping up the wheelbarrow and sliding it up.

"Uh, thanks."

"No problem, man," he said with a smile. "So like I was saying, it's really important that we talk about this wedding stuff. I've been planning to be Jay's best man for a long time, and I really don't want to screw it up for him. He's done a lot for me. We need to get this right. For Jemma."

"What is with you and Jill and this over-the-top need to make everything perfect for James? He's a simple guy."

I knew I'd fucked up the second Harry's eyes narrowed.

"Jill? What does Jill have to do with this? Have you been conspiring with her to oust me as co-best man? That is *not* okay. It's more than not okay. It's truly diabolical is what it is. I'm going to have to talk to Jemma about this, Ben."

He couldn't. Sure, James knew Jill and I were working together to take care of the flood. And I even figured he'd be alright with Jill and I eating dinner together. But I didn't trust Harry not to make my friendship with Jill sound like something...more. If he did that, James might ask more in-depth questions about my relationship with his sister, which might scare her off, which meant she might not want to continue our relationship anymore, and...my brain didn't want to follow that path.

"Harry, wait!" He stopped midway between our vehicles. "Jill and I haven't been talking about wedding stuff at all, so don't worry about that. We're...friends...now that we've gotten to know each other better while I'm helping with the yard."

He spun around and studied me closely. "You and Jill are friends?"

"Yes..."

"Are you sure about that?"

"I said it, didn't I?"

"That wasn't an answer."

"What are you, a detective now?"

He crossed his arms over his coveralls, his gaze taking on an uncharacteristic shrewdness. "I'm just a simple mechanic, Ben."

"What is happening right now?"

"That's an excellent question. What *is* happening with you and Jill?"

"I told you. We're friends."

"Okay, then tell me, what is Jill's favorite color?"

"This is stupid, Harry. I don't need to prove to you that Jill and I are actually friends."

"Another question dodged, Benjamin. Do I need to talk with Jill? Is this some weird delusion you have going on or something?"

He looked genuinely worried. If he brought this up to Jill and made her second-guess our arrangement... I had to give him *something*. "Jill's favorite color is pink, alright?"

"That question may have been too easy. It's pretty obvious Jill loves pink. How about...what did she study in college?"

He was being downright insulting if he thought I didn't know that. Granted, he didn't know I had paid *too much* attention to Jill over the years. "History," I said, crossing my arms over my chest. "But she was disappointed in the classes because they didn't focus enough on the *Ton* in Regency England."

Harry mirrored my posture. "I'm willing to give you that one. Maybe you and Jill really are friends now. But don't forget that she's been publicly claiming to hate you for over a year. Something is fishy here."

"Jill does not hate me. She mildly dislikes me."

"I'm highly skeptical. You look nervous."

"Who wouldn't be nervous while being interrogated?"

"This isn't an interrogation. It's a conversation. Does it *feel* like an interrogation to you? Do you have something to hide?"

I was done with this. If he didn't leave soon, I risked spilling my guts in sheer frustration, and that wasn't acceptable. I wouldn't compromise Jill's privacy that way. And I couldn't risk Harry and his loud mouth exposing us to James either. "Harry, Jill and I are adults, and we can do whatever we like together. She doesn't need your permission."

I could see in his body language that he had given up. *Finally.*

I swooped in, going in for the kill while he was vulnerable. "Now, let me make one thing absolutely clear. You will not bother Jill the way you're bothering me about this. And if I hear that you do, I will personally come to your apartment and kick your ass." I jabbed my index finger toward his face.

"You will not question her like she's done something wrong," I continued. "Don't forget who my mother is. She holds a lot of influence in this town. One word to her, and you might not have your gig at Canalside Auto anymore. Do you understand?"

Harry's face scrunched. For a second, I thought he might cry. A muffled sound—a sob?—came out of him, then another, until he dissolved into a fit of snorting laughter.

"Dude, you just threatened me! *You!*"

It wasn't meant to be *funny*. I was totally scary. The only people who seemed immune to my scare tactics were members of the Klein family.

"Hoo boy, let me catch my breath." He wiped away a tear. "Okay, I'm good now. And you have nothing to worry about. I love Jill, dude. She's my cousin, but she's more like my sister. I'm not going to bug her the way I bug you. Man, it's way too easy to get under your skin. I've gotta have fun with it."

Now he sounded exactly like Jill. Was I really so easy to tease?

"Yeah, well, it gets old fast."

"I'm sure it does. Anyway, now that I know you're not trying to shoehorn me out of the wedding, I should get going. Wouldn't want the *big, scary mayor* to get me fired now, would I?"

I ignored the jab, continuing with laying down the stone.

"Ben."

I looked up from my work to see Harry's suddenly somber face.

"Yeah, Harry?" I asked wearily.

"Jill is a special person. If you hurt her, I'm not above some light threats myself. Got it?"

CHAPTER TWENTY-THREE

Jill

"**T**HAT'S THE LAST OF them, I think," I said to my coworker, Glenn, as I squatted down next to his wheeled cart. Glenn was the best of the clerks at Greyport Public Library—organized, and efficient, and willing to put up with my antics. It was an added bonus that he was kind, and funny, and kept me supplied with chai lattes at our monthly queer movie nights at Out Alliance.

"I really appreciate your help. I can't believe how many books those kids pulled off the shelves. I'm always tempted to ask them the help re-shelf them, but I know they'd do it wrong, and it would double my work."

"Seriously. It was a little nutty this morning." We usually got a handful of children for our summer reading event, but Emma had come up with the bright idea to work with G-State to offer free tickets to their summer concert series to any kid that showed up to read.

We hadn't expected the level of attendance. The ends of Glenn's chestnut hair curled with sweat. I wanted to go home and sleep, but I still had to pull a shift at Fantasy Dongs before meeting Ben for dinner.

"You're telling me. I can't wait for this shift to be over. Arjun is coming over tonight. I'm hoping I can convince him to give me a foot rub." Glenn's boyfriend was a successful accountant. He was tall and lanky and completely head over heels for my coworker. I had a feeling it wouldn't take much convincing.

"You know, if the two of you moved in together, you could have foot rubs every night. I don't know what you're waiting for."

"Please, I'm only twenty-three. I'm not about to push it too fast and mess up a good thing. Arjun is the first guy I've dated who my parents have actually liked. I'm afraid to ruin it."

"Sometimes I forget how young you are. Maybe because it makes me feel positively ancient."

"You're the youngest thirty-year-old I've ever met. You have nothing to worry about."

"Thanks for the reassurance. I always worry that I'm too much or too immature." Too flaky, too unserious. The list went on...and on.

"You're perfectly Jill, and I'm happy for it. If you're up for it, you should come hang out with us tonight. I can't promise you any foot rubs, but we could always drink wine and watch shitty reality shows. Apparently, a new one is filming soon where people find love on a cruise ship. It looks both trashy and delightful."

"I can't. I'm getting dinner at The Sticky Pig with a friend." I tried to sneak away with Glenn's cart, but he caught it with the toe of his sneaker.

"A friend?" One bushy brow rose.

"Yep." I attempted to shove the cart forward, but his skinny ass was deceptively strong.

"Uh-uh. You're not getting off that easily. If you were hanging out with Kristi or Emma, you would have just said that."

"Okay, Mr. *I'm Obsessed with True Crime Podcasts and Think I'm an Amateur Detective*."

"You're being deliberately vague. No detective skills required."

"I'm not being vague. I'm meeting Ben Till. We've become friends recently."

"Oh, I *see*. I'll forgive you for ditching me if you're going to dinner with Ben Till. That man is sexy as fuck. I respect your game, girl."

"One, I am not ditching you for anyone, seeing as we didn't have established plans. Two, Ben and I are *friends*. We're getting barbecue. If it were a non-friend date, we wouldn't be eating messy food." It was sound logic, and I was proud of it. The fact that I could not stop thinking about the man's perfect dick and the silver piercing that ran through its head was neither here nor there.

"That makes no sense. Arjun and I ate Italian food on our first date—both messy and bad-breath inducing. And then we made out hard-core afterward."

"I have never, and will never, make out with Ben." It was technically the truth. Mutual orgasms, yes. Kissing, no. But Glenn didn't require all those pesky details.

He sighed. "Sounds boring. But I'll stop bugging you about it. If you end up having a torrid hook-up, tell me everything. I'm a taken man, and I need to live vicariously through you."

"Yeah, yeah, yeah. You'll be waiting a long time for that."

I WORE A WHITE dress for dinner. I'd chosen it on purpose, knowing I would have to wear one of those silly paper bibs to guard the pale fabric from stains. No one would wear one of those on an actual date.

The dress swished around my knees as I stepped up to the host's stand and gave the young woman my name. One black-painted, chipped fingernail traced a line down the piece of paper as she searched.

"Here you are. Your date is already here. I'll take you back."

My wedge heels thudded along the plank wood floor. The Sticky Pig was rustic, like so many other businesses in this town, but the food was amazing. I considered it a step above the greasy burger and fries fare offered at Maven's, though it wasn't as formal as the local Italian place, Carmella's.

I caught Ben's eye from across the mostly empty restaurant floor as I walked. He sat in a corner booth, arms spread wide across the back, looking like he owned the place.

He didn't shift as I approached, just followed my path with his gaze, taking me in from head to toe, his blue irises burning. I flashed back to last night in his bedroom, to when I made him wild with need.

I was sexy, and strong, and reclaiming my sex life. I felt the lightness of that settling in as I moved, swishing my hips as I strutted down the long plank floor. One of the waiters stopped in his tracks, and I shot him a sultry smile before looking back at Ben.

"Your server will be with you shortly," the host said as we arrived at the table, placing two laminated menus down on its surface.

Ben sat lounging like some kind of depraved royal. I was surprised he didn't get up, didn't do the gentlemanly thing by ushering me into my seat.

"Shall I sit?" I finally asked.

He said nothing, but he did do that manly chin dip gesture, indicating the place to his left.

"Okay, then." I slid into the booth.

He made no effort to move, his tattooed arms stretched out along the expanse of the seat back. His thick thighs, encased in dark denim, encroached on my space, leaving me no choice but to sit pressed against the length of his side.

"What's up with the man spreading? Make some room, please." I gave him a hip bump, but he didn't budge.

His body heat seeped through the fabric of his jeans and my thin dress. A shoulder-wracking shiver traveled up my body.

"You cold?" he asked—the first words he'd said to me all night.

Not at all. But there was no polite way to explain that my body was humming with the memory of him straddling me, so close but never close enough. What would he do if I returned the favor right now and threw my knees around either side of those hips? Brought my center down atop what I now knew he was hiding in those jeans? Could I break him again, the way I had last night, or was my newfound confidence just a fluke?

"Nope." I settled in with a smile.

His brow furrowed. "How—"

"Good evening! I'm Troy, and I'll be helping you tonight. Can I start you out with anything to drink?"

It was the waiter I'd passed on my strut to the table. He was on the young side—a G-State student, if I had to guess—with a mess of floppy blond hair. Cute, if not a bit overeager.

Ben continued to sit like a sexy statue.

"Hi, Troy," I said. "You'll have to forgive my friend here. He must have forgotten his manners at home. I'll have some water with lemon, please." I smiled sweetly, hoping to dilute some of Ben's sour.

"A Coke," he said with a grunt.

Troy wrote our orders down dutifully, his lips moving as he scribbled, before striding off toward the kitchen.

"What is your problem?" I hissed at my table mate.

He slid one arm down from the back of the seat to reach for a menu, the move brushing my shoulder blades. "I don't have a problem," he mumbled as he stared intently at the list of food options.

"You're not very good at faking it. You're being a total dick to Troy. Did he do something heinous before I got here? Wait, don't tell me, did he say that landscaping was stupid and people should replace their lawns with concrete slabs?"

He snorted and kept his gaze on the menu. "Oh, it's *Troy* now, is it? Are you old friends?"

"That is literally the man's name, Ben. I wouldn't have pegged you for the kind of guy who is rude to service staff." I let my disappointment shine through. If there was one thing I wouldn't tolerate after Oliver, it was meanness.

The hard plastic corners of the menu clicked as Ben snapped it shut and hit me with an arctic blast from those ice-blues. "Good old Troy wouldn't stop checking you out the second you walked in. For all he knows, you're mine. So, I'm sending him a message, and he'd better fucking listen."

I didn't *want* to find Ben's possessiveness attractive, and I certainly didn't welcome the tingling feeling it induced, but it appealed to a primal part of me. It was regressive and wrong but somehow hit just right.

I cleared my throat as Troy approached again, his gaze fixed on the wobbly drink tray that carried Ben's Coke and my water.

"Thank you," I said as he slid my glass to me.

Ben remained quiet.

"Do you need more time to look over the menu?"

"Nope," Ben cut in. "I'll take the beef brisket and a baked potato." He flicked the menu across the wide table toward Troy. "Thanks," he tacked on at my chastising look.

"And I'll have the pulled pork with French fries, please."

Troy collected our menus and trotted back to the kitchen.

I whirled on Ben. "You are an absolute cave man."

His answering grunt was all the encouragement I needed.

"I'm being serious. You have no right to declare that I belong to you like a piece of property. This is a dinner between two friends. Even if Troy was checking me out, there would be no reason for me not to welcome the attention."

Ben leaned into my space, the scent of mint and fresh soil tickling my nostrils. "You aren't interested in that kid, not when I made you come all over my bed last night."

Oh, he was fighting dirty now. "Let's get one thing straight. *I* made myself come last night. And you were right there with me, so if that gives you some sense of sick ownership over me, then I own you right the hell back, Benny Boy."

We were both leaning in, breathing each other's air. I couldn't stop looking at his mouth, wondering what it might taste like.

No. I sat back, reaching for a cold swig of water. There would be no kissing under any circumstances.

"That's the difference between you and me, I guess, Blossom. I'd be happy for someone to call me theirs. You look at it as a negative."

How had we spun this back to me? "Does your mom—an accomplished, ambitious woman—think she belongs to your father?"

He shrugged. "I've never asked. But she talks a lot about how she wouldn't have been able to do half the things she's done without his support. He feels a sense of pride in her accomplishments, and she's the same with his. I guess ownership isn't the right word, but it doesn't have to be a bad thing."

It sounded good when he put it that way. I twirled the thin silver ring on my pinky. "You're lucky—in having them, I mean. That's so rare as to be unbelievable. I never had an example of a healthy, mutual relationship growing up. Maybe it broke me when it comes to love."

"Because your dad was never in your life?"

I huffed out a laugh. "What dad? He was barely around. I think Mom was only with him because she wanted kids. Once she had her boy and girl, she was just as done with him as he was with us."

"When was the last time you saw him?"

"He made an appearance at Mom's funeral and then fucked off back to wherever he lives. Idaho, or something. I think he was worried he would have to be responsible for me after she passed, but James made all the legal arrangements so I wouldn't have to uproot my life."

"That sucks."

As hard as I searched, it wasn't pity I found in Ben's face.

"Yeah. It does."

He reached out a hand to calm my fussing fingers, the ones still twisting that bit of silver around and around. "I think you're wrong, though."

"Wrong about what?"

"Being broken. You and James share a father. Do you think he and Emma won't make it because of that?"

"You know I don't think that. My brother was born to be a husband and partner. That isn't me."

"Do you want it to be you?"

I paused. No one had ever asked me that before. I'd been mixed up for so long since Oliver and then so content to be alone after that. Everyone—myself included—assumed that was my nature. But what if I could be a partner after all?

"I'm not sure," I said honestly. "I doubt it will happen, even if I wanted it."

"You can do anything you set your mind to, Blossom."

I wanted to believe he meant it. Ben's faith in me had once felt like a given, but after what I'd heard from him last year, I wasn't so sure.

Chapter Twenty-Four

Ben

I WANTED TO KISS her so badly. I wanted to boost her up on the railing of the balcony outside her studio apartment and feel the squeeze of those long legs around my hips while I tasted her pink lips.

Jill thought eating a pulled pork sandwich would be a turnoff. Instead, I was discovering I had a new kink for red-tinged, sauce-covered cheeks and napkin bibs.

Troy hadn't been able to stop his wandering eyes from dipping down when Jill had tucked the paper bib into the neckline of her white dress. Everything she did was sexy, and she had no idea.

I would never get over her at this rate. Was there any point in trying?

"Do you want to come in?" she asked as she keyed open the door to her apartment.

Considering my current realization that my Jill infatuation was terminal, I should have said no, but...

"Yeah."

⁂

J ILL SAT CROSS-LEGGED ON the floor at my feet, laughing up in my face as I stared, agog, at the chest full of sex toys she had just unearthed from under her bed. After we'd entered her apartment, she'd gotten a devilish look on her face and this was the result.

"What do you think?" she asked with a barely suppressed giggle.

"Uh, it's...quite the collection."

I'd never seen so many cock-shaped objects in my life. A small satin draw-string bag in the corner caught my attention, and I wondered what was inside. I had my suspicions, but I would let her lead the way.

"It's beautiful, right?"

I rubbed the back of my neck. "If you say so." I was sure my grin looked more like a grimace.

Her fingers curled over the lip of the chest, hesitating a beat, before she dove in. She hovered over the toys one at a time, like she was playing an internal, naughty version of *eeny, meeny, miny, moe.*

My cock grew harder in my pants as her fingers brushed over each toy. I could imagine those fingers around me, gripping and tugging without a trace of self-consciousness, the way she had rubbed tight circles on her clit while we'd been writhing on my bed together.

It had been beautiful, watching her lose her worries and forget about her past.

She decided on a purple vibrator, holding it at my eye level. "This is your basic wand vibrator with a variety of settings and speeds. Nothing fancy, but you can't go wrong with a classic. It's the same brand as the one you have at your place. The company makes really great products. You did your research."

"I, um...looked up some reviews on the site we used to fill out those questions."

"Oh my god, don't they have great resources?! The founder started out as an adult film actress, but she's branched out with her own production company and now the website. She's incredibly smart and ambitious—and also ridiculously hot, so there's that." She placed the silicone shaft gently back into the chest and clapped her hands together. "Which one do you want to see next?"

"Oh, is that what we're doing here? Pretending this sex toy demonstration was my idea?"

She smiled, and I wanted to fist pump the air. Fuck, I needed to tone it down.

"I get these crazy ideas sometimes," she said. "I thought this might be a fun way to break up the tension from dinner. Sorry if it's too much."

I sat up straighter and looked her in the eyes. "Don't apologize for that. You're in your element. Did our conversation earlier get too heavy? If you were uncomfortable, I'll dial it back."

She rose to her knees and scooted closer to rest her hands on my thighs. "No, Ben. It was okay. I don't mind talking to you about that stuff at all. It's just that I think the silly stuff is equally as important."

I nodded, disappointed when she sat back on her heels. I had been enjoying the sight of her kneeling between my legs a little too much.

Relax, I told myself. We would get to the physical part of the night, but that wasn't the focus right now. Jill's well-being needed to remain front and center.

"You call the shots, Blossom."

"For now. We can take turns—so long as you don't pull that possessive act again like you did before."

Yeah, that had been a little over the top. Jealousy wasn't a skin I wore comfortably, but once I'd slipped it on, it had been hard to take off. "I apologized to Troy, didn't I?"

"You did. But you're not off the hook with me until you pick the next toy you want to see."

I rubbed my hands together, getting my head in the game. The wicked grin on Jill's face had me wanting to play with her, if only to hear her giggle some more. "Alright, let's go with the one with green glitter." It was bright, large, and had varying bumps and patterns along the shaft.

"Excellent choice, Benny Boy. This is one of my favorites." She whipped out the monstrosity—and monstrous it was—in a smooth, brandishing motion.

"What the hell is that?"

Her tinkling laugh reverberated in my chest. "It's a dragon dick. It was Fantasy Dongs' best seller last year. Isn't it super realistic? I especially like the textures they chose."

"How is it realistic? Dragons aren't real, so how would we know what their dicks look like?"

She cocked her head to the side, tapping her chin with the wide tip of the sparkling appendage. "You make a good point. It taps into a fantasy, I suppose."

"Are dragons a common fantasy?"

"The idea of being held as part of a dragon's hoard? Cherished like that? Absolutely."

"So, it's less about being attracted to an actual dragon and more about the fantasy scenario?"

Her face brightened, and I felt like a rock star. "Yes, you get it! I rarely picture an actual dragon, but more, like, a dragon that shape-shifts into a really hot person. I don't know, if I think about it too much, it gets weird. But then again, sex can be weird sometimes, right? Not in a bad way. As long as everyone is consenting, and no one's being taken advantage of, I won't yuck anyone's yum."

"You're really great at this."

"At what?" she asked as she placed the dragon dick back in its rightful place.

"Talking about this, helping people feel comfortable speaking about their fantasies. Your passion for it shows."

"Oh. Thank you."

The fair skin along her cheekbones reddened. She was unfazed talking about every type of sex toy under the sun, but a compliment threw her.

"Do you have any other creature dicks—would Fantasy Dongs be the proper term?—in that bag of tricks?"

She practically shook with excited energy, and I let loose a smile that stretched my cheeks. "You know, I'm one of the top reps at Fantasy Dongs, even with a part-time schedule. I might have you so enamored with these products that you go out and buy some yourself."

"I admire your ambition, but dongs don't do much for me, creature or otherwise."

"Oh yes, I remember from when you filled out our questions. But I will point out that you did have a distinctly phallic-shaped object in your nightstand drawer the other night."

I snickered. When I'd been glaring bullets in the side of Troy's skull back at The Sticky Pig, possessive and pissed off at myself for feeling that way, I never would have predicted that the night would end like this—with us having so much damn *fun*.

There was a lot I was learning about Jill, and I liked almost all of it.

"You know I bought that specifically for you, don't you?"

Her nose crinkled the tiniest bit. "I would hope so. The thought of using a toy that's been used by someone else...Yuck." She shrugged. "Guess I should have asked that before putting it inside me, but what's done is done."

"You're fine. It was definitely not used. You're the only one I'll be using it with."

She smiled up at me shyly, biting her lip. The bashful look worked for her.

Who was I kidding? I found everything this woman did appealing.

It was suddenly important to me she knew that. "Jill?"

She peered up at me as she rearranged the purple dragon dick in her hoard. "Yeah?"

I shifted forward a fraction, leaning my upper body the barest inch closer to her. "We didn't really talk about it much, but the other night was great for me. I hope it was great for you too. You were really, really beautiful."

She looked away, tucking a stray bit of light hair behind her ear. "It was. Great, that is. And thank you."

"Whenever you're ready for more, you let me know, okay? I'm here for you to use in any way you like." *And happily. Forever.*

Whoa.

Forever? Had I really just thought that? I was doing this so that I could finally stop fixating on Jill, not fall even deeper into...whatever this was. The thought of ending this thing, here and now, crossed my mind, but I dismissed it immediately.

Truth was, I suspected it was too late for me—even before vibrators got involved.

Jill nodded once, efficiently, before she closed the lid on her box and snapped the locks on each side. She slid it under the daybed before setting both palms on her thighs with a smack.

"I'm ready."

Well, I certainly wasn't going to let her down now.

Chapter Twenty-Five

Jill

WE WERE ABOUT TO find out if last night was a fluke, and suddenly all that bravado I'd felt at dinner had abandoned me. Ben had *said* our first time together was good for him, but what if he was just lying, humoring me?

I watched his mind work for a moment before he settled back and asked, "If you're ready, why did you put the box away?"

"If you mean for this to be another night where we don't touch each other, I might have to kill you. A lot of people in Greyport will be very disappointed when their flower beds wind up looking like shit next spring."

He softened. I suspected he knew I was joking to mask my nerves. "Relax, Blossom, we're going to do plenty of touching. But that doesn't mean we can't incorporate...other things...as part of the fun."

"I'm not sure when you decided I needed some cutesy little nickname, but I'll overlook it. I take it you're not threatened by my wealth of sex toys? Some people I've been with—men, specifically—haven't always liked using them during intercourse." Oliver wasn't the only man I'd encountered over the years who'd offered his opinion where it wasn't needed.

His brows rose, and my fingers tingled with the need to smooth out the lines in his forehead. "Who said we're having intercourse tonight? And even if we were, the toys aren't a threat. As long as it's you and me and you're coming, I don't care how we get there."

I swallowed hard, studying him. He hadn't moved much since he sat on my pale-pink bedspread, looking stiff and out of place amongst the shimmery throw pillows. "Sit back," I said. "Get comfortable."

He lowered his upper body back against the layer of pillows pressed against the metal frame of the bed. He was tall enough that his feet still rested on the floor, his big boots stretched on either side of where I sat beneath him. Lifting to my knees, I kneeled between his legs, transfixed by the way his jaw tightened.

"Can I touch you?" I asked in a whisper.

He lowered his chin in agreement.

I ran my hands up his jean-clad calves, past the hard ridges of his kneecaps, and over his strong thighs. When I reached his hips, I placed my palms on either side of the mattress before using my leverage on the bed to come to a standing position. Ben's dark gaze followed my motion, his lips parting.

He'd talked of claiming me earlier, but right now, he was mine.

I moved a hand to the hem of my dress, the other to one of the thin straps at my shoulder. With a slow brush of my finger, I lowered the strap until it dangled against my tricep. I reached across and repeated the motion on the other shoulder. The white bodice drooped, held in place only by the round curves of my upper breasts.

I was dizzy from the sound of Ben's heavy breathing. Heady and loose, like getting to the bottom of a glass of wine. The sight of his thick fingers curling into my girlish comforter had me tipsy.

I twisted my fingers in the frilly skirt of the dress, tugging the fabric up inch by inch to the soft skin of my upper thighs. A tortured groan emanated from Ben's chest, and I bit my lip on a smile.

Deciding to put him out of his misery, I straddled him, the pale skirt floating between us a flimsy barrier. The hard press of his cock at my center had me fighting the urge to grind on him, but we weren't there yet.

I steadied myself on his broad shoulders, bringing my breasts closer to his face before trailing a hand over his buzzed scalp and around to the back of his head. If his hair was longer, I would have tugged on the strands, but I settled for pinching my fingers together around the short fuzz. Just enough for him to feel the pull.

His neck went slack, those ice-blue eyes drifting shut.

I slid my hand down to the base of his skull and pressed my thumb and forefinger to the small knots of muscle at the base, bringing him close.

"Eyes on me, Ben," I said, the words coming from a place deep inside me.

He obeyed, lifting his lids as if they were the heaviest things in the world.

"What are you doing to me, Blossom?" His mouth inched closer and closer to mine as I played in his hair, squeezing my thighs tight around him.

"Using you," I whispered, the barest hint of air between our lips.

I felt him grip the sides of my legs then bring his palms under my skirt to the curves of my bottom. His fingertips rasped against the sheer fabric of my underwear, and my hips rocked of their own accord.

"You better not kiss me," I reminded him as our breath mingled.

"You'd better not kiss me either," he said, giving the cheeks of my ass a rough squeeze in his palms as he tilted his hips up.

I smiled, bringing my head down, dragging my bottom lip along the hard edge of his jaw and across to his ear. He shivered below me. I took the lobe in my teeth and bit down, allowing him to feel the pressure before I gave the skin a soothing suck.

"Fuck, Jill," he said, giving me another nudge with his hard cock.

"Am I turning you on, Ben?"

We rolled our hips into each other again and again, dry humping like two teenagers first discovering sex.

He groaned. "You know exactly what you're doing to me."

I laughed, surprising even myself with how deliciously wicked I sounded. Maybe I really was good at this.

"Tell me what you want to do to me, how you want to touch me," I ordered. "And then I might let you do those things."

He brought his eyes up to mine. There was scarcely a hint of blue left. "You're an evil woman, you know that?"

Evil, but sexy. Powerful. "At least I'm letting you touch me...unlike the way you played me at your house."

That crooked incisor flashed. "I didn't hear any complaints when you were filling up that cunt with my cum. I'm pretty sure you liked that game."

I had, and he knew exactly how much. But this was my house, and we were playing my way, especially after he'd thrown that little tantrum with the waiter.

I brought my mouth close to his ear again. "Come on, Benny Boy. Quit stalling. Tell me what you want to do."

His blunt fingertips bit into my hips. "I wanna tear this dress off is what I want to do."

"Hmm, I'm not sure about that. I spent good money on this dress. What would you do after that?" He continued that steady push and pull with the tight hold he had on my ass, the thick head of his cock bumping up into me in just the right spot.

"I'd devour those tits. I didn't get to see them very well last night, but I saw enough to know they're beautiful."

"Would you lick them or suck on them?" His hips bucked. I moaned when I felt the scrape of his teeth along my neck.

"I'd do whatever you told me to do, Blossom, as long as you let me in."

The sensation that ripped through me at his words had me on the edge already. I didn't know if it was the power play or Ben or both. But I knew I wanted more.

"You're such a good boy, Ben. For that, I think you deserve a reward."

I shrugged my shoulders so the bodice of my dress slipped down over my breasts. The material caught briefly on the stiff peaks of my nipples before falling to my waist. I reached behind me for Ben's large hands before placing them over my breasts.

I was just big enough for him to cup. I'd never been busty, but my boobs were perky and round, and I'd always found them cute. And Ben didn't seem to mind their size if his panting was anything to go by.

"Touch them how you've been imagining," I said, removing my grip.

It had been dark the night before, but he must have been paying attention to how I'd pinched my nipples, tugged them between my fingers. He imitated my moves now, his work-roughened fingertips creating a sensation better than any I'd ever managed on my own.

"Have you ever used nipple clamps before?" I asked.

He shook his head in denial, continuing the onslaught of my delicate tips.

"Me neither. Wanna try them sometime?"

"Yes," he said through gritted teeth.

I loved that he was so hard up, yet he still humored me. "You have permission to taste them now." I'd kept him waiting long enough.

He wasted no time, leaning his head down as he lifted me to his mouth. He kissed across the mound of my cleavage first, then dipped his tongue in the valley between before focusing on a stiff peak. His lips closed over the tip while he thrummed his thumb along the other, pinching and rolling it. He worried it between his lips, releasing it with a wet suctioning sound before moving his attention to the other breast. I jerked when I felt the sharpness of his teeth around the delicate skin, reaching for his head to hold him in place.

That set him off, like the slight hold I had on him made him wild. Ben was bigger than me, was certainly far stronger than me, but in this moment, I had complete and utter control over him.

I was drunk on that power, words spilling out of me. "You're doing such a good job, Ben. I can see how much you love this. But surely this isn't where your fantasies stop, is it?"

The popping sound that filled my studio as he lifted his mouth was obscene. His lips were swollen and shiny.

"No," he said.

"What happens next?"

"We get rid of this dress." He fingered the layer of fabric covering our laps. "And you take these off." He slid his hand up and around the back of the skirt to rub his palm across the backside of my cheeky panties.

"And then?"

"Then I'll lie down, and you'll fuck my face."

I could picture it. I was already so wet from everything we'd done so far I might drown him. Would he like that? Oliver never had.

"You think you deserve that, do you?"

"Oh, I know I don't deserve it. But you do."

I quirked a brow, enjoying our back and forth. "Sounds pretty cocky to me. Are you that good?"

His hand twisted in the back of my underwear, the elastic digging into my skin. "Never had any complaints."

Maybe no one had ever complained about him, but they had about me.

Before he could react, I hopped off his lap and slipped my dress the rest of the way off, struggling to shed the bolt of insecurity I felt bubbling up. "Get on your back and grab the bed rails. Don't move unless I tell you to."

Chapter Twenty-Six

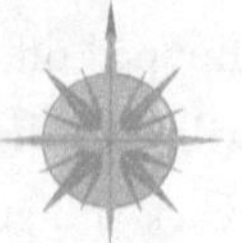

Jill

B EN TILL, FULLY DRESSED and barely controlled, lay splayed out on my bed. It would have been ridiculous—him with his tattooed, buzzed-head, badass look on my girly bedspread—if it weren't so mindbogglingly sexy. Slightly larger than a twin, the mattress bordered on too small, but when he bent his knees, he fit just right.

His eyes were wide, his face slack as he took in my naked body. Forget my stupid inner voice that was sounding more and more like Oliver's by the second. A man as delicious as Ben wanted *me*. Oliver could get fucked.

The ink on Ben's knuckles shifted as he clutched the metal frame above his head. I regretted not keeping a set of restraints in my box of toys, but since I wasn't interested in using them on my own, I had never gotten around to it.

"You gonna make me wait all night to taste you?" he taunted.

I clucked my tongue. "You're not calling the shots, Benny Boy. For that, I should make you wait even longer."

He attempted to shrug while still gripping the bed frame, the motion emphasizing the muscles of his shoulders. A vein in his forearm popped. I wanted to lick it.

"You're only punishing yourself," he said, noticing the way my eyes flared.

"Naughty boy." I trailed my fingers down my stomach, dipping into the waistband of my panties. I held Ben's gaze as I stroked the tips of two fingers into my slick center. Part of me wanted to get myself off in front of him, to wind him up until he went wild, but I wanted to fulfill his fantasy more.

That's right, face-sitting had been front and center on Ben's survey answers. It was only right that I returned the favor after my cream-pie dream had come true last night.

I removed two wet, shiny fingers from my underwear, bringing them to Ben's lips. His mouth dropped open, but he paused before taking them in, seeking my permission.

"Go ahead."

His tongue darted out first, curling around each digit, savoring the taste, before he sucked them into the damp heat of his mouth. By the time he finished, we were both breathing hard.

"You like that," I said. His lips were shiny, and I watched, transfixed, as he slicked his tongue over them.

"Because you're fucking delicious." His hands clenched and released around the metal framework.

"I suppose I've tortured you long enough. You have been an excellent listener." My nonchalance was belied by how shaky my legs were. As fun as our power play was, I was ready to ride his tongue.

I shoved my panties down my legs, kicking them off when they tangled around my ankles. I swung a leg up onto the bed then shifted some more until I was basically hovering above Ben's chest.

Leaning forward, I placed my hands between Ben's on the bars of the bed frame. The iron was cool to the touch, a stark contrast with the heat of his body.

"Why are you wasting so much time, Blossom?" he said as his hips bucked beneath me. "Get that beautiful ass up here."

"How bad do you want it?"

His upper lip curled. "I'm two seconds from coming, Jill. How bad do you think I want it? I need you. Please."

The begging was what did it. I lowered myself onto his eager, waiting face, feeling strong and sexy and free of self-judgment.

He let me set the pace. I slid myself along his tongue, directing it from my hot center to my clit, grinding on his chin. I was using him selfishly, but the sounds he was making told me he was enjoying this just as much as I was.

I felt the orgasm building, my muscles contracting to the point of near pain. Ben's tongue curled around my clit. My hips bucked. My limbs were locked up and achy. I needed this orgasm, *needed* it so badly. It was so close. I was going to get there.

Your pussy lips are so gross. They're way too big.

No. No, no, no. Oliver would *not* fuck this up for me tonight. Not when we were fulfilling Ben's fantasy.

Did Ben find me gross too? I glanced down. He looked...blissed out. But my labia *were* a little large, weren't they? He couldn't *really* want them all over his face, right?

Have you thought about getting plastic surgery for it? There's a local surgeon who does it.

I screamed in frustration, throwing my leg up and over Ben's head and hopping off the daybed. Me, and Oliver, and my stupid insecurities had ruined sex for me—again.

"Whoa, whoa, whoa, what just happened?" Ben asked, taking his hands off the bed frame. I stepped back until my calves pressed against the edge of the coffee table.

He sat up, reaching out to wrap an arm around my bare waist. "Is it okay to touch you?"

I nodded.

"Talk to me," he said, drawing me in close.

I squeezed my legs together. "This is what I always do. I remember all the shitty things my ex used to say to tear me down, and then I get in my head and can't come. It's like I get caught in this vicious loop. And now your sexual fantasy is ruined. *This* is why I'm bad at sex."

He was shaking his head before I even finished, hugging me tight. "Jill, you're not bad at sex. Trust me. You were with a straight up dick who lied to you, okay? I don't know every last word he said, but I know he was lying. Because nothing I've seen the last two nights with you says that you're bad at sex. I love your body and the way it reacts to me. I—" He stopped, gathering himself for a moment. "You've been treated poorly, and now you're getting stuck in an old pattern. What we need to do is find a way to break that pattern."

He'd said *we,* and that made a world of difference. I was part of a team, and Ben was competent as hell. But the doubt still pulled along my frayed edges. "What if it never happens?"

"We have time to figure it out, Blossom. This was the purpose of your *friends with benefits* plan, remember? We have a connection and a level of comfort with each other that will allow us—you, I mean—to open up and let go more easily. It may not all be smooth sailing, but it's going to work. I believe in you."

"How are you so certain?" I asked quietly. It scared me that I believed him right now, because I didn't know how far his faith in me went.

He buried his head in my stomach. "Because you're Jill. You don't give up, not ever."

I cupped his cheek, tilting his face up to me. "Don't lie, Ben."

I *had* given up in the past, and he knew it. First on myself, after the Oliver debacle, then on countless career attempts, several of which Ben had been witness to. That wasn't counting the things he hadn't seen—the cruise I'd planned with college friends only to bail at the last minute because boats made me twitchy, the time I was supposed to feed my coworker's goldfish only to get locked out and slowly watch the fish turn ghost-white through a window with each passing day.

A muscle in his jaw twitched. "Why do you think that's a lie?"

I definitely wasn't ready to talk to him about overhearing that phone call. Not because I feared his reaction, but because I was too afraid to admit how much he'd hurt me.

I imbued my next words with an air of casualness. "Call it woman's intuition. I've got to keep some secrets."

He scrubbed a hand over his face, as if washing away his visible concern. When he came up for air, it was with that charming smirk. "I could make you tell me, you know."

"As if you could do that. I call the shots, or did you forget?" I took my nails and dragged a trail up his back, not deep enough to leave a mark, but enough that he could feel it.

Something flared in his gaze. "I figured we could take turns." The hand around my waist drifted down to the bottom of my ass cheek, the rough pads of his fingertips settling at the dip of my thigh.

I smiled. "I can live with that."

He placed a delicate, close-mouthed kiss just above my belly button. I shivered because it felt so fucking *nice*.

"Hey, Ben?"

He hit me with those ice blues.

"Yeah?"

"Would you hate me if I didn't want to do anything else tonight? Like, sexually?"

He stiffened. "What? No, I wouldn't hate you. We do what you want to do, Jill. Always."

"I don't want you to think I'm selfish or that I don't care about your pleasure and fantasies too. I don't want it to be all about me all the time."

"First, getting you off gets me off. I share your pleasure. And second, if you aren't in the mood to do something, the last thing I want to hear is that you're forcing yourself out of some sense of obligation to me. Because if you're not one hundred percent with me, I don't want it."

I rubbed his scalp, the short hairs itching under my palm in the most satisfying way. "That was...a perfect answer."

He gave my butt a small pinch. It was too gentle to hurt, but I still yelped, making a show of it.

"So, do you want me to head out?" he asked.

I didn't want him to leave at all. "Would you like to stay to watch a movie?"

I could have sworn he looked shocked for a split second. "You sure? No pressure. I'm good if you want me out of here."

"I'm sure. We're friends, right? Friends watch movies together."

"Okay, yeah," he said, bobbing his head up and down. "What are we watching?"

I powered on the TV and navigated to my favorite streaming service. "You pick."

"Only if you go put some clothes on. My dick needs to calm down, and you're seriously not helping."

I made a show of bending down to grab a pair of sweats from my dresser before strutting into the bathroom to pee and wash off my makeup. When I came back out, Ben had a movie cued up, ready to push play.

I snickered when I saw what he'd chosen. "*American Psycho*, really?"

"Hey, you're the one who brought it up. I figured it was a favorite."

"Hardly," I scoffed.

I sat down anyway, curling up under a fuzzy blanket, the window air conditioning unit blasting the tip of my nose.

Ben left after midnight, and I pretended I wasn't worried that he was never coming back.

Chapter Twenty-Seven

Ben

"**W**HAT'S GOING ON WITH you and James Klein's sister?"

I stared daggers at Dany as he raked a layer of mulch. Two of my summer crew members, Corbin and Avery, perked up from their side of the garden bed. They were nineteen and lived for gossip and tales of sordid hookups.

"Keep your voice down," I hissed at Dany. "Nothing is going on."

"Oh, alright. I'm fully convinced now that you just had that *totally normal* reaction to my question. Am I right, boys?" Dany directed toward our younger crew mates.

Avery laughed, his tanned face growing splotchy when I sent him a glare. He wisely shut up.

Corbin wasn't so astute. "Yeah, Boss, you sounded, like, crazy defensive."

"See!" Dany said, doing a strange, gyrating dance move with his rake. "Word on the street is the two of you have been seen all over town getting cozy. So, what's the deal?"

We could hardly be considered cozy, much to my chagrin. It had been a week since Jill and I had dinner at The Sticky Pig—and I had Jill for dessert. She'd been busy with Velvet, and I'd been working crazy hours, so we'd barely had time for much more than coffee at Greyport Grinds and a walk along the canal towpath. Both times I'd seen her, she'd been distracted and disconnected.

I sensed Jill was afraid to try again after what had happened last time, but I knew putting too much pressure on her would only make matters worse.

I didn't dignify Dany and my nosy crewmembers with a response as I ripped a slice into a bag of mulch with a utility knife, the tearing sound tickling my brain.

"One of my friends is a line cook down at The Sticky Pig. He said they were there last week, and Ben looked like he wanted to kick the shit out of a waiter who checked Jill out," Corbin said.

"No shit? *Ben?* This is what I like to hear." I glanced up to see Dany rubbing his hands together like some sort of comical villain.

"I saw them taking a walk this week!" Avery chimed in.

I stuck the knife into another bag as I kept my gaze glued to the younger man. The canvas tore with a loud *zip* and Avery paled, clamping his mouth shut again.

"You about done being menacing over there? It might work on young Avery here, but I know you better than that. You're a big softie," Dany teased.

"Maybe I'll stop being scary when you're done gossiping like a bunch of high school girls."

I wouldn't reveal anything about my relationship with Jill to Dany and a crew of teenagers—not when I was feeling shaky as it was about my status with her.

No matter how hard I tried to convince myself that the physical side of our relationship was going to help me get over her, it wasn't working. I wanted her just as much, if not more, than I had before. And she wouldn't even allow a kiss, let alone a commitment.

"That's sexist," Dany said, referencing my *high school girls* comment. "Men like to gossip just as much as women, and you'll never convince me otherwise."

"Maybe. Don't tell our mothers that I said that," I mumbled. Ma would have my head if she heard that.

He cackled. "I won't. So long as you tell me what's going on."

"Are you trying to blackmail me?"

"I'm trying to make conversation and find out what's new in my friend's life. I do actually care, believe it or not."

Well, now I felt guilty for snapping at him.

"Jill and I are friends," I said with a sigh. "We've gotten closer since I've been helping her with Velvet's lawn."

"And how does James feel about that?"

"He...doesn't care. Why would he? Like I said, Jill and I are friends. Do you check in with the siblings of everyone who you're friends with?"

Between wedding planning, his custom furniture orders, and my summer schedule, I hadn't talked much to James since our night out at Maven's. Our friendship wasn't the kind that needed constant communication to stay strong. I could not talk with James for a full calendar year, call him up begging for help, and he would be there, no questions asked.

Was Dany right, though? *Would* James care if he found out that Jill and I were growing closer? And if he did, would I care enough to stop wanting to be near her at every opportunity?

A voice in the base of my skull said no, that I would pick being with Jill over anything else, and that was something I wasn't yet willing to confront.

Dany gave a brief hum as he considered my statement. "It does seem a little strange that you're spending more time with your best friend's sister than with your best friend himself. And said sister is extremely attractive."

It was hard to pull off a shrug as I faced him. "I haven't noticed her attractiveness. It's not like that with us."

My friend smiled smugly before turning to our other crewmembers and motioning them closer. "Corbin! Please do share more about your line cook friend and what he witnessed at The Sticky Pig."

The younger man slicked a bead of sweat off his brow. "Um, sure, okay. I mean, there wasn't much detail because, like, what do I care about what some thirty-year-olds are doing, right?" His breathless tone said he very much did care. "So, my buddy said they sat all close to each other, and Ben had his arm around Jill the whole time. And like I said, Ben was about ready to kill the waiter who looked at Jill's legs. But I can't really blame the guy. It's kind of hard not to notice her, you know? She's always wearing those dresses and skirts and shit. One time, she wore this dress and had her hair in braids, and I think I went home and looked up milkmaid porn for a straight month."

I choked on my spit. The group went quiet, and Corbin looked around, his face proclaiming innocence. "Did I say something wrong?"

My ears were hot—and not from the sun beating down on us. "If I ever hear you talk about masturbating to Jill Klein again, you'll be lucky to even have a dick. In fact, delete her from your spank bank entirely." I gave the knife in my hand a little flip, catching it by the handle before snapping it shut.

"Got it," Corbin said, his voice a squeak.

"Yep, totally just friends, huh?"

"Fuck off, Dany."

I WAVED OFF THE three other men when we finished up the job. The sun was only just beginning to set, belying the late hour. The summer season was backbreaking, but I would miss it by the time January and February came around.

My phone buzzed in my pocket as I heaved my tired body into my work truck. It was Jill sending a meme about landscaping. It was both stupid and funny at the same time. The laugh that rumbled out of me was almost painful.

Taking a stab in the dark, I made a move.

Ben: Want to hang out tonight?

That sounded casual enough. Not at all like I was itching to see her again.

Jill: Sorry, I can't. James and I finally finished sanding the floors at Velvet, so I'm busy vacuuming up all the wood dust.

I shoved down my disappointment and steered my car back toward town. Halfway through the drive, I decided it wouldn't hurt to stop by Velvet, just as a friendly gesture to help out. Nothing more, nothing less. I swung a quick U-turn and angled for Jill.

The truck bumped down the country road, slowing as the tires hit the gravel lot outside Velvet. It was empty, Jill's SUV nowhere to be found. She wasn't here vacuuming sawdust or doing anything else.

It was the confirmation I needed. She was officially dodging me—and lying about it too.

Laying my head back against the headrest, I surveyed the building—the one my mom had such a complicated relationship with. The connection I still hadn't mustered the courage to mention to Jill.

It already looked different—and better—since my last visit. There were visible patches in the worn clapboard siding that I knew would eventually be covered in a fresh coat of paint. The windows had all been replaced, no longer covered in brown film.

Jill was kicking ass at this renovation in an undeniable way. Others had helped, but this place *was* Jill, and I wasn't sure if she even recognized what an amazing job she was doing. How amazing *she* was, even in the face of scrutiny and doubt.

It hit me hard that I had been one of her doubters too, but she continuously proved me wrong. It was probably past time I gave her credit where it was due.

I rolled my window down as I pulled out of the lot, swearing I could smell Jill's moonflower scent in the surrounding air. I inhaled deeply and let it out in a big puff.

The ball was in her court. I couldn't keep chasing her.

CHAPTER TWENTY-EIGHT

Jill

I WAS BEING A creep—or worse, a stalker—as I stared at Ben's house. I huddled in my SUV, parked across the street. A warm, foil-wrapped tray of brownies rested on the passenger seat, the delicious smell filling the vehicle's interior.

At least I wouldn't go hungry if I ended up losing my nerve and stayed out here all night.

Losing my nerve had been the theme of my life over the last week and a half. Like when Ben had asked if I wanted to grill up some steaks at his house after our walk along the canal. I'd made up some bullshit excuse about meeting a delivery person at Velvet. Then, when we'd met for coffee at Greyport Grinds, I'd ducked out after twenty minutes, telling him I was scheduled for a non-existent shift at Fantasy Dongs.

He had stopped reaching out after I'd refused him again a few nights ago, making up yet another lie about needing to clean up sawdust.

I knew he would want to talk about what had happened back at my apartment. And then he would probably want to try again to help me get my confidence back. I wasn't opposed to that logic—it *had* been the point of my plan in the first place—but my embarrassment was still an open wound.

I was infuriated with myself. Ben wasn't Oliver, and I wasn't the girl who'd dated Oliver. I'd had one successful orgasm with Ben, and I wanted more of them. It was time to put on my big-girl pants and handle my nonsense.

I grabbed the brownie tray and hopped out of the SUV, marching up the driveway toward Ben's house. The garage door was open again, and I could see the interior door, but it seemed too presumptuous to use it.

I waffled back and forth, one foot angled toward the garage and the other toward the path bordered by wildflowers that led to the front door. A trail of sweat dripped down the nape of my neck, and my palms were slick under the warm tray I held.

"Thanks a bunch, Ben!" a cheery, feminine voice called out. I watched in horror as the garage door opened.

I froze as an attractive, brunette woman turned toward the man in the door frame and wrapped her arms around him in a hug that lasted two seconds too long to be anything but personal.

"You're welcome, honey. See you soon."

Honey?

I needed to leave—now. They hadn't looked my way yet. There was still time. But my feet couldn't seem to move, and my stomach was lurching like I'd just stepped off the spinning teacups at the local amusement park.

I convinced my right leg to take a big step backward when the brownies fell, slipping out of my damp hand. I watched in horror as the pan careened toward the blacktop in slow-motion.

The metal dish landed on one corner, then tilted to the other, back and forth and back again in a hideous clang.

"Jill?"

Fuck.

I squatted down, collecting the fallen dessert before sneaking a momentary glance up at Ben. He looked so fucking handsome and so fucking confused. It was painful.

I really needed to go.

My quads burned as I shot to my feet, already inching away down the driveway.

"Uh, hey, Ben and...Ben's friend. I was just, um, bringing over something for you. James made dinner, and there were leftovers, so...you know. Just being courteous and all that. I definitely did not bake these myself. But I can see you're busy, so yeah, I'll mosey on home and—"

"Jill, this is Honey Martin. I don't think the two of you have met."

I paused. Her *name* was Honey? That made some sense, but it didn't explain the lingering hug. Not that I cared who was hugging Ben and for how long. It was only that a heads up that he'd moved on would have been nice.

"Hi, Jill. It's nice to meet you." Honey smiled widely. She looked really nice, and I liked her emerald-green halter neck romper. She was perfectly perfect for a perfect guy like Ben. They would probably get married and have a billion babies by next year.

I was sure the smile I returned made me look nauseated. "You too. Sorry to interrupt."

"Oh, it's not a problem! I was heading out anyway. I hope to see you again soon!" Honey walked smoothly down the blacktop, her tan wedge heels clicking as she went.

She was stunning—and kind, to boot. It was hard to fault Ben for being interested in a woman like her.

I bet Honey didn't have a questionable job history. She looked like she had her shit together and had never missed a rent payment in her life. She probably didn't have the voice of an evil ex in her head all the time or a dozen sexual hangups either.

I spun on my heel and aimed for my SUV.

"Jill."

I paused at the sound of Ben's voice.

"Those are my brownies. I want them. Come on."

B EN LEANED UP AGAINST the kitchen counter next to me, crossing one ankle over the other as he held the neck of a beer bottle in a loose grip.

I slid a plate with two brownies to him, tipping my chin down to his drink of choice. "That's not going to be a good combo. Beer and chocolate? *Yuck.*"

He ignored me, picking up the brownie and taking a big bite. The way the muscles of his jaw moved as he chewed was more fascinating to me than it should have been. If he was done with me and my issues and ready to move on, then I needed to do the same. Noticing his muscles, and his jaw, and his eyes, and his...everything...wasn't good for me.

He swallowed, took a swig of beer, then locked eyes with me. "Tastes fine to me." I wanted to lick a stray crumb of chocolate off his lips.

"Good. That's...good. I'm glad the whole pan wasn't ruined when it fell." I scooted toward his fridge, taking out a jug of milk. "Is this expired?" I asked, rotating the opaque plastic until I found the square black numbers on the bottom curve.

"What was the point in asking if you were going to check anyway?"

I shot him a dark look as I poured the white liquid into a small cup. I only ever drank milk if I was eating cookies or brownies. Otherwise, it reminded me too much of the school cafeteria. "What crawled up your ass?" I asked.

He set his beer down with a clink and crossed his arms. He looked relaxed at first glance—all leaning, lion-like grace—but upon closer inspection, I could see the tension in his body.

"Am I not allowed to be annoyed that you've been ignoring me for over a week? Now you show up here with dessert as if that should make everything better."

A direct hit. "I didn't ignore you—not entirely."

He scoffed. "That's splitting hairs, and you know it. And I know you lied at least once too. I swung by Velvet after work a couple nights ago when you said you were working late. You weren't there. That's a shit thing to do. I thought we were friends again. The least you could have done was tell me you were done with me."

"Because I wasn't! I mean, I'm not. Done with you, that is." Not like he was with me.

"Could have fooled me."

"Oh, please. It's not like you wasted any time getting over it."

He uncrossed his arms, lowering them to the counter's edge in a white-knuckled grip. "What are you talking about?"

"Playing dumb doesn't suit you, Benny Boy." I kept my tone deliberately casual, hoping he wasn't paying mind to the pulse beating out a wild rhythm in my throat. "Honey seems cool. I was...surprised to find you with someone else. But I'm happy for the two of you."

Ben scowled. "Honey is my friend."

"Well, I'm your friend, and I sat on your face a week and a half ago. So, forgive me if I'm not sure how you define friendship."

He exploded off the counter, pacing a step into the middle of the kitchen before spinning around to face me where I stood at the refrigerator. "You're driving me *insane*, Jill! I'm friends with Honey because she's been dating Danylo, my coworker, for five years, and I'm helping her plan a surprise party for him. No one is sitting on my face besides you, but since you clearly don't want to do that anymore, I don't see how it's any of your business."

We were both breathing hard, our faces a scant distance apart. The heat of his exhalations brushed my cheek. I leaned in...

The ice maker behind me kicked on, and I leaped about a foot in the air. I used the opportunity to step back from the near-kiss, bringing my shoulder blades flush against the refrigerator. We weren't doing *that*, and I needed to remember that.

"Nothing to say?" Ben asked.

"I—I'm thinking." I was an idiot—first, for my embarrassment over Ben having witnessed my freakout in my apartment, and now, for making assumptions. It was my own fault my fledgling connection with Ben was at risk.

He smirked but drifted a step closer to me despite his obvious annoyance. "Why did you come here tonight, Jill?"

I swallowed. "To apologize. And bring you brownies."

He deliberately stepped into my space and leaned down to brace one arm above my head on the fridge. He reached down with his other hand, and I waited to feel that firm touch on my hip, waited for him to pull me in close so we could burn off the heat of this anger.

Instead, he snatched a mangled brownie from the tray and ripped a bite off in his teeth.

"Apology not accepted. Go home." The fact that his mouth was full made the command that much more insulting. Like I didn't even deserve basic manners.

Oh, hell no. I would not let him eat my apology treats and order me around and not even hear me out. I handed him my glass of milk as he finished chewing. He chugged the rest and placed the glass on the counter.

I crossed my arms, my elbows brushing the soft cotton of his t-shirt. "No."

"No, what?" He lowered his head until our foreheads were almost touching, but I refused to be intimidated.

"I mean, no, I am not leaving. You haven't even heard my apology yet. Plus, I'll need that tray back."

"You know, most of the time, people start with some variation of the words 'I'm sorry' when they're making an apology. Instead, I get mediocre dessert and accusations of making moves on my friend's girlfriend."

"Mediocre?!" I placed both hands on Ben's big chest and pushed. I shouldn't have been able to budge him, but the move caught him off guard, and he stumbled back.

"Oh, fuck, I'm so sorry." I reached out to grab his forearms to steady him.

He caught my wrists at the same time, the pale skin of my lower arms entwining with his colorful palette.

"Jill." That word—my name—was like a plea. I looked up. Ben's eyes were dark, almost like he'd...liked that I'd pushed him.

"Ben. I am sorry." I swallowed before asking, "Is this alright?"

He nodded once before loosening his grip on my wrists.

I moved quickly, afraid that I would lose the small ounce of courage I'd gathered if I hesitated, and twisted my fingers in the fabric of his shirt. I dragged him close. If I thought for a moment about the physics at play, it was obvious that Ben came willingly, allowing me the power to push and prod.

"Do you really think my food is mediocre?" I asked, my lips hovering close to his ear.

He shivered, as if waiting for me to bite down on the soft lobe. "I thought you said your brother made the brownies."

I tamped down my laugh. I was such a shit liar. "We both know that was an excuse. Now tell me, did you like what I made you?"

His muscles bunched in my hold as we held our strange position, me backed up to the fridge with him curled over me, caught up in my grip. "They were alright."

"Just alright?"

"I could think of things I'd rather eat more...if you'd let me."

I clucked my tongue. "Tonight isn't about me. Tonight is about me making amends to you."

"What if that's what I want most?" He was practically panting for it, and if that wasn't gratifying, I didn't know what was.

"Maybe later," I said with a wicked grin before I pivoted, my hold on Ben's shirt taking him with me until our positions were reversed. Now he was pressed up against the refrigerator. "For now, you'll have to learn exactly how good I am at apologizing."

I lowered to my knees on his hard kitchen floor.

Chapter Twenty-Nine

Ben

I WOULD NEVER RECOVER from the visual of Jill kneeling at my feet, staring up at me with that chaotic grin on her face. Her blonde hair was a mess from her running her pink-tipped fingers through it, and one sleeve of her lilac-colored dress was slipping off her shoulder.

She looked so amazing and beautiful and powerful that I almost forgot that I was still mad at her.

All I could think as she reached for the buckle of my brown belt was that I was so happy she was here with me. It was so heady I had to squeeze my eyes closed, sighing at the clang of the metal buckle opening, the pop of the button on my jeans, and the rasp of the zipper as she tugged it down.

I had missed her so much.

"You're missing the best part," she said, startling me as I felt her exhalation across my lower abs where she'd raised up my shirt.

I choked out a laugh. "Not sure if this is the best part, Blossom."

My skin pinched slightly as she curled her fingers in the waistline of my pants and boxer briefs, and my stomach clenched as I waited for her to drag them down.

"The anticipation is *always* the best part."

My eyes flew open as my pants and boxers hit the floor with a swoop. Jill sat back on her heels, taking in the sight of my dick like it was her next meal.

Still, she hesitated, reminding me of the way she'd tensed up while riding my face back at her apartment. I wanted to help—knew I *needed* to help her. It was what I was here for, after all. To serve Jill, to let her use me to meet her needs.

I needed to step it the fuck up.

"You're doing great," I tried.

"I know, Ben," she said, her voice a snarl.

Okay, the pep talk route wasn't it. I cast my mind back to the questions she'd answered, the ones about roles and dirty talk and power exchange. Right now, Jill was in charge, and we both liked it. I thought we'd both been shocked at just how much. But one thing she had noted was that she liked a back and forth, almost a fight for the lead.

I moved my hand that was plastered flat onto the fridge and traced her cheek, sliding it into the back of her hair. My fingers twisted in the fine strands, forming a ponytail of sorts.

"What are you waiting for, Blossom? Suck my cock."

Her eyes lit from within, and I knew I'd done it. Those smooth hands slid up my quads, and she grabbed hold of my dick in one hand while the other landed at the side of my ass. I felt the change in texture that was her little pinky ring—the one that spelled out *Fuck*—as she gave me three firm strokes.

"Like that?" she asked, even though she already knew the answer from the way I was basically humping the air.

I gave her scalp a squeeze, delicate but notable. "I want your mouth, Blossom."

She shot me a raised-brow look, her grip tightening by a degree.

"Please," I said.

She hummed once before taking me into the warm, wet heat of that distracting mouth. It was heaven and torturous hell at once. She kept hold of the base of my cock with her fist and brought her lips down to meet her hand. I groaned when I felt her tongue curl around the head, moving the ball of my piercing. She was playing, experimenting.

"You ever been with someone with one of those before?"

She pulled off and met my gaze as she kept up steady strokes over my saliva-soaked cock. "Nope. Why? Am I an expert?"

I was mad for this woman. She was a complete contradiction in every way. A teasing, cocky vixen with a secret shy side. A commitment-averse serial non-dater who showed me more and more of her fierce heart with each moment I spent with her.

"You should teach classes," I said with a gasp as she swallowed me down again.

It wasn't long before I was close to coming, Jill's fingers digging into the clenched muscles of my hip. I loved the way she smelled, loved the sounds she made as she licked and sucked, loved the way her hair tangled in my fingers.

She released her hold on my dick but kept going with slow, deep sucks. She reached for the hand I had tangled in her hair, placing her own over the top of it before pulling up enough to speak.

"Fuck my face."

Holy hell.

Obviously, I listened, grabbing the back of her head in both palms and thrusting.

This was a dream, and I didn't want to wake up. But I couldn't last forever, especially as the head of my cock pressed over and over against the back of Jill's throat as I followed her command. The inner muscles of her mouth clenched around me, and I was done for.

"Coming," I managed to grunt, loosening my fingers from her hair so she had the option to pull off if she wanted. She hadn't gotten very specific about swallowing in those questions, only saying it depended on her mood.

Apparently, she was in the mood as she timed her swallows with each jerk of my cock, a blissed out look on her face. I went limp against the fridge, registering the magnet shaped like Saint Sophia Cathedral poking into my shoulder blade.

Jill looked up with a smile as she rose to her feet, bringing my pants and boxer briefs with her. I sent her a grateful look as I tugged the fabric back in place.

"So," she said, all cheeky confidence and flushed skin. "Still think I'm bad at apologies?"

I smoothed a palm over her cascading locks, tucking the mess behind an ear. "Your apology sucked."

That earned the bawdy laugh I had been hoping for. "Literally," she said as she leaned into my hand. I doubted she even knew she was doing it, seeking me out like a cat wanting affection.

"I think your apology is still missing something, though."

Her fair brows pinched together. "What's that?"

I slowly spun us around until Jill's lower back rested against the lip of the kitchen counter. "I had another sort of dessert in mind."

I watched as her face fell. The change was minuscule, but I paid so much attention to Jill's every move that I clocked it right away.

"Oh, uh, I'm not—I mean, are you sure?"

I placed my palms around her waist and boosted her onto the speckled laminate counter. She was at eye-level now, a hairsbreadth away physically, but her head was somewhere else again. I knew she was embarrassed and worried about failing, but I could also see how badly she needed this.

I swooped the heavy fall of her hair over her shoulder, cupping my hand at the side of her neck. I tilted her face up to look at me.

"If this doesn't work, I'll turn on a movie and make some popcorn. Fuck, I'll go get that toy I bought for you out of my drawer again and leave you to it. You can let me watch or tell me to leave you the hell alone. I don't care. But I think we should try."

"This night is supposed to be for you, though. How is it fair for me to make you eat me out when it might be a lost cause in the end?"

I gave her a little shake. "First off, you're not *making* me do anything. I'll lick your pussy eight days a week if you allow me that privilege. And second, I think if your last memory is of this not working, you're going to keep having trouble. Like a self-fulfilling prophecy or whatever they call it."

Her body quaked with a chuckle. "You sound like Kristi."

"She's a wise woman. I'll take that as a compliment," I said as I ran my thumb along her pulse point.

"You think so? You don't think she's strange or anything?"

"Nah." I spoke the word next to her ear before tracing my tongue along the path my thumb took moments before.

Jill shivered, her legs coming up to wrap around my hips.

"Really?" Her breath hitched as I licked across her collarbone. "Some people think she is, but she's truly—"

I lifted my head and pressed a finger to her pretty rose-colored lips. "Jill? Let's stop talking about your friend now, okay?"

She bobbed her head up and down. I felt her thighs clench in an unconscious effort to bring me closer.

I hid my smile in the curve of her shoulder as my heart clenched. It hurt to be this happy.

CHAPTER THIRTY

Jill

B EN TILL GAVE OFF pheromones, because the man had essentially shushed me, and I found it sexy. To his credit, I *had* been babbling.

He was right. We needed to make another attempt. I didn't want my last memory of cunnilingus to feature a running monologue from my douchey ex-boyfriend.

Ben's hand at my nape tightened a fraction, pulling me back into the present. He fixed those silver eyes on my mouth, and for a split second, I thought—hoped, for some odd reason—that he might kiss me.

Instead, he used the finger at my lips to tug the thicker bottom one down, exposing my teeth. A second digit joined the first, and he placed the tips of each just inside my mouth, pressing at the flat of my tongue.

I opened fully, accepting the entry, and sucked his fingers deep, laving them with my tongue the same way I'd treated his cock.

"You're so good at that. You know that, right? You sucked me so well, Blossom."

I was wet remembering the way he'd shot his cum down my throat, and his words made me even wetter. The praise meant something, especially after hearing only critical words for so long—from Oliver, but more from myself.

He took his fingers out and glanced down at them. "Perfect," he whispered, almost to himself.

"You ready?" he asked as he settled on the floor between my legs. Even with me perched on the counter, he was so tall that his head was level with my hips—the ideal position for what he planned to do.

I nodded shakily. A split second later, he was pressing my knees apart and ducking beneath my lilac-colored skirt.

His hot breath drifted across my inner thighs and over the silk fabric covering my clit. I stiffened, not out of nervousness this time, but out of anticipation. I couldn't see Ben, but I could feel him everywhere all at once, and I loved it. I loved the pressure of his broad shoulders forcing my legs wide. I loved the way the heat of his exhalations sent tingles up my body. I loved the way his teeth nipped at the thin skin at my hip and the way he nuzzled the same spot afterward, his clean-shaven face rough with end-of-day stubble.

I whimpered when he moved his damp fingers, sliding them into the sides of my panties. He rubbed the backs of his knuckles slowly down my slick labia, teasing and toying until my hips began to move involuntarily, seeking him out.

I didn't have time to worry about his opinion of my vulva before he switched things up. With a quick twist of his hand, he changed angles, grabbing the waistband of my underwear in a tight fist and pulling until the material tore. I couldn't contain my gasp, and my thighs clenched on instinct, pressing firmly into his ears.

He groaned, pulling out from under my skirt to look at me. His blue gaze bore into mine, cold as ice but on fire for me.

"I liked that," he said.

"I could tell," I said. And I could. Ben wasn't judging me, or my pussy, or the way I'd almost choked him out with my thighs.

"Don't be afraid to grab my head. Put me right where you want me, okay?"

"Okay."

"I mean it, Jill. Don't be gentle."

With that, he dove back under, taking one long, hard lick straight up my center, lingering on my clit for a moment, before repeating the move twice more. His fingers curled into the flesh of my outer thigh, making me shiver in delight at the thought of the bruises I might find in the morning.

I dragged a foot up, placing the arch on one of Ben's wide shoulders, opening myself up for him. I couldn't see him, but the sense of near anonymity eased some of my self-consciousness, allowing me to focus on my body and how good this felt.

Ben wasn't satisfied, though. He grabbed that foot, all the while continuing his onslaught on my pussy, and placed it level with my hips on the counter. Taking the other foot, the one still dangling, he did the same thing. He stretched me as far as possible without restraints. Next, he reached for the hand that was white-knuckling the lip of the countertop and placed it atop his head over my dress. I wasn't touching him directly, but I could feel the warmth of his skin through the thin fabric.

The whole time, he kept up a steady pace with lips and tongue, and I was embarrassingly close already—if I could ever get there.

I wondered afterward if Ben had felt the change in my body language when the thought ran through my head, because he changed his approach again, sliding two large fingers inside me and covering my clit with his mouth. He went faster now too, and my brain couldn't keep up with the steady speed of his sucking lips and thrusting fingers. I held him to me with both hands. If he moved an inch, it would be ruined.

When his teeth scraped over my sensitive flesh, it was over. My foot slipped along the counter as all the muscles in my body clenched and released in pulsating waves, making contact with the pan of brownies. The metal tray fell to the floor with a clatter, its contents spilling across the pale laminate.

Ben sat up straight, pulling out from under my dress with a bewildered look on his face. When he looked back at me in wonder, I burst out laughing.

If someone had asked me if I could have ever envisioned myself spread out on Ben Till's kitchen counter, his lips and chin covered in the proof of my arousal while we laughed over spilled brownies, I would have called bullshit. Laughter and orgasms weren't something I had associated with one another in a very long time.

"Well, damn," he said as our echoing chuckles petered out. "My apology brownies are ruined."

I snorted as he stood up, wrapping his arms around my waist to help me down off the counter.

"Those brownies were barely hanging on anyway. Besides, don't you think the blow job was a better way to say I'm sorry, anyway?"

Ben slicked his tongue over his lips. "I'm not sure; the brownies were pretty damn good."

"Oh, really?" I said in mock offense. "I thought you said they were mediocre. You're not trying to imply that my oral skills are sub-par, are you?"

"Why, do you wanna practice some more?"

I shrugged, shoving down the new wave of desire that flowed through me. As amazing as Ben had made me feel, the joy I'd derived from making him come was almost better.

"That could be arranged. You'd have to be a very good boy, though."

His eyes crinkled at the corners as he looked down at me. I was still in his embrace, my back pressed up against the countertop, and neither of us seemed inclined to move.

If we had that sort of relationship, I would have stood up on my tiptoes to give him a kiss. But since we weren't doing that, I settled for laying my head on his chest, the rhythmic *thud-thud* of his heart matching the beat of mine.

He gave a full-body sigh, sliding the hand at my waist up to rest between my shoulder blades. We stayed that way until the ice maker kicked on again, jolting me once more.

"Should we talk?" he asked.

"About what?"

He stepped away, and I wanted to tug him right back in. "Maybe we can have dinner? Talk while we cook. Keep our hands busy, since I get the sense that jumping straight into an emotional conversation without any distractions isn't going to work for us. Then we can watch some TV after, if you still want to hang out." He paused, his throat bobbing. "You don't have to stay. It's totally up to you. But please don't turn into a ghost again."

"Okay, but you have to promise to go easy on me."

"Only if you'll return the favor."

CHAPTER THIRTY-ONE

Ben

THE STEAK SIZZLED AS I flipped it on the grill.

Jill opened the sliding glass door, carrying a large mixing bowl with an uncut watermelon inside. In the other hand, she held a cutting board and a large kitchen knife.

"That smells good," she said as she set herself up at my picnic table.

"Thanks. I've had the steaks in the freezer for a while, so I'm glad to have an excuse to make them."

"It's really nice out here," she said as she cast her gaze around the backyard. I'd used native plants—wild grasses and flowers that attracted pollinators. It was my sanctuary, and it made me profusely happy that Jill liked it. "I'm guessing you did the work yourself?"

"You'd be right. It took a long time to get it exactly how I wanted. I had to fit the work into my schedule over the course of like, three summers. Didn't get much sleep those seasons."

"Kind of like how you fit me and Velvet into your plans this year?" She made the opening cut into the watermelon, the crisp crunch mingling with the sound of buzzing bees and a distant lawnmower.

I closed the grill and turned fully. The last thing I wanted was for her to think she was an obligation.

"What I'm doing to help with the flooding isn't a hardship. The digging is fairly easy, and your help made a difference."

"You would never admit otherwise, would you?"

"I am a gentleman." One who just wanted to be around this woman.

I moved to the table to sit next to her. She sent me a dirty look when I stole a piece of fruit from the ever-filling bowl.

"Watch yourself, Benny Boy." She cheekily aimed the knife tip toward me.

I threw my hands up in a defensive gesture. "I come in peace."

"If there isn't any watermelon left to go with dinner, you'll be sorry. Plus, cutting things up is about as far as my cooking skills go, so I'm gonna need you to let me play pretend chef over here."

"If you don't cook, what was that dessert earlier?"

"I *can* read basic directions. Add water and an egg and set a timer. When you insulted those brownies earlier, you were actually insulting Betty Crocker. She can take the heat, I'm sure."

I moved back to the grill as we chatted, checking to make sure the steaks weren't getting overdone.

"You want anything else with this? A salad or something?" I asked.

"Do you have corn on the cob? Corn on the grill is amazing, and I haven't had it in forever."

"Nope. But I can pick some up at the grocery store tomorrow if you want."

"I'll grab it on my way over since I don't have to put in any hours at Fantasy Dongs. That makes it a little easier on you, doesn't it?"

"Yeah, thank you."

I plated the four steaks and smiled as I kept my focus on the bumpy concrete. Jill and I hadn't had a conversation about doing anything the next day, but somehow, we had both settled into that arrangement. I worried if I called even the barest amount of attention to our growing domesticity, she would run off again.

"The meat needs to rest. You want to slice up those veggies while I grab a head of lettuce from the fridge?" I tipped my chin toward the small basket on the table. It was filled with fresh vegetables I had picked from my garden while waiting for the grill to heat up.

Jill agreed, and I ran back into the house to grab everything we needed to finish dinner prep.

"**S**o," I said as I slid into the seat across from Jill. She was chopping sweet peppers with a very serious tongue tip between her teeth. I was tempted to bite it. Gently, though. "I just want to put it out that there you seemed to enjoy yourself tonight."

She looked up from the cutting board with raised brows but said nothing.

"That's a good thing...right?" I was getting mildly terrified.

She flicked the knife down hard into the red flesh of a pepper. "It is."

"Then why do you seem mad right now?"

She peeked up at me over her lashes so I could spot her hidden grin.

"You're messing with me!"

"Of course I am! I can't have you getting too big a head now, can I?"

"You're evil."

"I'm just a girl, Benny Boy."

"Yeah, you're a girl who ignored my ass for almost two weeks."

"Oh, we're moving straight into the more serious topics for the night, are we?"

"Someone's gotta get serious."

She set the knife down on the cutting board, tossed the peppers into a large mixing bowl filled with lettuce and cucumbers, and brushed her hands together.

"Ghosting you was a shit move. I am genuinely sorry."

"I mean, on some level, I get it. You were vulnerable, and I saw it. I'm a reminder of that vulnerability. But I don't want you to forget that we're friends too. I don't judge my friends. We knew going into this that it would involve some trial and error. The errors aren't fun, but if we just stop trying every time we hit a sticky spot, we'll never move forward." And I was selfishly desperate to keep going with her.

"You are, like, disturbingly in touch with your emotions, Benny."

I chuckled, pushing back from the bench of the table to check on the steaks. If only she knew how off-kilter my emotions toward her had been over the years.

"That's a compliment, I think?"

"Oh, it is. But it's also intimidating as fuck. Because I definitely don't measure up in that department."

I shook my head as I placed a hand on her slumped shoulder. "We're not gonna play the comparison game." I took a chance and leaned down to press my lips to the delicate skin at the base of her neck. "First, because I think you're giving yourself too little credit, and second, because communication and self-reflection are skills like any other. They take time to development. Maybe I've just had more practice."

She twisted in her seat to catch my eye. "You're not helping me feel less intimidated here, just so you know." She said it with a smile, though. A real one.

I drifted away, reluctantly, to plate the meat and grab utensils. Jill did a wiggling dance as she added watermelon and salad to her dish.

"I'm so excited for food. I hadn't realized how hungry I was until you started talking about dinner."

"You didn't get enough to eat when we were in the kitchen?" I teased.

"Wh—oh, come on, Ben, seriously? I know you can do better than that."

"It was low-hanging fruit. I had to."

She chewed, her cheeks puffed out like a chipmunk. "This is fun," she said as she swallowed.

"What is?"

"Eating, hanging out, making jokes with you. I *guess* I can see why my brother has kept you around for so long."

I cleared the sudden catch in my throat at the mention of my best friend. "Do you, uh...think he'll still like me if he ever finds out about this? Us, I mean?"

Jill speared a cucumber slice and popped it into her mouth before answering. "Why would he ever find out? It's not like we're doing anything he would need to know about."

My mouth went dry. I chewed a chunk of steak for what seemed like a solid minute before I got the strength to swallow. She was right. The only reason for James to know about me and Jill was if we were more than a hookup.

"Are you okay?" she asked.

"Huh?" I had zoned out.

"You got quiet all of a sudden. I just asked if you were okay."

"Uh, yeah. I'm good. Just thinking about what you said. About how James doesn't have a reason to know about us."

"Right. We're both consenting adults. My brother has never cared to ask who I've slept with before, so I don't see why it should matter now."

"You're right, but…"

"But what?"

"Well, it's not like we've been subtle. I don't want to make a big deal of it, but some of the guys on my crew were asking questions. Apparently, there has been some gossip. And, well, I imagine Honey has her suspicions now too."

The ridge of Jill's cheekbones turned a soft petal pink. "I assume you told your crew members that we're just friends, right?"

"I did. But I'm not sure if they believed it."

She sighed. "I suppose there isn't anything we can do about it at this point. The more we try to deny it, the more suspicious it'll look."

"Yeah. Probably." I told myself I didn't care that she sounded so…unenthusiastic…about the idea of people knowing about us. I *shouldn't* care. I was supposed to be getting over her.

"There's nothing more to it, in that case," she said. "We just keep doing what we're doing, and fuck whoever has an opinion. It's not like it'll last forever."

Fuck. Me.

I chugged the last of my iced tea, choking on the final gulp. "Do you still want to be friends after we're finished with the benefits?"

She drummed her glossy fingernails on the grainy wood surface of the table. "I really don't know, Ben."

I forced myself to stay seated, even though all I wanted to do was jump up and run for the hills. Anything to burn off this unnamable feeling.

Because I still wanted Jill, and it was apparent now that no number of hookups was going to make me stop wanting her. It would probably last forever at this point.

She was already looking for a way out.

I gritted my teeth before responding. "Why not? I don't want another rehash of you ghosting me and lying to me about it this last week. That hurt, Jill."

"I told you I was sorry! And you said you understood why I did it! So, was that not the case?"

"It was—it *is* the case. But if you were really sorry, you wouldn't imply that you're about to do the same thing to me again. What gives? Because to me, we established that this relationship would involve sex, but at its core, we would be *friends*. If that's not where your head is at anymore, tell me now."

I did stand up this time, shooting up from my seat and bashing my kneecap on the wood underside of the table. "Shit," I muttered as I stalked toward the sliding-glass door, my empty plate in hand.

"Ben, stop."

I paused because I was the worst sort of masochist with this woman. I could make out the vague lines of her face in the reflection of the sliding-glass door.

"It isn't that I don't want to be friends with you after we stop having sex. It's that...fuck, this open and vulnerable communication shit is hard." I heard a sniffle from her direction and started to turn. "No, don't look at me! It's easier to get this out if I can't see you." I heard her shoes scrape on the patio close behind me. "The reason I don't know if we can continue being friends after these next few months is because I know you'll move on."

"Jill, what are you—"

"Please don't interrupt. I need to get this out." She let out a shuddering breath that I longed to feel on my skin. I wanted to take her in my arms and soothe what was bothering her so much. But I couldn't do the work for her. "Okay, so you clearly want a serious, long-term relationship, right?"

"Right," I said stiffly.

"Well, when you do find your person, what's she going to think about you being friends with a woman you have a sexual history with? I don't want to get in the way. I don't want to be a weird, awkward reminder of that time you pity-fucked me for a summer—"

I whirled around, and she was in my arms in two steps, my palms clasping her damp cheeks. "Let me make one thing absolutely clear: I don't pity you. When we finally fuck—and believe me, we *will*—there will be no place for pity. I'll be fucking you because you're beautiful and sexy and funny. For no other reason than the fact that you turn me on, and I *want* to be with you. Do you understand?"

It was as real as I was willing to get with her. Any further confession would scare her away for good.

She closed her eyes briefly and gave a brief nod.

"As for your other concern, what sense does it make to get worried about something that isn't even happening? What mysterious, amazing girlfriend do you think I'm going to suddenly find? You act as if I'm going to meet my wife tomorrow."

"You might, though."

It was the worst feeling in the world that I was beginning to think I already had. Wasn't being in love supposed to feel good? Euphoric?

"So what?" The words came out like I'd swallowed shards of glass. "You're my friend, and whoever I'm with in the future will have to accept that."

She smiled through tremulous lips that I wanted to take deep, sipping pulls from. If only that wouldn't violate her firm boundary. "That's deliciously naive, Benny Boy."

"If it's a problem, we'll evaluate as it happens. For now, I don't want to borrow trouble. Do you want to be my friend, Blossom?"

"Yes, I do." Her accompanying nod was emphatic.

"So, let's go inside, clean up, and throw on the TV for a while. Just don't run away on me again, alright?"

"Alright."

"You promise?"

"Yeah. I promise, Ben."

If I could convince Jill to stick around longer, to spend more time with me, then she might give this a real shot. I would have to play it cooler than anything I'd ever done, but I could do it.

I had a mission now.

Jill

THE FOLLOWING WEEKS PASSED in a whirlwind of Velvet repairs, work, and Ben. It was odd the way we had settled into this comfortable domestic routine. Neither of us had mentioned it, almost as if we were afraid to ruin whatever fantasies we'd built up in our heads about what this was. We ate dinner together and watched reality TV shows nearly every night of the week—and for a guy who insisted he hated reality shows, Ben had *thoughts* about which contestants were there for love versus fame.

If he had to work a late job, we skipped the dinner portion of the night and just hung out on his couch with popcorn and a shitty movie.

And sometimes, Ben ate me out so well and for so long that I felt like I needed an I.V. to rehydrate.

The only thing I could reasonably complain about was that we still hadn't had penetrative sex. We'd done plenty of other things, and I wasn't in the business of claiming that P-in-V sex was the only *real* way to do it—hell, I could attest that much fun could be had with no penises involved—but I was frustrated that he was still holding back. Because I wanted to take that step with Ben, wanted to see if the orgasms he'd coaxed from me would carry over into other acts. Most of all, I wanted to feel what that damn cock piercing could do when it hit me just right.

I was slightly embarrassed about how many times I'd looked up different types of piercings and their benefits. Apparently, Ben's choice of jewelry, the apadravya, was said to feel particularly good for the wearer's partner, and I wanted to test that for myself.

For science.

That night wouldn't be this one, much to my chagrin. My period had started, and I'd woken up with a lingering headache and cramps. Over-the-counter painkillers had taken the edge off enough to make it through my shift at the library, but all I wanted now was my bed and a heating pad. If a magical fairy showed up with dark chocolate and an iced coffee, I wouldn't be upset.

I had messaged Ben this morning to let him know I would be temporarily out of commission. He had been fine with it, telling me to let him know if I needed anything. When I had apologized that we wouldn't be able to take advantage of the benefits aspect of our friendship, he assured me it was no big deal and that he had plans for the night anyway.

I was still trying to get a handle on the wave of disappointment that had hit when he told me. It was stupid and made no sense. Ben and I were casual. Casual wasn't seeing each other every single night for weeks. Casual wasn't making grocery lists together. Casual wasn't inside jokes and back rubs and looking up plant facts on my lunch break to impress Ben.

Maybe a break tonight was exactly what I needed.

I was cleaning up scraps of construction paper when Kristi and Emma sauntered over from the hallway that housed their offices. Kristi had a large canvas tote bag hoisted over one shoulder with stray items poking out the top. Emma carried her purse with no strange objects in sight.

"Hey," Kristi said. "Want some help with the rest of this mess? Glitter is a bitch to clean up."

"No, thanks. I'm good. This is the last of it," I said as I swept the remaining craft supply mix into a plastic bag. "I've just got to take this to the dumpster, and then I'm out of here too."

"Want to come over to my place tonight?" Emma asked as the three of us walked out the back door. "Kris and I were talking about it earlier. James is hanging out at Maven's with Ben, so we have the house to ourselves."

The swaying plastic bag tangled in my legs when I heard Ben's name, and I would have gone down if it hadn't been for Emma's bracing grip on my elbow.

"Is everything okay with you?" she asked.

I avoided Kristi's knowing gaze. I had been keeping mum on the new developments from the Ben front, but the woman was the most observant person I knew.

"Yep! Never better." That sounded appropriately convincing—I hoped.

Kristi coughed—a muffled laugh—and I shot her a withering look.

"Don't look at her, Jill. That wasn't even subtle. Now you have to come to the house and fill us in," Emma said with a smile.

I launched the garbage bag up into the dumpster, where it fell with a satisfying rattle. "There's nothing to share. I just have my period, and I'm feeling off. Nothing more to it."

Emma clicked her car's key fob. A short beep sounded in the back lot. "I've been around you when you've had your period before, and it doesn't explain the cryptic looks and the general weirdness. Do *you* know what's going on?" she asked, turning to Kristi.

My friend smoothed a hand over her purple hair, the silver bangles on her wrist catching the light. "I do, but we shouldn't talk about it here."

Emma's brow lowered over her eyes. "Why not? We're the only ones—oh, hi Mayor Till!"

Ben's mom, all five intimidating feet of her, strode out the rear entrance of the town hall. The town offices and the library shared the same building, as well as the dumpster we were all huddled around.

"Good evening, ladies! Don't stay out too late. I've heard a raccoon likes to make a ruckus back here."

She was around the corner and hopping into her sporty black car a minute later. The goldenrod and sky-blue flag decal on her back window caught a ray of sun as she made a left turn onto the side street.

"I want to be her when I grow up," I said with a sigh.

"I don't know. She's cool and all, but that could get really fucking weird for Ben, don't you think?" Kristi said.

"Kristi! What the hell!"

"Alright, we are going back to my house right now, and the two of you are going to tell me what is going on," Emma said, linking a firm arm around my elbow and the other around Kristi's. "I'll drag you there if I have to."

❧ ❧ ❧ ❧ ❧ ❧ ❧ ❧ ❧

"I THOUGHT HE WAS never going to leave," Emma said as she detailed how long it took to get James out of the house.

"Is the honeymoon period over already?" I pocketed two Tylenol tablets in my cheek.

She smiled shyly, as if holding in a happy secret. "Not at all. But sometimes I need to miss him so I appreciate him more."

"Don't let her lie to you. She just wants the hot gossip, and she knows you won't talk with your brother around."

"Kristi! I feel called out." Emma flicked on the switch for the ceiling fan before settling in next to me on the couch. I grabbed one of the down-filled throw pillows, placed it on her thighs, then shifted to plop my head down on her lap.

I let out a relieved sigh as the muscles in my lower back loosened.

"You sure you're alright?" Kristi asked. She was curled up in a brocade arm-chair.

"I'm fine. Just crampy and cranky."

"Do you need anything? Water? A banana? A heating pad?" I could feel Emma shifting below me, ready to leap into action.

"No, no, don't get up. I'm finally getting comfy." I was half tempted to close my eyes and fall asleep. Something about being in James and Emma's old Victorian house—my childhood home—made me feel warm and safe. It was the one place that felt like my mom.

Emma patted my head and curled back into the sofa. "You let me know if you change your mind. I'm not being entirely selfless, so don't get it twisted. I'm hoping if you feel better, you'll be more likely to talk."

I groaned and buried my face in the pillow. "There isn't much to tell. Ben and I are friends now."

She was vibrating under me. I got the sense that she was struggling not to hop off the couch and start pacing the living room.

"*Just* friends?"

I'd debated making up a lie on the way over. Emma's ultimate loyalty was to my brother, after all. But in the end, I'd decided to trust her.

"There are...occasional benefits involved," I said, still muffled into the pillow.

I felt her take a deep inhale. "Did you know about this?" She shot the question at Kristi.

"Sort of. I knew Jill was thinking about it, but I didn't know for certain that things had changed until now."

I sat up slowly, my body protesting. "It was only something I was considering until a few weeks ago. I've kept it to myself until tonight."

"Were you scared to tell me because I'm marrying your brother?" Emma asked. "I don't want you to censor your conversations with me because of that. We were friends before I got with James."

I placed a gentling hand on hers. I'd made the choice to trust Emma with this secret, and I needed to trust her and Kristi with my fears and worries too.

"I can't say it didn't cross my mind, but I realized as I drove over here that you two are my people. If I can't be open with you, then I can't be open with anyone." Emma's eyes softened. Kristi gave me a reassuring smile.

"I haven't dated anyone in so long that I think I've forgotten how to talk about it. And even when I did date, things were so bad that I felt like a sad-sap bringing it up. Like I was putting a burden on my friends by even mentioning it."

"Are things...bad...with you and Ben?" Emma asked carefully. She always knew when to push and when to let me lead.

"Not at all! It's been...well, pretty wonderful if I'm being honest." So wonderful that it was freaking me out. My walls were slowly eroding. I didn't know what would happen if I let Ben all the way in again and got hurt.

"So, what exactly is this thing you and Ben are doing? Are you dating?"

"Definitely not. It's strictly sex and friendship." I spoke the words quickly. Firmly.

"How did it get to this point?" she asked. "You've been talking about how much you hate Ben practically since I met you."

My efforts to hate Ben had failed in spectacular, orgasmic proportion. I was practicing opening up to my friends, but I wasn't ready to dive into the reason I had been so upset with Ben. "I worked it out. He helped with the yard flood, we got close, and now he's helping me get my groove back, so to speak. I want to feel more confident about sex before Velvet opens."

"*You* aren't confident about sex?" Emma asked incredulously.

I let out a light laugh. "Remember that shitty dating history I brought up earlier? Let's just say that it left a mark, and sex with a partner has been a challenge for me ever since. But Ben's the opposite of my ex, and he's hot, so..."

"True, he does have that sexy yet simultaneously sweet thing going on, doesn't he? It's just that...no, forget it."

"You can't start a sentence like that and then say forget it, Emma."

"Don't take this the wrong way, but you've gotten a little, shall we say, *touchy*, with the Ben subject in the past, so I'm taking that into account before I really unleash my thoughts."

I crossed my arms and made a *hmph* sound. "I am not touchy about Ben."

"Sure you're not." Emma tipped her head toward Kristi, who had thus far been quietly watching our back and forth, her eyes following the verbal volley like a tennis match. "What do you think, Kris? Touchy or not touchy?"

"One hundred percent touchy."

"Oh my god, can we stop saying touchy?! I would kick you out, but this is your house."

Emma shimmied her shoulders in delight. "That's right, isn't it? You're stuck with me for life."

I got back into position with my head on her lap, keeping my arms fastened over my chest as I watched the blades of the ceiling fan rotate.

"I promise I won't bite your head off about whatever it is you're about to say. Chances are I've already said it to myself anyway."

"Well, it just seems to me that your preexisting connections to Ben—the whole brother's-best-friend thing—make him an odd choice as the guy helping you gain sexual confidence. There are a lot of potential complications, and you're putting yourselves in that position for what? Something casual? Unless you have a very good reason for it, it sounds risky. Why Ben? He's hot, but so are lots of other people. People without all the extra...baggage...that Ben brings to the table."

My back was stiffening up again, despite my relaxed position on the sofa. "The extra baggage is Jimbo. And since Ben and I are only casual, he never needs to know. Besides, even if we were serious, it wouldn't be any of James' business. The whole idea of a woman's brother thinking he has the right to decide who she's with is so stupid it's mind-boggling."

"Oh, I agree. Don't get it twisted. For the record, I don't think James would be upset that you and Ben were together—not exactly. But you know how he worries. I think he would be scared of one of you getting hurt if things didn't work out."

"There isn't anything to work out or not work out. We're friends who occasionally get physical. No big deal."

"How often are you and Ben hanging out and getting physical?" Kristi asked.

"A normal amount. Like I said, we're actual friends now."

"What's a normal amount? Because you're one of my best friends, and lately, if I don't see you at work, we probably only hang out every other week."

That was true. I'd been so overwhelmed that I'd started a slow slide off the friendship train lately. "I'm sorry, guys. Things have been hectic for me, but I should be making more time to see you both."

"I don't care about that. Not to say I wouldn't love to see more of you, but I get it. You're working two jobs and opening a business. I don't take it personally, and I'm pretty sure Emma doesn't either."

I flicked my gaze up to see Emma bobbing her head in agreement.

"But my point is this," Kristi continued. "You have all these things going on, but you're making time for Ben. You dodged my question, so I have to assume you're seeing him quite a bit. And before you get all worked up, that is a *good* thing. But it does make me wonder just how casual this really is. Are you keeping firm with your boundaries?"

"Yes. No kissing. No sleepovers. We haven't done either of those."

"Well, damn, never mind," Emma said. "I was going to ask if Ben was a good kisser. He looks like he would be."

"Ugh, I know right?" I blurted out.

Kristi raised her dark brows. I hid my face in my hands.

CHAPTER THIRTY-THREE

Ben

JAMES SLAMMED THE DRIVER'S side door of his truck shut as I came around the other side.

"You sure I can stay? Don't want Emma to get put out."

"Nah, she won't mind. Tomorrow is her day off, so it's all good. We've got the spare room since Harry moved out."

"Thanks, man."

I'd left my truck in the Maven's lot. I didn't make a habit of overdoing it at the bar, but tonight I'd had one too many. Driving was a risk I didn't want to take. James would give me a ride back to the truck in the morning after I slept it off.

The house was quiet as we tiptoed in through the front entry. He shot me an irritated look when I closed the glass-paned front door a touch too hard, rattling the frame.

"Sorry," I said, holding in a low-pitched snicker.

A dim light above the oven offered enough illumination for me to start my trek up the stairs.

"I'm gonna get a glass of water before I head up. You need anything?" he asked.

"Spare toothbrushes in the bathroom?"

"Yep. Emma got a fancy new basket for them, under the sink on the left-hand side."

I giggled as I brushed, thinking about how I almost could have had it all—free toothbrushes for life. Though I wasn't sure how Dr. Casey would have liked this tipsy, goofy version of me. Probably not as much as Jill liked it. Not that Jill had seen me tipsy, but she'd definitely seen the silly during our recent hang-outs.

Lately, we had become obsessed with finding the perfect popcorn seasoning. Jill liked the classic butter-and-salt combo, while I was all about trying new flavors, my latest favorite being a mix of Buffalo and garlic. We usually started with our own bowls but always split them half and half by the end of the night.

I dried my face and caught a glimpse of my bloodshot eyes. Before leaving the bathroom, I sent off a quick goodnight message to Jill. Sleep was calling my name, but I didn't want her thinking I'd forgotten about her. She had said she wasn't feeling the greatest. If my plans with James hadn't already been set, I might have stopped by her apartment with a bucket of our favorite snack.

As if I'd conjured it with a thought, the scent of moonflowers filled my nostrils when I pushed open the guest room door. Jill's blonde hair spread across the pillows of the double bed, a gorgeous surprise. Her phone sat on the nightstand, lit up by my goodnight message. I waited a beat to see if she was stirring, but her soft, steady breathing was the only sound in the room. The floorboards creaked as I slowly made my way toward the bed. There was no way James knew she was here, no way he would have sent me to this room if he knew she was here.

I slowly sat on the edge of the mattress, level with her hip.

"Blossom," I whispered, giving the cap of her shoulder a gentle nudge.

She shifted, her head lolling in my direction. Her eyes opened to small slits. "Ben?"

"Hey," I said.

She looked confused, and my face hurt from grinning. I was about to get a Jill-filled night after all.

"What are you doing here? And why do you smell like nasty beer?"

A snort emanated from the back of my throat. "Maven's. Too much tonight. Your brother told me I could crash here. Don't think he realized you were already in here."

"Emma wrangled Kristi and me after work for an unexpected girls' night. We parked on the street. Kristi is on the couch. You probably missed her."

I liked Kristi Margarucci just fine, but I didn't care where she spent the night, not like I did with the woman in front of me.

Jill scooted farther toward the wall and lifted the blanket, inviting me inside. "Come on."

"Are you sure? Is there enough space in there for both of us?" My tongue slurred over all the *S* sounds in that sentence. Maybe I was drunker than I realized.

Her laugh tinkled like one of the wind chimes in my garden. "Get in, Ben."

Not wasting a second, I ripped my t-shirt over my head and stripped down to my boxer briefs. She cocked a brow at me.

"I sleep hot. Sorry."

I wasn't sorry at all when I felt the press of her skin, warm from the cocoon of the bed, on mine. The double bed left little space to maneuver.

I could have Jill cuddles all night long.

The prospect sent a thrill up my spine—and down my dick. I needed to get that under control. There would be no funny business tonight. Jill had mentioned feeling achy and having a headache.

"Get some sleep," I whispered in her ear as I settled my arm around her, just under the curve of her breasts.

"You too." She tugged my hand to the center of her chest. The steady thumping of her heart caused my own to skip a beat.

This is perfect, I thought as the rest of the world went dark.

"BEN."

I shoved my face into the pillow, pressing my ear into the plush surface.

"Ben," the voice said again, this time with more urgency. "I need to pee. Can you let me up?"

A layer of dust caked my eyes as I forced them open. Jill's brown eyes stared back, up close and personal. I registered the soft weight of her in my arms. She'd turned in the night. Our legs were tangled and wrapped around each other, like a horizontal hug.

"Good morning." That was the understatement of my life. Waking up with Jill made for a *great* morning.

"It's not morning yet, you doofus. At least, I don't think it is. Jimbo and Emma didn't think to put a clock in here, and I can't find my phone to check the time. But it's still dark, so I think we're okay. No one knows we're both in here."

I loosened my hold on her and turned onto my back. She slipped out of the bed and pulled on a pair of loose cotton shorts I hadn't noticed sitting on a dresser.

"Come back when you're done?" I asked, keeping my gaze carefully diverted. I was already afraid she would hear the stark desperation in my voice.

She didn't answer, and I couldn't resist twisting at the neck. Her only response was a slight twitch at the left corner of her mouth as she sidestepped into the hallway and closed the door softly behind her.

MY BODY JERKED AS I felt the heat of another body settle in next to me. I relaxed a second later when my nose registered that Jill smell.

"How long were you gone?" I grumbled.

Her back pressed into my chest, and she hooked a foot around my ankle. I let loose a great sigh into the mattress.

"Ten minutes, tops. I ran downstairs for a glass of water." She ran the smooth tips of her fingernails along my forearms.

"Shit. I didn't think I would fall back asleep that fast."

"You were a little tipsy. That probably didn't help."

"Yeah, I guess so."

"Did you and James have fun?"

Had we? Maybe we had. But all I could think about was what was happening right now, in this moment. "I think so. We hung out with some local guys for bit. Played some darts. I lost."

I felt the quake of her body rather than heard her small puff of laughter. "I would judge you for being bad at darts, but I'm awful too."

"I'm not *awful*. It's just that Scott Watson is a menace. I lost actual money."

She patted my wrist. "You'll be fine, Benny Boy. From what Tracey says, Scott is hyper-competitive. He even puts Harry to shame." Scott was married to Jill's boss at the library. "The first year he played Santa for our children's event, he was determined to see more kids than the Santa the previous year had. I swear he had a tally sheet. You could see him running the numbers in his head. It's admirable, actually."

"Yeah, well, he can play darts with some other sucker next time. I'm not made of money."

She squeezed my fingers before pressing a close-mouthed kiss to the tattoo inked across the back of my hand. My breath hitched, and I hoped she didn't notice.

I swallowed. "What was that for?"

"I—I missed you tonight. I've gotten used to it being the two of us the last few weeks. Is that weird?"

I shoved down the swell of emotion building in my chest. "Not weird. I missed you too. When we were out, I kept thinking you would give me such crap for getting drunk off three beers. Or how you would have messed with your brother for staring at pictures of Emma all night."

Her quiet chuckle shook the bed. "Stop, did he really do that?"

"All night. A woman came up to him—just making conversation—and he practically shoved his phone in her face to show off their engagement pictures."

"Is it a sign of personal growth that I kinda love that he's so happy? If you *ever* tell him that, I might have to come to your house and cut all the heads off your flowers."

"That's deranged, Blossom. Have you considered talking to someone about those wicked thoughts you've got floating around in your head?"

She lifted my hand to her mouth and took a nip from the pad of my thumb. "Don't be funny. It turns me on, and I am temporarily out of commission."

I moved my palm down to settle on her lower belly. I didn't know precisely where the uterus was, anatomically speaking, but I figured I was on the right path.

"How are you feeling?" I asked as I drew a big circle into her warm skin.

"Not bad. The cramps come and go. Headache isn't so bad at the moment."

"Tell me if you need anything, yeah?"

"Yeah."

"Jill, does this count?"

"As what?"

"As a sleepover."

She stiffened. The word fell like a bomb in the middle of our safe place.

I'd ruined it—and after being so careful not to go too fast.

"No. It doesn't, because I'm going home now anyway. It only counts if we wake up, and it's the morning."

She moved in a flash, tearing out of my hold. She still had on her green shorts.

"Jill," I said, stopping her as she reached for the brass doorknob.

"Yeah?"

"Don't forget your phone."

I snatched it off the nightstand and held it out to her. She stepped forward, inching her way toward me.

"I won't bite. Just take the damn thing."

Her shoulders dropped away from her neck as she approached the edge of the bed. She hesitated for a moment before leaning over me and grazing her lips over my cheek. "Thank you, Ben. I'll see you tomorrow."

Then she was gone, taking my heart with her.

Chapter Thirty-Four

Jill

I SLAMMED THE HAMMER down on the split framework at the lower corner of the bar. It was sticking out strangely, and with the now-pristine floors buffed and polished with dark stain, it looked out of place. The noise of crunchy guitars and double-kick drum beats filled the air. Kristi had recommended me her favorite angry-girl play list, and I had to say it fit my mood.

"Jill!"

"Holy shit!" I threw the hammer toward the booming voice, belatedly realizing my mistake in giving up my only weapon.

My brother ducked out of the way in the nick of time.

"What the fuck? You almost killed me!"

"It would have served you right for sneaking up on me like that!"

"I said your name five times. Plus, you really think my big ass can sneak anywhere? I'm six foot five. Fuck. And leave my bar alone. You're going to ruin it."

"It's not your bar. It's my bar."

"I built it."

"It's in my building."

He stooped to scoop the hammer off the floor. "Show me what you were doing."

I rolled my eyes but gestured to the imperfection in the corner.

"This? Really? I told you that spot was giving me trouble, and I would be back to adjust it once the crew finished with the flooring. Why didn't you wait?"

"In case you haven't noticed, Jimbo, I have a shit-ton of work to do. I don't have all the time in the world to wait around for you to become available."

"You know you don't have to do this all on your own, Jilly Bean."

Maybe I didn't have to, but I wanted to. James was so competent and giving that he made it damned hard not to want to rely on him for every little thing. My annoyance wasn't with him, but with myself for falling into the habit of letting him take over again and again.

I squared my shoulders before responding. "I'm the one who put my name and my money on the line here, so I sort of do. I'm not going to use you, or Ben, or anyone else for that matter, more than I have to."

"Well, what if we *want* to help? Do you think I'm only doing this because I feel obligated? I've been after you for years to come up with a serious plan for the rest of your life. You've been floundering in part-time, gig jobs since you graduated from college, and I've hated seeing it. You're smart and passionate, and you've finally found a way to channel that. You think I won't do everything possible to support you?"

My brother wasn't typically a talker, so I knew he meant what he said. I sniffled, mentally blaming it on the dust. "I haven't heard you string that many sentences together since the night you first told me about you and Emma."

He tugged me into his broad chest with a mitt-like hand. "Call me next time, got it?"

I would, especially after that speech, but not before I tried my own hand at solving the problem first.

"Fine," I said, my voice muffled against his shirt. "Ugh, you stink." I pushed off him. "When was the last time you showered?"

"I was at the gym and then had to make a delivery in Merlin Heights. I drove by and saw your SUV, so I decided to stop. Sorry to offend your nose."

"Whatever, just get to work on the bar. You know, if you'd built it right in the first place, there wouldn't be a problem now."

He flipped the hammer in his hand, an impressive feat, though I would never admit that to him. "Go...paint something, or whatever it is you have to do."

Leaving James in the speakeasy, I walked to the front of the building, where I planned to finish installing the shelves that would display inventory in the sex toy shop section of Velvet. I'd spent much of last week painting the walls a vibrant bubblegum pink. The shelves would help break up the color so it wouldn't be too blinding.

I pressed the play button on my phone, kicking my angry playlist back on. A clatter sounded from the other side of the building.

"Warn me next time, asshole!"

"You're a baby!" I yelled back with a laugh.

It was the first time I had cracked a smile all day. I was tired, overwhelmed, and my fluctuating hormones weren't helping my mood. I also hadn't heard from Ben at all today. Our normal routine was to connect around Ben's lunch time—when he forced himself to take a break—to come up with evening plans.

It had been radio silence since our moment last night at James and Emma's.

Did Ben think I was running away again? Sure, I had freaked out when he'd mentioned the sleepover thing, but only because I hadn't even thought of it until he'd said something. It was my boundary, my rule, and I had completely forgotten. I'd even kissed him—on the cheek, but *still*.

A stray thought formed in my head...that maybe Ben *did* understand what was going on with me, and he'd run out of patience.

I slapped the floating shelf onto the pegs I'd placed into the wall before stepping back to survey my work. It looked good, but I had a lot more to get done.

Taking a risk, I snapped a photo of the shelf with my phone and sent it off to Ben. If he responded, great. If not, that was great too. I was a big girl, and I would manage just fine without his input.

It wasn't like he hadn't disappointed me before.

I walked to the opposite wall, carrying the supplies to install the next shelf under my arm. My phone vibrated in the hip pocket of my tennis skirt, and I forced myself to wait thirty seconds, timing it with twists of my pinky ring, before opening the message.

Ben: Looks great. Have you been there long?

Jill: Thank you! I'm proud of how it turned out. I've been here for a while. Got here around ten this morning.

Ben: That's a long day. You didn't get much sleep last night.

Jill: You're one to talk. I was asleep before you rolled in smelling like a brewery.

Ben: It wasn't that bad, was it?

Ben: Did I actually smell terrible? You would tell me if I did, right? And if I did, I'm sorry.

I sent him three laughing face emojis in a row. He was so easily riled up.

Jill: It was a mild beer odor, nothing major. No worries.

Ben: You live to mess with me, don't you?

Jill: Surely you know this by now.

"What's got you smiling like that? Is it a funny cat video?"

I fumbled with the phone as I leaped back about a foot. "Jimbo, you need to cool it with the stealth moves. Fuck."

"Damn, you're jumpy as hell today. Now let me see what was so funny." He made a little grabbing motion with his fingers.

I brought the phone closer to my chest. "First off, cat videos are not a thing anymore. You're about ten to fifteen internet years behind. And second, there's nothing to show. I just got a nice message from a friend complimenting the shelves."

James looked like he wanted to ask more, but I was grateful when he moved on. I did not want to get into specifics with him about why his best friend had me grinning like a giddy teenager.

It was enough that I'd asked his fiancée to cover for me by not telling him I'd been sleeping in the guest room last night. The room he'd also sent his best friend to sleep in. All these secretive hijinks were going to give me an ulcer.

"Those shelves do look good. You want help with that one?"

"I've got it, but there are two more that need installing if you want to get on it. I was planning to put one between each window for right now. If they work well for inventory, I'll order more."

"Nah, I can make these out of scrap wood in about five minutes. Not sure why you didn't ask me to do that in the first place."

"I wasn't sure I'd like them, and I didn't want to bug you with yet another thing. But if you're willing to make them, I accept. I...get what you were saying earlier...about not looking at every favor as an obligation I have to repay. And thank you."

He rubbed a hand down his beard. "No problem."

We worked in companionable silence until the shelves were up. I had to admit, the job went much faster with someone else to share the load, even if that person was my overbearing older brother.

"You good if I head out?" he asked as I swept up a layer of dust along the baseboards. "I've got a project to finish before the end of the week. I should probably make a dent in it."

"All good. I'm gonna stay a bit longer." I'd noted some spots on the baseboards that needed another coat of paint while I was sweeping.

"Lock this door behind me, okay? I worry about you out here all alone, especially when you have that music on so loud you can't hear anything around you."

"I'll turn it down. I'll only stay a half hour at most."

I could tell he wanted to keep arguing, but he refrained. "Shoot me or Emma a message when you get home?"

"I can do that."

"Thanks, Jilly Bean. And hey."

"Yeah?"

"The place is coming around. Can't say I ever envisioned you owning a sex toy boutique, but you're killing this remodel. I'm proud of you."

"Minus the flooding, things have been okay, haven't they?"

"And you and Ben got that under control pretty fast, all things considered."

We'd finished the drainage swale—I was slowly mastering the landscaping terminology—two weeks ago, and Ben was nearly done sprucing up the rest of the property. Seeing shrubs and flowers I knew he had planted along the edge of the building made it feel like Ben was all around me, even when he was on the other side of town. It was...nice.

James gave me an awkward pat on the back before I tugged him in for a real hug. He hugs were rare, but they were the best. His enormous arms had always made me feel secure, and he did this squeezing thing that was both calming and energizing at the same time.

My brother was irritating, but I wouldn't trade him for the world. A peal of thunder rumbled in the distance as the front door drifted shut behind him.

It was strange. It wasn't even raining, and the sky had been clear only minutes before. I walked to the window to peer out, now noticing the dark clouds that had formed above. James' black truck made the turn out of the lot onto the county road back toward the town center, moving in the opposite direction from the storm.

I reached for the broom as my phone started ringing.

Ben's picture lit the screen, a goofy photo I had snapped of him one night when we'd done avocado face masks while we'd gotten ready to watch a movie.

We rarely chatted on the phone, so this was a surprise. Our friendship existed mainly in text messages and in-person hangouts.

"Hi?" I greeted uncertainly.

Static filled the other end of the line before his rushed voice came on. "Hey! Are you still at Velvet?"

"Yeah. James just left, but I'm sticking around a bit longer. Why?"

"We got rained out. A crazy storm started at the property we were working on, and one of my windshield wiper blades is shredded. I can barely see, and Velvet's a lot closer to where I am. Mind some company?"

"Oh my god, you don't have to ask. How far out are you?" My stomach dove as I thought about Ben driving in this weather with a poor view of the road.

"About five minutes, give or take."

"Okay. Don't rush. Just get here in one piece. Do you want me to stay on the phone with you?"

His warm chuckle sent a wave of goosebumps cascading across my skin. "Nah, I'm alright. Truthfully, it's probably safer if I let you go so I can focus on driving. I'll see you soon."

The call went silent right as a deluge of raindrops started coming down outside. Ben—if he made it here safe and sound—and I were in for a wild night.

Chapter Thirty-Five

Jill

HE MADE IT IN ten minutes. Every second of those five minutes over his indicated timeframe was excruciating. I kept picturing him flying off the country road into a ditch because he couldn't see the turnoff. Or driving straight into a utility pole.

Somehow, I heard a vehicle door slamming over the hammering of my heart. I raced to the window, watching as Ben sprinted toward me from his truck. His big boots made waves through the growing puddles in the parking lot. Suddenly, he stopped in the middle of the lot, looked off into the distance, then turned back to me with a wide smile.

He was soaking wet and absolutely insane.

I threw the door open, keeping all but my arm tucked in from the rain.

"What are you doing?! You're soaked!"

That smile got impossibly wider, his crooked incisor catching my eye. I'd bet he had hated that slight imperfection when he was younger, but it only made him that much more handsome to me. "The backyard looks great. No sign of flooding at all. The system we set up is working!"

He stepped into the doorway, his blue jeans so wet they looked almost black. I tipped my head back to look at him.

"You're a landscaping nerd."

He speared a damp hand through the chunk of my hair that was slipping over my cheek, tucking it behind my ear. A drop of water slipped from his cheek down the side of my neck. "And you're unbelievably gorgeous."

If we were doing the kissing thing—and we were *not*—this would have been it. Our first kiss. I could see it so clearly: his clothes dampening the front of my dress, heavy boots on either side of my thin sandals, tongues tasting of rainwater and each other.

He leaned in, bypassing my lips and instead brushing the tip of his nose up the slope of mine. "I'm getting you all wet."

Yeah, he was. "Mmm, I know."

"C'mon."

"**S**O, I WAS LAYING down the new paving stones when Dany shows up with a huge cookie cake. It had *Happy Birthday* written across it in blue frosting. The first thing he says is, 'Since none of you assholes bothered doing anything for my birthday, I figured I had to do something for myself.' And then he proceeded to eat the entire cake for lunch without even offering to share."

"An *entire* cookie cake? And wait...I thought you were helping Honey plan a party for him?"

"You would be correct. I even pre-paid for a round of drinks and food at the country club that's hosting the party. The least he could have done was share one measly piece. He knows cookie cake is my favorite."

"In Dany's defense, isn't the party a surprise? He doesn't know it's happening."

"Oh, he knows. He just wanted an excuse to eat cake for lunch and rub it in my face."

"What do you mean, he knows?"

"Honey told me the other day that she caught him snooping. She's pretty sure he suspects something."

"Isn't that going to ruin the party? That could be disappointing for Honey, what with all the work she's put into planning."

Ben had kept me apprised of the plans. Dany's long-time girlfriend was pulling out all the stops. She had even planned the party long enough after his actual birthday in hopes that he would be less suspicious.

"Nah, Dany won't let her be disappointed. He's going to show up and put on the most over-the-top, dramatic, surprised act the world has ever seen in order to make her happy."

I smiled to myself. "Make sure you film that for me."

Ben wiped a droplet of water off his face with the hem of his shirt. He didn't get any drier since the fabric was probably wetter than the rest of him. "Do you mind?" He lifted the bottom of the shirt to just above his hip bone. The fraction of skin on display had me feeling like a chaste Victorian thirsting for a glimpse of an ankle.

I swallowed. "Go ahead."

He reached behind his neck and did that attractive man thing, tugging the maroon t-shirt over his head from the back before draping the garment over the edge of the bar.

"Much better," he said as he rolled his shoulders. Muscles danced under his inked skin, stretching hypnotically.

"Going back to your earlier point," he said.

"Huh?"

He smirked. He knew exactly why I was distracted. "Filming Dany's reaction to the non-surprise party."

"What about it?" I had more important things to do than think about Dany's fake shock act—important things like ogling my fuck buddy.

"Why don't you come with me? See the show up close and personal instead of through a phone screen. It's at the end of the month, so you have three weeks to get the time off work if you need it."

Ben and I hadn't been out together in public since before I'd shown up with my apology brownies. Things between us had been…different…since that night. Close, and domestic, and undeniably intimate. Was this just a friendly outing, like when we'd walked around Fair Street Park or ate at The Sticky Pig?

Or did Ben want it to be more? And more importantly, did I?

"I can see the wheels spinning in your head." He leaned forward, placing one elbow on the flat of the bar top. "It's only as complicated as you make it, Blossom," he said, the soft words rattling in my ears.

I fiddled with my pinky ring as I avoided meeting his eyes. Those silvery blues had a way of staring straight through me. "I'm not overcomplicating things on purpose. I don't like being this way."

"I never said you were. But you're forgetting one very key part of our arrangement."

"What's that?"

"Friendship. We are friends. Aren't we?"

"Of course we are." There were days he felt like my *best* friend.

Ben's jaw bunched and released. "It wasn't all that long ago you were claiming you hated me."

Sometimes I wished I did. Because he was always challenging me, and he was nearly always right, and I wanted so badly not to want him. The sex was one thing, but if I went further with Ben, it meant putting myself at risk.

That overheard conversation had been a blow—one that still smarted. If I invested more into him, allowed myself to *feel* more, how deep would his lack of faith cut?

Tonight, I brushed it off. "Well, things change, I suppose."

"So, will you come to the party with me? Like the pair of great friends we are?"

"Will James be there?" I knew my brother hung out with the rest of Ben's group occasionally.

"Yep."

It really wouldn't be a date if Jimbo was around. Ben wouldn't want him getting the wrong idea. "Won't he find it strange that we're there together?"

"Nope. He knows we're friends now. Don't make this weirder than it needs to be, Blossom."

I would have to remind him to tone it down with the pet names in front of my brother. I was thawing toward the nickname, but I doubted Jimbo would see it the same way. "Ugh. Fine. You've convinced me."

He cracked a smile. "Sound more excited, why don't you. I'll send you the details. Now, want to make me a drink, bartender?"

"**Y**OU HAVE TO PRETEND that's gin, Ben! You wouldn't be able to drink it that fast." Rain battered the sides of the building as I made 'cocktails' for Ben. In reality, I was pouring water from an oversized bottle into the same red plastic cup over and over, miming pouring liquor shots. I wouldn't stock the Velvet bar until closer to opening.

"You don't know that. I could be a gin connoisseur who's so experienced in drinking it that I toss it back like water. And we need to test your bartending skills."

"That makes no sense. A gin connoisseur would take time to appreciate the drink. They wouldn't just take it like a shot."

"You're only saying that because you're slow."

"I'm no slower than Eleanor." The Maven's bartender had worked there for years. She was grumpy and stern, but she was a town staple. Even the G-State students, who mostly stuck to the businesses and bars up on the hill, knew of Eleanor.

"Ah, yes, but she has *earned* the right to be slow. You're just a baby barkeep."

I snorted. "A *barkeep?* This is a 1920s era speakeasy, you know, not a medieval tavern."

"I've been meaning to tell you that you seriously need to re-think your business plan. Fantasy role play is big these days. Lean into the trend, make this the ultimate hangout for elves and wizards. You've already got the dragon dicks."

"Oh yeah? You want to front me the money to do a whole new remodel?"

"Will I get a cut of the profit? I expect it to be generous, given the fact that I came up with the tavern idea. You're welcome, by the way."

"I think I'll stick to my current plan."

"I bet I could manage this place too. I'm a smart guy." If his goofy grin hadn't betrayed his lack of seriousness, I would have been tempted to throw my water in his face.

"You wouldn't know the first thing about running a bar or a sex toy boutique if you tried. You'd probably blush and run away the minute someone asked you to recommend a strap-on."

"Well, that tracks, considering that I have no need for a strap-on. I've got the real deal right here." He gestured to his groin. I happened to know just how right he was, given my close personal relationship with said real deal.

I was still going to screw with him a little. "Who says the strap-on is for *you* to wear? Maybe you might be up for some pegging action."

He blanched. "I'm pretty sure I remember checking the *Not Interested* toggle on that portion of the survey."

I laughed as I poured him another shot of water and slid it across the bar. "Don't worry, I remember. Not really something I'm interested in either. Want to try another drink?"

"Hit me."

Ben accepted the water shot and took it back in a single gulp. "When do you plan on stocking this place with the genuine stuff?"

I sighed. It was a sore subject. "I'm trying to reason with myself on that one."

"What do you mean?" Ben asked as I gave him another pour of water.

"The liquor distributor quoted me a ridiculous price for the package I was hoping for. As much as I want to invest in what's on the shelves here, I just can't afford it."

"You can charge more for higher quality drinks, though, right?"

"It's hard to count on that. Even though I've put so much into this place, there's no guarantee it will pan out. People might not show up, or they might show up and think a sex toy shop, speakeasy combo is stupid and never come back. So, unfortunately, the bar stock will be on the lower end of my budget for now."

Ben's eyes were soft, but I couldn't hold them anymore. Not when I knew he agreed with the assessment that I'd probably fail.

"Well, I can't say that isn't smart of you."

He would say that.

"I was thinking of doing era-themed cocktails," I said, switching the subject. "I found one called The Bee's Knees. It's gin, lemon juice, and honey."

"Sounds...medicinal." I giggled when he twisted his mouth in mock disgust.

"It's a good thing I plan on hiring an actual bartender to help me craft the cocktail menu, then."

"Have you hired anyone yet?" I'd been venting to him about creating job postings for the bar and retail staff.

"One person. His name is Van. I managed to steal him from one of the college bars up by G-State. He was getting sick of the young clientele and shitty tippers."

He nodded slowly, running his thumbs along the curves of his red cup. "That's...cool. Good. I bet he's a fun guy."

I shot him a quizzical look, pouring myself a shot of water. "Does it bug you that I'll be working alongside a man or something? You do realize I'm attracted to both men and women, so if me working with people I could theoretically be attracted to is a problem, then this place will never be staffed. I'm down for exclusivity while we're hooking up, so the jealousy is unnecessary." I distracted myself by swiping a rag over liquid that was pooling on the bar top before braving a glance at him.

His face slackened, and he shook his head as if to clear it. "No. That doesn't bother me. I...didn't even think about it like that, to be honest with you. I know we're exclusive *friends with benefits*. Your sexual orientation doesn't factor into how much I trust you. And I do. Trust you, that is."

"Not every person sees it that way, you know."

"I do know, and that sucks. Galyna's wife, Carmen, is bisexual, and I know some of her past partners judged her for it. Like she couldn't possibly be happy with one partner and would inevitably cheat. Or that she was just confused and couldn't really be into both men and women. I guess that's why they're the ones in the past. Carmen being bisexual doesn't make her any less loyal or worthy as a partner. Her and my sister are rock solid."

I reached for his hand, stretching across the bar. His skin was cool.

"I appreciate you saying that, Ben. Not everyone is so open minded."

He twisted his grip, capturing my fingers in his own. "I don't deserve a medal for it."

"No, probably not. But it still means something to me."

"Jill? Can I be honest with you?"

I gulped. "Always."

"I am jealous. Not because I don't trust you, but because I'm never going to be as cool as a college bartender named Van. I like plants and popcorn and going to bed early. You'll eventually realize I'm boring and that you don't need my help with sex at all."

He was dead wrong. Ben wasn't boring at all. He—and my growing feelings for him—were more dangerous than the thunderstorm shaking the walls of the building.

I dragged my hand away. That was the easy part. I grinned, baring my teeth in a show of feigned nonchalance.

"You're not getting away from me that easily, Benny Boy. I still haven't even found out what that piercing feels like."

He shook his head and smirked at my stupid joke, the heaviness in the air dissipating.

Chapter Thirty-Six

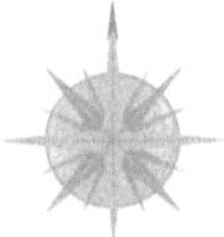

Ben

I T WAS THE NIGHT of Dany's party, and I wanted it to be a date. An *actual* date. Not one of the so-called friend dates Jill kept insisting were a thing.

I'd half-assed my attempt to bring it up to Jill when she was pouring me her fake drinks, chickening out in the end and assuring her it would be another one of our platonic outings. Every night since, I'd been too afraid to talk to her about it, even as she'd shared her worries about Velvet and her reliance on her brother. Even as we'd resumed the slow sexual burn of our relationship, I was still holding back.

I was determined that tonight would be different. Tonight, I was going to tell her how I felt and ask her if she wanted to give this thing we were doing a shot. Because somewhere in between nights spent eating buttery popcorn, and people-watching at the park, and digging holes, I'd realized that the infatuation I'd felt for Jill for years was something much, much deeper.

I was in love with Jill Klein. I'd spent so much time trying to find The One, so much time maintaining that Jill's quirks and flightiness were negative things, that I'd dismissed my true feelings.

I was done hiding, but I suspected Jill wasn't there yet.

So, I was enacting my plan and taking my time getting ready for Danylo's surprise party. Jill had dropped a hint a week or so back when we were watching a spy movie that she liked men in suits. Her exact phrasing had been that suits were lingerie for men. It made no sense to me—suits covered way more skin than most other men's attire, the opposite of lingerie—but I would take all the help I could get in convincing her to give me a chance.

I ran a set of clippers over my head, getting the buzz cut down as close to my scalp as possible before rubbing my hands over the top to dislodge any leftover hairs. I only needed to add the finishing touch below the belt: a new set of hot-pink studs for either side of my piercing. Jill's favorite color. I smirked as I spun the tiny balls onto the metal. I couldn't wait to see her face.

A subtle spritz of cologne later, and then I was stepping into the black suit. I'd foregone a tie, leaving the top two buttons of the dress shirt unbuttoned for a casual look.

Checking the time, I grabbed my wallet off the counter and headed to my red car, hanging the suit jacket on a hook so it wouldn't wrinkle. I had offered to pick Jill up for the party, fully expecting her to decline. Much to my surprise, she had agreed to ride with me. When I'd asked her how she would explain that to her brother, she'd simply replied that she would worry about that if the topic arose. Like it was no big deal.

I didn't have time to ruminate over her change in attitude, not when I was already running late, and Honey had pressed that time was of the essence. She'd convinced Dany to go shopping with her in

Merlin Heights as a diversion, but his patience with the errand would only last so long.

I drummed my fingers along the curve of the steering wheel as I waited in traffic along Main Street. G-State was holding a new student orientation, so the town was packed. I gave a cursory nod to one of my long-time landscaping clients who was stuck in the car across from me. She looked primed to roll down her window and strike up a conversation across the median, but the flow of traffic thankfully moved on. I had one singular goal tonight, and idle chit-chat wasn't on the menu.

I got bogged down again when I approached the lift bridge over the canal, the oxidized metal frame rising as a party barge floated below. My collar was damp with sweat when I finally reached the lot beside Jill's studio apartment. Now I was late, and I was probably going to stink. *Great.*

Jill streamed out the door of her apartment and rushed down the stairs that ran along the outside wall of the building. Her hair was loose with a slight wave to it as it flew behind her shoulders. She was wore a long, flowing yellow dress—the precise shade of my favorite moonflower variety—and those thin, lace-up sandals.

I shoved open the car door and stepped out. She came up short, the flats of her shoes skidding on the torn blacktop.

"That is seriously unfair of you," she said, still motionless several paces away.

I walked slowly closer, internally cheering. Mark the suit down as a win. "What's unfair?"

She gestured from my feet, up to my head, then back down again. "All of that. Where were you hiding all of this sexy suit goodness?"

I stalked forward, focused on the way her pupils widened and her chest rose and fell with each step I took.

"You like it?"

"Um. Yes. That's an understatement."

"Do you think I'll be overdressed for the party?"

"You were the one involved in the planning. You tell me."

"Probably will be. But I find I don't really care right now."

"Why is that?"

"This reaction from you."

She crossed her arms over her chest, forcing her breasts to jut out slightly. I doubt she realized she was doing it. "You think you're hot shit, huh? Was that the point of this?"

Glimpsing that sideways smile on her face was the point.

"Maybe. Or maybe I just want to show up Dany at his own party."

She let out a little laugh as she dropped her arms. "That does sound like fun."

"You have no idea."

I swept my arm toward the car, and Jill followed, her yellow skirt swaying. My fingers twitched as I resisted the urge to grab the fabric and tug her close. It was best to start our *Just Friends* act now, before we were out in public.

I crossed my fingers, hoping that tonight was the last night I ever had to pretend I wasn't madly in love with this woman.

W E WALKED UP THE tan pavement leading into the clubhouse of Eagle's Lodge Country Club, carefully keeping a few feet apart. The hedges along the path were well-maintained, and whoever had chosen the flowers had done it well. Maybe someday I could take Jill by the hand and point out the intricacies of the flower beds before sneaking off to the side of the clubhouse to kiss her up against a wall.

But we weren't there, not yet—and perhaps not ever. So, for now, we were walking like friendly acquaintances into the cabin-like building.

I had had my doubts when Honey told me she planned to hold the event at the country club, unsure that there was any way to get Dany to the location without arousing suspicion. But once she saw the large bay windows overlooking a picturesque man-made pond, her heart was set.

Jill's eyes bugged out as she craned her neck, taking in the room. Sets of deer antlers hung on either side of the double doors we'd just entered, and a huge bearskin rug took up a portion of the floor in front of a fireplace.

"Have you ever been here before?" I asked. I'd attended weddings here in the past, but none in the last couple of years.

"Nope. Has it always been so...on theme?"

"I think the rug is a recent addition."

"Should I be worried about the menu? I've never been brave enough to try wild game." She looked over at me with a grimace.

"Last time I was here, it was your basic chicken, beef, and fish. You should be good. The decor does not match the food options."

"Oh, thank god." She bumped me with a bare shoulder. "How about a drink while we wait for some more people to arrive?"

I placed a gentle palm on her bare back to steer her toward the long bar where a small group mingled.

"Hey, Boss!"

I sighed as I turned toward the pair of distinct voices, keeping a light touch on Jill's lower back. "Hello, Corbin. Avery."

"Aren't you going to introduce us?"

Jill looked up at me with a smile that I wanted to eat. There was no avoiding them. "Jill, these are two of my crew members. Corbin is the one in the striped shirt, and Avery is holding the beer."

"It's nice to meet you both."

I glared a hole in Corbin's head as he shook Jill's hand, lingering a touch too long. I hadn't forgotten the comment he'd made about milkmaid porn.

Tracing my pinky over the smooth surface of Jill's back, I dipped it below the fabric that covered the curve of her ass. She shivered, stepping away with a blush as she scooted up to the bar.

I tore my eyes off her and looked back at my two teenage employees.

"Speaking of holding beers, how did you snag that, Avery? You're underage."

The pasty nineteen-year-old reddened. "Uh, I just asked for it. They didn't check my ID."

"Finish it and don't order another. Got it?"

"Got it, Boss."

"So, Ben..." Corbin started. He was far braver than his friend. "I can call you Ben, can't I?"

I gave him a flat look but nodded once. I wasn't that much of a stickler. "You and Jill are just friends, correct?" He smoothed a hand down his red-and-white striped polo, straightening the fabric.

"Correct."

"Then you wouldn't mind if I asked her out? She looks gorgeous tonight, and she seems cool as hell."

I was fairly certain I had nothing to worry about—the last person Jill would be interested in was a kid in a polo shirt—but it didn't mean I wanted to encourage Corbin's interest.

"Weren't you the one who said you didn't care about what a couple of thirty-year-olds were doing with their time? This is a college town. There are plenty of age-appropriate women around Greyport you could go for."

Corbin wriggled his eyebrows in an unsettling fashion. "It's summer. The college won't be back in session for at least a month. I know Jill is older than me, but there was a spark there when she shook my hand. Right, Avery? There was a spark, right?" He nudged his shorter friend with an elbow.

"I'm not sure. She—" Corbin's lip curled as he gave Avery another, less gentle nudge. "Yep, yes, a definite spark!"

I glanced over my shoulder at Jill. She was at the bar now, chatting up the pink-haired woman slinging drinks. Did everyone want a shot with Jill tonight? She took two tumblers in hand and navigated around a couple waiting in line. I watched as she made her way back to me, biting her lip as she took in my attire.

Corbin, and the bartender, and whoever else, could try their best with her, but my suit was going to win me the girl.

I gave Corbin a smirk. "Do your worst."

CHAPTER THIRTY-SEVEN

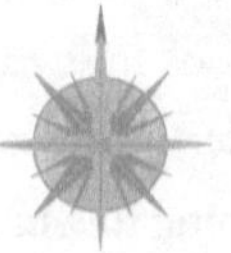

Jill

E VERYONE HUDDLED IN THE clubhouse's kitchen, the servers whispering off to the side as we tried our best to stay quiet. Honey and Dany were about to walk in the door, and we were supposed to pop out any minute. The room was teeming with energy, but the only thing I could focus on was Ben.

My brother and Emma arrived just in time and took positions opposite me, Ben, and Ben's two young crew members.

Corbin, the taller of the two, had found his way directly next to me. He was cute, albeit young, and had been flirting since Ben had introduced us. It was flattering to know I still held some appeal with college-aged people, though that demographic no longer interested me.

Ben's red face when he had seen Corbin brush a small bit of lint off the shoulder strap of my dress had been *delicious*, though. Ben was still holding out on me when it came to sex, and I wanted him and all that pent-up energy of his to be mine.

I stole a peek at him, biting my lip at the half-lidded look he directed at me. The suit, and the fresh shave, and the subtle cologne mixed with his natural fresh soil scent were about to kill me.

I must have let loose a nervous sound, because Corbin gave me a nudge. "They're coming in now," he said in a chastising whisper.

I nearly missed Ben giving the younger man a gentle cuff on the back of the neck, speaking low words in his ear. Whatever he said caused Corbin to stiffen and add an extra inch of space between him and me.

I bit my lip, tapping into this fight.

I shifted backward, brushing my ass against Ben's groin. He pulled back a fraction, placing both hands on either side of my waist as he nudged me forward, placing that safe cushion between us. I heard his teeth snap amongst the quiet titters in the room.

I snickered, and he gave my hip a soft tap. A subtle warning. He was right to give it, especially with all the people in the room with us.

"They're here. They're here!" came a man's voice. I thought it was Dany's father, a short, squat-looking man who Ben had introduced me to earlier, along with his wife, who was a friend of Ben's mother.

Mayor Till was out of town tonight. Otherwise, she would have been in attendance.

I tried to ignore the fact that Ben had pointedly invited me to an event his mother was guaranteed to miss. Sure, we'd dressed up, and he'd given me a ride here in his fancy car, but this was a *platonic* date. I was under no illusion that Ben wanted to take things further with me.

He'd been acting strangely all night, almost nervous, and not in the way he was when I teased him. On the car ride here, I'd caught him staring, but his only reaction when I'd asked him what was wrong was a cryptic smile.

I could have sworn he almost captured my hand in his when we'd walked the flowered path into the clubhouse tonight.

What if I took that step and reached for him first? Did I want to do that? Was I *ready* for that?

Ben and his cookie-cutter life weren't me. He was the ideal fit for a woman like the attractive blonde I had seen him with in that dive bar back at the start of summer. He'd since told me she was a successful dentist, smart, polished, beautiful. His mother had set the two of them up.

He'd said there was a reason he ended it with her, but that was the type of woman he deserved. One who wasn't riddled with hangups from a crappy ex-boyfriend. A woman with a successful career, who owned a home, and knew how to balance a checkbook.

As awful a person as Oliver had been, he had been more my speed. He'd lived the same sort of free-spirited, messy, casual-living kind of life I was used to.

I was a studio apartment, and Ben was a suburban ranch.

He probably wouldn't even trust me to water his plants if he went away for a weekend.

Dany's father got an alert on his watch—I was guessing a message from Honey giving the all clear—and gave us a hand signal. Everyone went quiet as he counted down on his fingers. When he put the last one down, we all funneled through two wide swinging doors in the main reception area of the clubhouse with a booming, "Surprise!"

Ben's voice shouted the loudest, or maybe he was the one I focused on the most.

Honey's face gleamed as she jumped up and down next to her boyfriend. I noticed the birthday boy shoot Ben a sly smirk, but to his credit, he made a great show of shock and awe, flapping his hands and letting out a great gasp.

Ben was right. It was far better in person than it would have been on video.

I hung back as Ben and Dany's other friends and family members greeted him with hugs and well-wishing slaps on the back.

"Hi, Jill."

I turned toward the sound of the woman's voice.

"Hi, Honey. How are you?"

She wore a stunning amber dress, her freckled skin glowing. She had been lovely when I'd seen her at Ben's house, even dressed casually, but tonight she had upped the game. It was half the dress and half the pure happiness she was radiating.

"I'm great. And so pleased you came tonight. Ben looks...really, really happy." Her eyes were warm with the weight of expectation.

I swallowed hard. Was it really possible that I made Ben that happy? "Oh, um, yes. He was super excited for the party."

"I don't think it's because of the party, Jill." Her implication was clear.

I flicked a quick look at Ben, now standing next to James, the two of them chatting with Honey's parents. "Ben and I are just friends, Honey."

One of her dark brows quirked. "Are you sure about that?"

"Last time I checked." The words sounded mangled.

"Huh. Well, things have a way of changing when you least expect." Her pensive look flipped back to bright and open. "Can I get you anything? A drink or something to eat? The appetizers should be coming out soon."

"I'm okay, but thank you."

When she moved on through the crowd, I breathed a sigh of relief. I liked Honey a lot, but I was afraid she could see right through me—and even more afraid that she would find me lacking. Because sure, she implied I was making Ben happy *now*, but surely that wouldn't last.

"Well, that reaction from Dany was worth getting dressed up for this party." Emma sidled over, clutching a copper mug.

"Right? He really sold that." My eyes drifted back to Ben. His face lit up as he hinged slightly at the waist in laughter. The move drew my attention toward the way his black suit pants hugged his thick thighs and round ass. He'd ditched the suit jacket on the back of a chair and rolled up the sleeves of his dress shirt. I wanted to take a bite out of those tattooed forearms.

Emma nudged me out of my Ben-trance. "I'm going to guess that Dany's fake surprise act isn't going to be the highlight of your night, given the way you're staring down your man."

"Not so loud," I hissed under my breath. "First, he's not my man. And second, my brother is here. Do you really want him to find out about me and Ben like that?"

"So, you do admit there's a you and Ben to tell him about? It's not just a casual, *friends with benefits* thing anymore?"

"I—I'm not really sure," I admitted. I was halfway to wanting more, but the other part of me was too terrified to take the leap.

Emma's brown eyes were warm as she draped an arm over my shoulder. "For what it's worth, I think the two of you are good together. But if you're still uncertain, I wouldn't mention it to James. Like I said the other night, he'll get worried, and it will become a whole thing."

I sipped from my now-lukewarm mule. "What made you decide it was worth a shot with James?"

"Honestly? It was you and Kristi who encouraged me to take the chance and work through my insecurities alongside him as opposed to going it alone. There will probably always be days when those feelings crop back up, but talking with James, and to my therapist, helps."

"I just— I never did tell you the reason I was so mad at Ben, did I?"

"You did not."

Her tone was relaxed, deliberately so.

My hands shook as I gripped my glass. "Please don't tell James. I know there's supposedly some sort of gossip pact between spouses where things are expected to be shared, but this is not one of those instances. Do you understand?"

Her brows flew up. "I've been keeping your thing with Ben a secret, haven't I? You don't have to worry about it. I think it would be best for you and Ben to tell your brother about your relationship yourself, if it ever does progress to that. I'll navigate James' feelings about me keeping it from him when the time comes."

"Are you sure? I would hate for Jimbo to get mad at you because of something I asked."

She waved her hand around, her oval engagement ring catching the light. "James and I trust each other. If things come out, he'll understand why I didn't tell him. He knows I'm friends with you and that our friendship isn't dependent on my relationship with him. He'd only be upset if I kept a secret the jeopardized your safety. Is Ben dicking you down so good your health is at stake?"

I sputtered, vodka and lime juice singing my nostrils. "You really just said that, huh? Right in front of this party?"

She shot me a cheeky grin. This was why my brother loved her—she gave him shit, and he ate it up with a spoon. Emma kept him from getting old and boring.

"Tell me why you're mad at Ben. Or used to be mad at Ben. Whichever it is at the moment."

I sighed and walked with her over to a round table covered in an off-white linen tablecloth, where we sat down. A tall vase filled with floating candles offered the illusion of privacy from the rest of the party-goers who gathered around the bar or near the hors d'oeuvres.

I clutched the fabric draped in my lap to hide the trembling in my fingers. "I haven't told anyone this, not even Kristi—although, knowing her, she's already figured it out."

Her brow scrunched. "You don't have to tell me before you're ready, Jill."

"I know!" I was tired of everyone just...rolling over and letting me avoid confronting my issues. It wasn't anyone's fault but my own, but the feeling was irrational. I bit my tongue, tamping down my frustration. "I know you would never pressure me into that. But I'm in over my head, and not talking about it hasn't helped me so far, so I'm trying something new."

"I can look away if you want me to. Maybe it will be easier if you think you're monologuing in your room."

"No, that would feel weird. This is a normal conversation, and we will talk about this in a normal fashion, like normal friends do."

"We've never been normal."

"But we can pretend, can't we? Let's start by not saying the word normal again. It's getting...not normal."

"Okay, go."

I took a deep breath and shot it out through my nose. James had once said breathing like that helped his anxiety. I wasn't sure it worked—I felt like a horse whinnying.

"Okay, so remember back when you and Harry were still fake dating? And how Jimbo arranged a time for me and Ben to chat about business stuff?"

"Yes. You were super defensive anytime someone asked you about it."

"Okay, judgy much? I wasn't defensive. I just didn't want to talk about it."

"I'm pretty sure you're being defensive right now."

She was not wrong. "Whatever. Anyway, Ben and I met up one afternoon between me working a shift at the library and logging some hours with Fantasy Dongs. Things were fine for the first fifteen minutes. He was patient with my questions and really knowledgeable."

I took a sip of my drink, forcing a pause before I got to the hard part.

"And then my realtor called."

"Fancy girl with a fancy realtor."

"Hardly. It was Lacy Snyder. She was a grade above me and wore cat ears to school every day in middle school. I asked her to keep an eye out for properties, but it was very casual at that point."

"But clearly it turned less casual."

"Clearly. She had found Velvet—or the building that is slowly becoming Velvet as we speak. I answered her call, and she was so excited on the phone, so then I got excited too. As soon as I hung up, I told Ben all about the building and how I wanted to go for it. He didn't seem to care one way or the other—or so I thought. Well, then, you know how when I get hyped up about something, it makes my bladder go crazy?"

"Yep. You're just like a dog that way."

"Thanks for that. Anyway, when I was walking back from the bathroom, Ben was on the phone. It sounded serious. And he was being...mean...saying my plan was silly, and the business would never last. How I would probably be closed in a year anyway. He never used my name, but it was clear as day that he was talking about me. And maybe Ben and I were never close like he is with James, but I always *liked* him. And I thought he liked me too—or at the very least respected me. Being wrong hurt." Bad enough that I'd been stewing for over a year.

Emma sat silent for a moment, her mauve-painted lips twisting. "Has Ben ever said anything like this to you, before or since? Or have you heard him say similar things about other people?"

I shook my head. "Not at all. It was so...out of character. I might have built it up in my head, but over the years, I'd always felt like Ben was, like, a silent wall of support in a way. When James came to all my events as a kid, Ben came too. When James had to come bail me out of one dumb plan after another, Ben was there, quiet and non-judgmental. I even met up with him again after—at James' urging—and he was nothing but kind the whole time. But I couldn't get his words out of my head, and everything he said after that rang hollow. How could I believe a thing he said was genuine after that? How could I trust that anything he'd ever said to me was real?"

"It's just...so unlike Ben." Emma squinted her brown eyes, looking across the large room toward where Ben was talking with Dany. It was as if she was trying to visualize him saying the words.

"I know. Even now, I can't quite reconcile it with the version of him who I've been spending time with this summer."

"And you're *positive* he was talking about you? It wasn't some sort of mix up or a miscommunication? Something that could be solved by one simple conversation?"

"Did you read another book with that plot line?"

"Don't deflect. I'm being serious! Sure, it sounds like a plot point, but human beings are shitty communicators in real life all the time. Have you broached this subject with him at all?"

"No. I've been...scared, I guess. I know deep down that he was talking about me. Now that Ben and I have become friends, it's almost worse knowing that he said all those things. That this friendship may not be rooted in respect. Sure, the lust factor is heavy, but if I found out that was Ben's sole motivation..." I trailed off because I didn't want to admit it, to say it out loud and give the thought even more power.

"Jill, you have to talk to him. Hear him out. Remember that, even if he did mean what he said then, he knows you differently now, right? You were just James' sister before, and now you're something more."

"I guess..."

"You're also kicking ass with Velvet, and I'm willing to bet he sees that too. What he said about you and your ideas was dead wrong. Give him a shot to prove to you that he knows how wrong it was."

What if he didn't think it was wrong, though? "Is there any point in inviting that hurt, if he and I are just going to go back to being casual acquaintances again soon? This won't last forever."

"Are you certain about that? Do you want to be done with Ben? Because watching him look at you tonight, I don't think he's going to be too keen on that."

I didn't have time to contemplate her words before I felt a tap on my shoulder. I turned toward the person behind me, spotting Corbin's obnoxiously shiny belt buckle at my eye level. He was clearly going for some cowboy-chic look and not quite hitting the mark. He deserved some credit for trying, at least.

"Care for a spin around the dance floor?"

He held out a smooth palm. His face was bright and his smile expectant.

"Why not?" I could use the distraction.

Chapter Thirty-Eight

Ben

I T WOULD BE BOTH immoral and illegal to break my coworker's hand.

I had to keep reminding myself of that every time I heard the bright peal of Jill's laughter from the dance floor and looked over—because I was weak, damn it—to see Corbin sending her into some spin move. My employee was good at dancing. Who knew?

"You good over here?" Dany sidled up, fresh drink in hand.

I tipped my chin down stiffly. Dany, the asshole, had the nerve to chuckle.

"What's so funny?" My jaw ached from clenching it so hard.

"You're not fooling anyone. Why don't you just ask her to dance?"

I flicked a look over at James. He was piling mini-meatballs on a plastic plate, not paying me a lick of attention. "It isn't that simple."

"Oh yeah? Seems like a pretty simple, five-word sentence to me. *Will you dance with me*? She responds, and there you have it."

"James would get suspicious."

"Would he?" Dany rubbed his chin like some kind of fucked-up philosopher. "Thought you and Jill were just friends. Friends dance."

I opened my mouth to object, but he cut in before I could get the first syllable out.

"Unless," he said, lifting an index finger. "The *way* you want to dance with Jill isn't in a friendly fashion. Now that would be...interesting, to say the least."

"You say that like you think the two of us are going to have sex in the middle of the dance floor at your birthday party or something."

"Hey, my mind didn't go toward sex. If yours did, that's all on you. There are many ways a dance could be taken as more than friendly. A brush of a hand across an arm. A meaningful gaze into a dance partner's eyes. A lingering sniff of the hair."

"Where are you coming up with this shit?"

"Honey and I watched a new historical romance series on TV. I was skeptical at first, but it ended up being really addicting. Before I knew it, I was sneak-watching episodes ahead of time. Oh, if I get any kind of hint that you told Honey that, I'll also tell James you're banging his little sister."

I choked on air. Dany slapped my back as I cleared out a cough.

"I'm not—"

"Don't bother denying it. That reaction confirmed it, but I was already suspicious. Honey was too. She said there was definite tension between the two of you when she met Jill. She filled me in tonight."

"Honey doesn't actually know anything, and neither do you, for that matter. Jill and I aren't fucking." Not *technically*, at least.

"Do you want to be?"

"What difference does it make?"

"That isn't a no."

I crossed my arms, leaning around Dany to check in on Jill and Corbin. They were standing near the DJ booth, and Jill was writing something down on a slip of paper while Corbin tried to act like he wasn't trying to look down the neckline of her dress.

I sighed. "It's not a no, but you cannot tell James. I don't give a damn about you sneaking episodes of a TV show, and I'm not going to say anything to your girlfriend about it."

Dany clapped me on the shoulder. I resisted the urge to shake him off. My patience was wearing thin between my friend and my employee's dance floor antics.

"I know you wouldn't. I trust you. But I am worried about you."

"What for?"

"You're invested. Like, you can't take your eyes off her tonight, even though you're at a kick-ass party with your best friends. Are you even having any fun?"

"I thought I was, until you started giving me the third degree and threatening to ruin my longest-standing friendship."

Dany waved his hand dismissively, the ice in his cocktail tilting wildly. "I wasn't serious. You know I live to provoke you. What use would you have for me otherwise?"

"I'm not really sure what use I have for you now, to be quite honest. Maybe I should fire you."

"And leave you with Corbin and what's-his-face as your only remaining workers? You'd be calling me to come back to work in two hours, max."

"Don't test it."

"It's my birthday. I'll do what I want. And as the birthday boy, I'd like to ask you an important question."

I mentally braced myself for whatever he was about to hit me with. "Go ahead. It's not like you need my permission. You'll say it anyway."

"Do you know what you're doing?"

I ripped my gaze from Jill and Corbin, who were now heading back to the center of the room to lead a coordinated line dance. Dany's face was somber, his silly smile markedly absent.

I didn't need to ask what he was getting at. I asked myself the same question almost every day. *Did* I know what I was doing with Jill? I loved her, but I still had no clue what she felt for me.

I stood silent, waiting for Dany to fill the quiet.

"Ben, the way I see it is that you're into Jill—as more than a friend."

"And what if I am?"

"What are you going to do about it? I say you ask her to be with you. Boyfriend, girlfriend, all the bells and whistles of being a couple."

"I...want to. I was planning to talk to her tonight. But...what if she doesn't want a relationship with me? She's been saying all summer that she doesn't want a commitment."

"Then you suck it up and move on. No sense in wasting your time."

"Jill could *never* be a waste of time."

Dany took a dancing step back. "Settle down, killer. I didn't mean it as an attack on her. All you've talked about for years is how you want to find the right person to settle down with. You tried it with Stef, but it didn't work out. When I met Honey, you said you wanted to find The One, and again when James and Emma started dating. And I get it. My girlfriend threw me this big, epic surprise party, and I've never been happier. I want that for you too. But if she doesn't want a commitment, where does Jill fit into that?"

As far as I was concerned, Jill *was* my future. I could picture her so clearly coming home from late nights at Velvet, me heating a special dinner for her before rubbing her feet and cuddling while we watched reality shows.

And that didn't even touch the filthy things I wanted to do to her—with her. How I wanted to fuck her with that little blue toy she loved so much before making her come all over my face. How I wanted to watch her pretty pink lips stretching around my cock as she tongued the balls of my piercing. How I wanted to fill her pussy the way I knew she was craving.

I'd been deliberately holding out on her with the last one. It was clear by now that Jill didn't need me to feel like she was good at sex. She had *always* been good at sex, despite what her douchebag of an ex had told her. I'd just happened to be the lucky guy in her path when she'd decided to own that power. If we had penetrative sex and it was great—as I suspected it would be—then she might have no further use for me.

But watching her tonight with Corbin and hearing what Dany was saying too, I was even more resolved that it was time to stop screwing around and let us both have what we wanted—each other with no restrictions.

It would be the best damn sex she had ever had in her life. I'd told her she could use me, and I would let her use me well.

And then I would tell her how I felt about her. And hope she felt the same way.

CHAPTER THIRTY-NINE

Jill

CORBIN PULLED ME OFF the dance floor by my elbow, leading me to a table with sauced meatballs and pigs-in-a-blanket.

I loaded up my plate and had the miniature biscuit-wrapped hot dog halfway to my mouth when Corbin went in for the kill.

"What are you up to tomorrow night?"

How did I kindly tell him I was way too old for him and also painfully uninterested?

"No set plans," I said around a mouthful of food.

He rubbed his palms together. "Would you like to come with me to the G-spot?"

I choked on a biscuit flake. "The what now?" I'd had a feeling he was gearing up to ask me out, but I didn't think he'd take it that far after a handful of casual dances. I'd had more sexual chemistry on my disaster date with John than I had with Corbin.

"The G-Spot. You know, the new music-and-waffles place up near G-State."

I had no idea what new businesses were popping up near the local college. Because I wasn't a college student, like him.

"I've never heard of it." Eager to keep my hands busy, I grabbed a small wooden toothpick and speared a meatball before plopping it onto a round plastic plate.

"It's supposed to be good. Avery went there last week. He listened to a sick jam band and ate chicken and waffles for hours. There's even a dispensary next door where he got edibles after."

"Wouldn't he want to eat the edibles first? Before gorging on waffles?"

"Huh. That's a good tip. I'll have to let him know. See, I knew you were chill."

I smiled tightly. "Thanks."

"So, what do you say? Waffles, weed, and jam sessions tomorrow night?"

He looked so earnest that I nearly felt guilty. "I don't think I'm your type, Corbin."

"Why, because you're old?"

I inhaled a piece of meatball and had to cough several times to clear it out.

"I'm not *old*. I'm older than you, but I'm only thirty."

"Yeah. That's what I meant. Thirty. Old."

No, it fucking wasn't what he'd meant. How did Ben tolerate this child on an almost daily basis? I guessed at nineteen, calling a woman chill was the epitome of romance.

It didn't hold a handle to Ben telling me I could do whatever I set my mind to.

"I'm going to have to decline."

"Aww, bro, really?"

"Really." The whining was highly unattractive.

He let out a gusty sigh, his shoulders slumping. Surely, he wasn't *that* interested. "Now I'm gonna have to tell Avery I lost the bet."

"What bet?"

"The one that said Ben would come over here and fire me within twenty minutes of me dancing and flirting with you. I kind of hate the job, but if I quit, my mom will stop paying my car insurance. My last-ditch effort before I hit the twenty-one-minute mark was asking you on a date."

"Are you kidding me? You and Avery had a bet going about Ben and me?" And how many other people had their own similar feelings about the two of us if these two dim-witted teenage boys could figure out something was going on?

With that thought in mind, I looked around for my brother. He was chatting with Dany's parents near the bar. I was safe for now.

"Did, uh...did Ben say anything to you or Avery? About me and him?"

"Nah. It's just incredibly obvious that he likes you a lot."

My insides were shimmering, like they were about to take off on glittered wings and leave my body behind.

I loved that Ben liked me enough that these two idiots could see it written plain as day on his face. Emma had pointed it out too.

But did he respect me? That was the one thing holding me back.

"Oh, okay. Well, as you can see, there's nothing to tell. Ben and I are friends."

Corbin snorted. "Yeah, sure. The two of you are kind of ridiculous, you know? I'm friends with some guys who work back of house at The Sticky Pig, and they said you could cut the sexual tension between you two with a knife. They were hoping they might get to see some public sex, but..." He trailed off with a wistful look. "It wasn't meant to be."

Oh, *ew.* "Look, whatever you or your friends think you've seen, it doesn't mean anything. It's casual. Nothing more. So whatever stakes you have on this bet, you can forget them."

"Does Ben know that?"

"Does Ben know what?"

"That things are casual with you guys. Because despite me hating my job, I like the guy. He's a good boss. If you hurt him, I might have to...I don't know...sign you up for a bunch of annoying marketing emails or something."

"Wow. You're a real wild card, aren't you?" Corbin was funny, in the way very young men could often be. I didn't know if he was right about me having the power to hurt Ben. I knew from experience that he had the power to hurt me, so it only made sense if the reverse was true.

"Hey, I could have threatened you with a glitter bomb. Or sent you a fake letter saying you donated a ton of money to your least favorite political candidate. I went easy on you."

"If you say so." I looked away, trying to catch Emma's eye so I could make a funny face at her.

"Jill, I am deathly serious," Corbin continued, lowering his voice to a harsh whisper. "If you hurt Ben, I—and everyone else in this town—will be very, very unhappy with you."

I blinked, caught wholly off guard. He wasn't kidding around. And the worst part was that the little shit was probably right.

Everyone loved Ben: the handsome son of the beloved mayor and her loving husband. The successful business owner who cared for the lawns of all the local not-for-profits free of charge. Ben hadn't told me that one himself, but I'd stumbled across it in an article about him in the town paper. I wasn't precisely *searching* for information on Ben, but I worked in a library. Sometimes the information found me.

"Do you understand?" Corbin asked, enforcing the point with a withering stare.

I gulped. The goofy, jam-band-loving teenager was gone. "Uh, yeah. I understand."

If Ben and I took things in a committed direction and it inevitably failed, I would surely be the one to blame in the eyes of Greyport. I was the one who couldn't hold down a steady, full-time job. The one who had never had a long-term relationship. The flaky one. The one who was starting up a business where I sold—*gasp*—sex toys.

That wasn't even including the blowback it would cause within my family. James was barely beginning to trust me to branch out and make smart choices without his input. A crash-and-burn that jeopardized his oldest friendship wouldn't do my relationship with my brother any favors.

I stole another glance at Ben. He was helping Honey move a set of chairs. I could practically hear him ordering her to go have fun while he took care of things. He was kind, chivalrous like that.

As if sensing my eyes on him, he looked over, sending me a small smile. I caught the tip of that crooked incisor peeking out as the corners of his eyes crinkled.

Suddenly, I didn't care at all how the town or my brother felt about me and Ben.

CHAPTER FORTY

Jill

As if sensing my mood, Corbin asked the DJ to play one of my requests and offered to take me for another spin on the dance floor. I declined, no longer feeling up to faking it, and returned to the table Emma and I had been sitting at earlier.

"Hey, Jilly Bean." Jimbo strolled over with a small plate of desserts. "I brought you something."

"Oh my god, you're the best brother ever. How did you know I needed some sugar therapy?"

James shrugged his broad shoulders. "Figured you'd need some carbs after working off all that energy dancing."

"Well, you were right. Where's Emma?" I glanced around for his fiancée.

"Bathroom. I think we're gonna head out. Emma's hurting after being on her feet all day, and I'm tired of being around people." I could see the scowl hiding under his beard.

"You're such a joy, you know that?" I said, teasing.

"Yeah, and you're a punk. How are you getting home? We can give you a ride if you need one."

Ben and I were supposed to have thought up a cover story for what we would tell my brother if he wondered why we were coming and going to this party together. Instead, we'd made awkward small talk with Ben's coworkers and given each other sidelong glances from across the building all night.

"Nope, I've got it from here," I said, sinking my teeth into a macaron and going with the vaguest answer possible. The more information I gave, the less likely James was to buy my story.

"You do? I didn't see your SUV out in the parking lot. Service isn't the best out here, so I'm not sure if any of the rideshare apps will work. You really can join us. Emma and I don't mind."

"I've got her covered."

Goosebumps pebbled my skin as I felt the smooth fabric of Ben's sleeve brush against my arm. I stole a peek at him from under my lashes, scared to look too long in front of my brother.

Ben stood solidly at my side, both hands tucked into the pockets of his black suit pants. He looked cool and casual, like he didn't have a care in the world.

"Thanks, man, I appreciate it." James looked over his shoulder at Emma's approach as she sidled up next to him. "Ready to go, pretty girl?"

My friend grinned sleepily up at my brother as they said their goodbyes, leaving me alone with Ben.

"I should be annoyed with you," I said.

"Oh yeah? Why's that?"

"You and my brother had some silent conversation where he basically handed me off to you like...I don't know...a prize pig or something."

"A pig?"

"I couldn't think of a good analogy. You know what I mean."

Ben shifted on his heels, the movement drawing my eye. Was he feeling nervous too? "James worries about you. You know that. I wanted to give him enough reassurance to get him off your back so he won't drive himself and you crazy. If you don't want to ride home with me, you don't have to. I'm sure Corbin would be more than happy to help."

I let out a choked laugh. "I won't be going home with Corbin, but I'm pleased to know you think I can still keep up with someone more than a decade younger than me."

"Blossom, you could keep up with anyone if you put your mind to it."

"Well, my mind's not on Corbin."

"You don't say."

I smirked, enjoying the back and forth. Bantering with Ben was nearly as much of a turn-on as his fingers strumming my clit.

Well, almost.

Ben didn't know it, but I'd decided that tonight was the night we were having sex. And if he was interested, I was considering breaking some of my rules. I had already come dangerously close to breaking the sleepover boundary when we'd stayed at James and Emma's house, and there were moments when all I wanted was to kiss this man.

"What's going on in that head of yours?" he asked, his voice gentle, like I was an animal he was trying not to spook.

I met his eyes, those ice blues flashing with heat and care and something else I couldn't identify.

The music slowed to a popular ballad, and we watched as the dance floor filled with couples. I noticed Corbin nodding at Avery before taking a step toward Ben and me.

Ben's head whipped toward his employee and halted him in his tracks.

"Want to dance?" Ben asked, one pale brow raised in question.

"Won't people start to wonder?"

"Wonder about what?"

"That we're...you know. Together."

"Does it matter if they think we're together?"

I took a big breath, letting it settle in my diaphragm. There was a challenge in Ben's question, one that was less about a dance and more about where we were going in the future. Despite our best intentions not to grow attached to each other, we'd ended up here anyway. Now, I had to decide.

I released the air from my lungs and smiled up at him, free and without restraint. "Let's do this." I took three strides toward the shiny tile floor before I felt the warmth of Ben's rough hand on my wrist.

"We don't have to rush. I want to take my time with you." His lazy smile set my insides alight.

When we made it to the dancefloor, I let him lead. His steps and spins were graceful as he pulled me in close.

"You're a good dancer," I said.

"Ma made me take lessons when I was younger. It's not the same kind of dancing, but I used to perform with the troupe at the Ukrainian Festival when I was little. It was fun."

"Please tell me she has home videos of that. I want to see Baby Benny Boy in action."

"Oh, believe me, there are plenty. Galyna is tech-savvy and helped her modernize the video collection last year, so those moments are now preserved for eternity. I'm sure she'll show you if you ask."

Now we were talking about me spending time with Ben's family, looking at baby photos. We needed to have a conversation. A real one. With words, not just heavy eye contact and touches.

I trembled against Ben, unmoored and shaky with the weight of my feelings.

"Cold?" He dragged his pinky finger under the strap of my dress where it tied at my neck.

"No," I whispered.

"You want to get out of here?"

"Please."

He tugged me by the hand toward the table where I'd stashed my purse, tapping his toe impatiently while I gathered my items.

"Hey, asshole!" I heard Dany yell from a distance as Ben maneuvered me toward the door. "Way to leave without saying goodbye!"

Ben didn't give him a backward glance, instead shooting the hand not holding mine into the air, middle finger raised. A roar of laughter rang out as we walked into the night air, only to be cut off as the door swung shut.

There was a slight chill in the air—an early glimpse of autumn—when we rounded the corner of the building. The path was illuminated with lights set along the pavers, the only sound that of crickets chirping.

"Ben, I—"

My words were cut off as I found myself pressed against the outer wall of the building. I only had a fraction of a second to focus on the scrape of the wood against my shoulder blades before all I could see was Ben.

"Jill." He brought my hand up to his face, pressing the flat of my palm onto his cheek, and turned into it, nuzzling like a contented cat. He twined the fingers of his other hand in the strap at my neck again. The slight pull of the fabric bit into my skin.

I leaned into the feeling, robbed of speech.

Ben closed his eyes, the corners creasing with effort. I took my free hand and wrapped it around his broad back. I pulled him close until his hips were pressed between my legs.

His eyes flicked open, blue nearly gone as the black of his pupils overtook the pale irises.

"What are we doing?" he said.

"You started it," I shot back.

He shook his head, his forehead rolling against mine. "Nah. You've been driving me crazy for a long, long time, Blossom."

How long was a long time? Ben and I had been teasing one another since the start of summer, but that wasn't that long ago—not in the grand scheme of things.

He released my hand, but I kept it tight to his cheek, smoothing my thumb over his skin. He'd shaved before picking me up. His face wasn't usually so smooth this late in the day. I knew because I had felt the late-night rasp of his stubble between my thighs. I knew because I knew Ben.

"Is this what torture feels like?" His breath brushed my lips. We were so close but still so far because of the limits I had placed on us.

"If it is, those spy movies you've been making me watch are doing it all wrong."

He laughed, and I felt the reverberation throughout my body. The thick length pressed between my legs twitched, and I stifled an audible groan.

"God, you're beautiful," he said. "You just bit your lip. I've never wanted to be someone's lip so bad before."

I slipped my fingers across his cheekbone and ran the pad of my ring and forefinger along his plump bottom lip.

"I think you should kiss me," I said on a breath.

We had been building up to this all night, since the moment I had seen Ben stride up to my apartment in that suit. Since the moment he had confronted me outside that dive bar.

He startled, rearing back a fraction.

"But that's one of your hard boundaries. No sleepovers, no kissing. Are you—"

"I'm sure, Ben." I hoped he realized what this meant. That I was opening myself up to him for real. That Ben was the exception to my aversion to commitment.

"Fuck. Okay. Just... Let me get myself together for a second, alright?"

His chest rose and fell with effort. He slipped his fingers free of my dress and tucked a stray bit of hair behind my ears, his movements tense and shaky.

"Ben, are you—"

"Fuck it," he said, swooping in and silencing the rest of my sentence with his mouth on mine.

CHAPTER FORTY-ONE

Ben

I COULDN'T BELIEVE IT. I was kissing Jill. I was *kissing* Jill. I was kissing *Jill.*

Later, I could puzzle over the fact that she had barreled right past her boundary, full steam ahead. But right now, my mind was too overwhelmed with her, and her moonflower scent, and the touch of her lips on mine.

They were smooth and tasted vaguely fruity from the lip balm I'd seen her slicking over them throughout the evening. I liked it.

But not as much as I liked the pure taste of her. I was dying for more.

Her fingertips pressing into my back muscles told me she felt the same as she pulled me closer until my hips were tight between hers against the building's wall.

What if I hadn't seen her out on that lousy date? Had never stopped her in that parking lot and offered to let her use me. I would have missed this moment, the one where I got to hear the sweet, rasping whimpers coming from the back of her throat. The one where I got to feel the slick heat of her tongue rubbing against my own.

I might have missed the moment where I realized I'd been in love with her since I'd hugged her at her college graduation and smelled her hair. It had only taken me eight years, give or take, to figure it out. I could have spent another eight lonely years dismissing my feelings as an inconvenient infatuation.

We never had to do anything more than kiss, and I could die happy.

I slid my hand down from her neck to the smooth curve of her ass. The material of her dress was slippery under my palm as I tugged it up, little by little, until there was enough room for Jill to widen her legs to make more room for me. She sighed in relief as my hard length pressed into her warm center.

I bent slightly at the knees then straightened as I thrust up toward the spot where I knew she needed me the most. Our movements slowed as we ground against the side of the building, mouths teasing and playing.

When we had walked out the door of the country club, I'd had some inkling of how we would end this night—naked, sweaty, and quivering in release—but I would never have guessed it would begin with us making out and dry humping like a couple of horny teenagers in public.

In public.

Fuck, this was insane. Some of my oldest friends were right inside the building and could walk out at any moment. Hell, if Emma and James left something behind, they could be walking up this very path.

"Jill," I said, tearing my lips from hers.

"Yeah?" Her eyes were glassy and unfocused. The last time I'd seen her looking like that, she had been seconds away from coming while I ate her out on my living room couch.

"We have to stop." It took a monumental effort to step back.

She slumped against the wall and looked up at me with a scowl. "You suck."

"Get in the car, Blossom. I'm gonna take you home where we can do this properly. If I've finally got you, I'm not risking any interruptions." I was getting dangerously close to confessing all to her, and I needed to tamp that down. I would tell her tonight, but this was not the moment.

"Are you so certain I'm a sure thing?" she said, biting down on her swollen lower lip.

I shook my head. If only I was certain about that. But she'd kissed me, so that had to count for something. "You're about as far from a sure thing as it gets. I've never been kept on my toes like this before."

Her eyes widened, and her movements stilled.

"Are you surprised to hear that?" I asked, tugging her hand to get her moving toward my car. We needed to get somewhere private—and fast.

"I—I guess I am. You have dated a lot of incredible women. I find it hard to believe that I'm that special."

"Are you keeping tabs on my dating history, then?" I wanted to puff up my chest and preen like a peacock. I should have worn this suit weeks ago.

She gave me a light thwack on the upper arm with the back of her fingers. "I'm not keeping tabs. I mean, you *were* on a date the night I told you I needed a *friend with benefits.*"

I threw open the passenger door to the car and gestured for her to slide in. I closed the door securely behind her and hustled around to my side as she buckled up.

Jill groaned, tipping her head back against the headrest as I pulled out of the parking lot.

"What's that noise for?" I glanced at her from the corner of my eye, lingering on the smooth column of her throat and planning my strategy for where I would kiss it first.

"Do I sound hideously jealous?" she asked, her gaze still averted.

"Not hideously so," I replied, unable to keep the shit-eating grin off my face.

Her husky laugh sounded as if it came from deep within her throat.

I reached across the center console, finding her hand in her lap. On instinct, she flipped her palm until it was flush with mine, entwining our fingers.

"You're incredible, too, you know?"

She squeezed my hand. A silent thank you.

"Where are we going? Your place or mine?"

"Your place," Jill said decisively. "I want some of that churro-flavored popcorn you bought the other week."

"I've got that one and the other flavor you wanted to try. The barbeque one."

I stole a side glance at her and found her grinning at me, all teeth and bright cheeks. I bit back my own smile. "What? I have it on good authority that I'm a great listener."

"We'll see about that." Her smile held a wicked promise.

Jill

I WAS GOING TO die at the hands of Ben Till.

Halfway through the car ride home, our handholding had changed to him having his hand on my leg, the tips of his big fingers resting on my inner thigh, dangerously close to the source of my longing.

I unclipped my seatbelt and threw open the car door as soon as he pulled into his garage and shifted into park.

"You in a hurry for something?" he asked as my shoes scuffed on the concrete floor.

I ignored him, taking the two steps to the door and twisting the knob.

It didn't open. I jiggled it again.

"It's locked, Jill. Hold on."

He ambled over and spent what felt like an eternity digging in his pocket for his house key. When he finally found it, he brought it up to the keyhole, missing the mark not once, but twice.

"Holy shit, Ben," I said, snatching it from his grip and unlocking the door myself. I shouldered my way inside. Turning, I made eye contact with Ben, who was still on the other side of the threshold.

"What are you waiting for?" I asked with a quirk of a brow, daring him to answer.

He moved his head from side to side, like he was clearing out cobwebs. "I'm nervous, I guess. Didn't think I would be."

He was adorable. And sexy as fuck as he blushed and rubbed the back of his neck.

"Ben?" I slowly stepped toward him to lean a shoulder on the door frame, popping out my hip. Now that Ben had admitted to his nerves, mine had gone out the window. I felt like the most powerful femme fatale. All I needed was a slinky red dress and one of those long cigarette holders.

"You said you're a good listener, right?" I licked my lips. His blue eyes darkened as his gaze shifted down, lingering over my curves.

"Uh-huh."

"Then listen to what I'm about to say. Get inside this house, and fuck me. That's an order."

He was on me in an instant, his hands wrapping around my waist as he bent me backward in the door frame and placed his lips on mine.

Our tongues and teeth clashed as we fought for dominance. He spun us around and walked me backward as I held his face and neck in a tight grip.

Ben had said he wanted to take me somewhere without risk of interruption, and I wanted the same. I wanted to make him mine, at least for tonight, and maybe, if I was brave enough to trust him, for good.

I struggled to kick my shoes off as we made our way through the kitchen. When Ben sank to a knee in front of me in the middle of the room, I protested the loss of his lips. He chuckled darkly as he propped one foot on his thigh, slipping it free of my heel before doing the same to the other. I shivered as he ran his fingertips along the arch before holding it up to drop a soft kiss there.

He flicked his eyes up to mine with a goofy grin. "We both said 'maybe' to feet stuff on that survey."

I burst out laughing, not breaking the moment but heightening it.

Since Oliver, laughter and sex weren't things that went hand in hand. Anxiety and tension? Sure. But never the sheer joy that being with Ben delivered.

The man at my feet challenged every one of my assumptions about him more and more with every minute we spent together.

As my laughter died down, I tipped my head forward to look at Ben, still perched on bended knee below me. It was a pose of vulnerability and supplication, but there wasn't a hint of weakness in him.

He looked confident, and strong, and willing to dive into all the messy, sticky, hard places with me.

If I was ready to go there with him, we needed to clear the air about what I had overheard him saying about me and my plans for Velvet. That resentment and fear couldn't linger any longer, not if we wanted to build something healthy, whether it was a romantic relationship or just a friendship.

That conversation would have to wait because Ben was unbuttoning the cuffs of his dress shirt. My mouth fell open as he pulled the shirt from his waistband and got to work on the buttons trailing down his middle, baring more inked skin as he went.

He was still on the floor, though, and that was a problem. Now that I knew what it was like to kiss Ben Till, I was addicted to his lips, and I wanted them back on mine.

Ben, apparently, had other ideas as he shrugged off his shirt, letting it flutter to the gray vinyl floor. I lowered a shaky hand to his bare shoulder as he nuzzled into my lower belly.

"Ben," I said on a gasp as he started working his head under the skirt of my yellow dress, nipping at my inner thighs. "I don't want that tonight."

"Hmm? Don't want what?" he mumbled.

"Your mouth. I want your cock."

He ducked out from under my dress, his blue eyes turned liquid black. "Why not both?" He slid his palm from the outside of my leg and around to the crease of my thigh, tracing the edge of my panty line before dipping the fingertip beneath the fabric.

"Um." I panted as he moved that finger up a fraction of an inch, never taking his gaze off my face. "I just...don't want you to feel...obligated."

He removed his finger—damn him—only to change the angle on his wrist so he was cupping me entirely. I couldn't contain my gasp.

"Let's get one thing straight, Blossom. Eating this pussy is never an obligation. Make it my breakfast, lunch, and dinner, and I'll die happy with blue balls. But if you don't want it right now, I don't either. You're in charge here. So, how do you want me?"

The possibilities were endless. The power dynamics at play between Ben and me made it so even the most vanilla of sexual acts had me keyed up. Sex with us was a mental game, and he and I played it well.

"I think...we should go to your bedroom." Most of our hookups since that first night had taken place in his living room while we watched TV.

"Do you *think* you want that, or do you actually want that?"

I brought my hand down to his bare shoulder and dug my fingernails in. In my mind, I was scratching the word *Mine* on his back with the sharpened tips.

I bet he'd let me do it if I asked.

"Take me to your bedroom, Ben."

In one smooth motion, he was on his feet and tossing me over his shoulder, the air shooting out of my lungs.

"Careful," I said with a giggle. His only response was a playful slap to the back of my thigh as he speed-walked down the narrow hall to his room.

I let out a screech as my head narrowly missed the door frame when he turned to shut the bedroom door behind us. A moment later, I was flat on my back on his bed.

He followed me down, one suited leg between my thighs as he held himself above me with his hands bracketing my head.

"Can I kiss you again?"

I nodded, my lips falling open in anticipation.

The kiss was wet and dirty, no hesitation for us to learn each other this time. He tasted better now than he had against the wall of the country club.

He thrusted his hips against mine, and I swore I could feel the metal ball of his piercing hitting me just right.

"Fuck." He grasped the outside of my leg and bent my knee up to make more space for himself between my thighs. God knew he was big enough to need it.

The fabric of my dress protested the movement, stretching until my leg wouldn't go any farther.

"Dress. Off." I wiggled desperately under Ben.

He ignored my request, instead gliding his hand down to the hem to lift the skirt higher.

That wouldn't do at all.

I reached up to clutch his throat in a loose hand.

He lifted his head to look at me. His face was slack, but his eyes were on fire.

"I am the one calling the shots tonight, aren't I?"

I experimented with a small pulse of my fist around the thick muscles of his neck. His cock jumped in response, like I had wrapped that hand around it instead.

"Do you like that?" I asked.

"Yeah," he grunted.

"Do you trust me to make us both feel good?"

He nodded as I released my hold on him, then he lowered his head to run his tongue along the curves of cleavage bared by my dress.

"Why won't you take my clothes off, then?"

He nipped the skin at my collarbone before looking up at me.

"Because you and these dresses have been driving me crazy for months. I may or may not have a fantasy about fucking you while you're wearing one."

"We can do that next time. This dress is *dry clean only*. Very expensive. I can't be getting cum on the fabric. And you *do* want to come, right?"

"Fuck, yes, I want to come." He thrust his hips up again, letting me feel him at my center. The head of his cock bumped against my clit, leaving me panting as he repeated the motion twice more.

We needed to get this show on the road before he finished in his pants, and I lost out on the full cream-pie experience.

I found the slope of Ben's ankle with my foot, wrapping my lower leg around his. Using my leverage, I shifted him off me with a twist of my hips, leaving him lying stunned on his side, facing me.

"Where are you going?" he asked with wide eyes as I sat up on the bed.

I found the bow at the nape of my neck that held the halter straps of my dress together. Slowly tugging the strip of fabric, I watched as Ben followed the motion of my hand before settling on the skin bared by the falling silk. The built-in bra cups in the bodice kept it from slipping off my breasts, but the sagging fabric was hanging on for dear life. Ben looked like a man who had just caught his first glimpse of a meal after weeks of starvation.

"Would you like to take it the rest of the way off?"

It was the least I could do, seeing as I was about to use and abuse him for the rest of the night. Somehow, I didn't think he would mind.

His throat bobbed as he pushed up on one arm to hook a tattooed finger into the shadow at my breastbone. The material at my back tightened as he dragged the dress down and down and down. My nipples stiffened as the rush of silk slid over them, baring them to the air-conditioned room. Ben slowly sat up, as if mesmerized, and dipped his chin like he was about to take a bite.

I placed my forefinger across his lips. "Did I say you could put your mouth on them?"

His silver eyes were hazy, and there were deep furrows in his forehead. "Can I? Please?"

"Just a taste."

His lips opened, and he slicked his tongue over them. I inhaled sharply as he took one nipple between his teeth. The soft pinch was just on the other side of painful until he released the bite to caress it with a gentle tongue. He pulled off with a wet pop before moving to the other bud and sucking it deep.

"You're wasting time." I aimed for stern, but my breathlessness belied my tone.

"Never a waste with you," he responded as he found the hem of my dress with searching fingers and clawed it up and over my head.

Since I hadn't needed a bra, I'd chosen my underwear with care, hoping that Ben might see it. It was for him, but it was also for me.

"Did I ever tell you that yellow is my favorite color?"

"How fitting, then." I smirked as I lay back down on the bed, placing my feet flat on the dark comforter.

"God, you're pretty spread out on my bed."

I cast my mind back to when Ben and I had started this, when my head was still filled with Oliver's ugly words. The only thing I could hear in this moment was Ben's voice, and it was beautiful.

"Thank you," I said, accepting the compliment I knew I deserved. "Now what do you plan to do about it?" I asked.

"You giving me the control now?"

"As if."

Ben chuckled as he collapsed back into me, holding my face between his palms as we kissed.

I slid a hand between us, taking hold of his length through his pants and boxers. "We forgot to take your pants off," I said, tearing my lips from his.

"Fuck, I know. What were we thinking?"

"We weren't."

He laughed as he rolled away, undoing his belt buckle and whipping the leather strap from the loops at his waist. I bit my lip. The move was sexy as hell.

He twisted the belt into a loose coil and set it next to my head on the mattress. I stole a peek at it as he kicked his way out of his pants, standing above me in only a pair of black boxer briefs. We would come back to that narrow slice of leather later. But now...now I had other plans in mind. Plans that included removing our underwear.

I slicked my tongue over my lower lip, and Ben pulled the waistband of his boxer briefs slowly down below one hip bone and then the other. His thick, erect length slowed him down as he maneuvered the fabric the rest of the way off.

His quads were taut as he stood over me at the foot of the bed. He was hanging on by a thread, and I was itching to unravel him.

"You can take mine off if you want." I tipped my chin toward the scrap of yellow lace, the only thing left dividing us.

He fisted his erection, and I watched, rapt, as his wicked barbell piercing appeared and disappeared in his grip while he stroked.

On a downstroke of his fist, I noticed the ball ends of the piercing. They were pink. Hot pink. My favorite color.

"Did you do that for me?" I shifted closer to get a better look.

Light pressure on my sternum pushed me back down on the mattress.

"You know I did it for you. Look your fill later. I want to savor this a little longer. You, spread out so pretty on my bed like this. Like sunshine on an overcast day."

I squirmed. "I want to get fucked, Ben. We can do the savoring later. Unless..."

I turned to reach for the nightstand and opened the drawer, searching blindly for the blue vibrator I had used for our first time together.

Striking gold, I held the shaft aloft. "I could always do it myself." I powered the vibrator on, feeling the minute shivers from my fingertips to my elbows.

Ben was no longer standing at the edge of the bed. He was crawling up the mattress toward me. I wasn't certain if I was the predator who had enticed the prey in close before I snapped, or if I was the one being hunted.

With Ben and me, it could switch on a dime.

Before him, I'd never been in sync with a partner. It should have been obvious what I was missing in the past, even before things had gone sideways with Oliver. I needed someone who I felt comfortable enough to be myself with. Someone who I could stop and laugh with in the middle of sex.

I could have met countless people through My Cup, been on thousands of dates, and I never would have found what Ben and I had. The thought was both terrifying and exhilarating all at once.

He settled himself low between my thighs, kissing the soft skin near my panty line. Casual as could be, he snaked a hand up and snatched the vibrator out of my grip, tossing it to the side.

"That was rather bold of you, assuming I don't need that," I said, my breath hitching as he continued to lay butterfly-soft kisses across the yellow lace of my underwear.

"Do you? Need it?" He nipped the thin skin at my hip bone.

I dropped my hand to his head, drawing small circles with my thumb over the lobe of his ear.

"Maybe later," I said, giving in on a sigh.

He grinned. "Definitely later."

I didn't know which one of us removed my underwear in the end. Maybe it was both of us, hand over hand. Either way, the job was done, and then Ben was above me, kissing me, and he tasted so good.

He broke the kiss to look at me, his lids low. "Jill," he said, panting, "tell me what to do. Please."

I shifted my lower body until I felt the head of his thick cock notch at my opening, begging for entry but not yet pushing inside. It was delicious torture.

I suddenly felt the urge for something more, something different. I needed to reclaim the moment I'd had with him on that first night in my apartment. The one where I'd allowed Oliver to creep in. That asshole had no place in my relationship with Ben, and I was ready to kick him out of my head for good. "On your back. Now."

He rolled onto his back, reversing our positions. His cock didn't move an inch.

I stared down at him, in awe, as I hovered above him on shaking muscles. "Okay, that was seriously impressive. Big-muscle dudes aren't supposed to be that graceful."

When he started to laugh, I sank down fully, taking his length all the way in. The laugh morphed into a moan, mixing with my own noisy sigh.

Finally. Fucking *finally*.

I would gloat later, I decided, as Ben brought his hands to my waist as my hips rocked involuntarily. Clucking my tongue at him, I reached for his wrists to pull them off me. I wasn't strong enough to restrain him, not really, but Ben allowed it, just like he allowed me to tilt my body forward and press his wrists to the bed, crisscrossed over each other.

I leaned in close, letting him taste the words on his lips. "Don't move unless I tell you to. I'm going to use you now."

CHAPTER FORTY-THREE

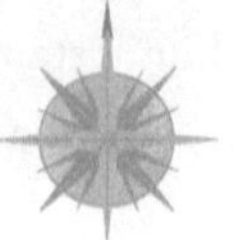

Ben

I'D BEEN HEARING JILL say those words in my head every time I'd jacked off for months—ever since that night at that dive bar.

I pressed the backs of my hands flat onto the mattress and gave a testing push back against Jill's grip. I didn't intend to shake her loose, but I wanted her to feel the power she had over me, to know all the strength within me was hers to command.

She gave me an answering grin, letting me register her weight on my wrists, and then squeezed the inner muscles of her pussy around me.

I groaned, my cock feeling like it was caught in a fucking vise.

"Shit, that was mean, Blossom." I barely got the words out.

"Was it? And here I would have thought you liked the feel of my pussy choking the life out of you."

That filthy mouth of hers was going to be the death of me...along with that gorgeous smile. God, I loved this woman so much it was ridiculous.

"Can you take more?" she asked, giving me another strangling squeeze.

I nodded, but it was more of a thrashing of my head back and forth against the mattress. If I had hair, it would have been wild with static.

She tilted her hips a few times, finding her rhythm. I was bigger than average—or so I had been told—and I could tell she was adjusting to the sensation of the barbell inside her.

Her body stiffened above me, losing the languid freedom. I had to step it up, make this good for so she could forget about her dickhead of an ex and all the bad experiences that had come after him. It was up to me to jolt her out of her head now. I was the one she'd picked to be her *friend with benefits*. I was the one who cared about her, listened to her, *loved* her. No one else was qualified to make this woman come the way I was.

I twitched my fingers as far as I could, brushing her inner wrist. "Stop thinking so much, Blossom. You're perfect. Now, *use me*."

Her brown eyes flashed, and her teeth snapped. My girl was feral, and I was obsessed.

She rose off my cock a fraction and lowered back down. We both moaned.

"There you go," I said. "Treat this cock like it's your favorite toy. Its sole purpose in life is to get you off, Blossom. If you don't let me do it, I'm gonna be mad."

She breathed out a burst of laughter, but there was heat behind it. "You think your dick is so magical it'll get me off as well as a vibrator with clitoral suction?"

I bit my lip as she moved her hips in a circle. "Nah," I managed finally. "I think *you're* so magical you're gonna get yourself off with me as your personal prop. You up for that?"

There was a rush of fluid as I felt her pussy grow wetter. Leave it to Jill to get turned on by being challenged.

"Oh, it's on, Benny Boy." She dragged her hands from my wrists to my shoulder, leaning into my lips. She licked across them once, then twice. I opened for her, sensing what she wanted, and met her tongue with mine.

Her pussy slid up and down again, her movements larger, gaining speed. It felt criminally good. I fought the urge to thrust up into her, to match her rhythm with my hips. She was using me, and I needed to let her.

She kept going, and I shut up, content to watch her face contort in pleasure as she rode me, up and down, grinding her clit into my pelvis with each rolling thrust of her hips.

Jill was in control, and I wasn't complaining. I would gladly allow her that for the rest of my life, if that was what she needed.

My fingers searched for purpose as we continued to kiss, slow and sensual, at odds with the speed of our lower bodies. She bore down, her pace hard, fast, and steady.

"I'm so close, Ben," she whimpered.

I wanted to touch her—*had* to touch her—so badly my palms itched.

"Me too," I said.

"Touch me now, please, please, *please*."

Thank fuck.

My arms were numb, but the pins and needles only heightened the sensation when I reached down to the round curve of Jill's ass with both hands. With her sitting on top of me, the flesh felt bigger, more substantial, than when we were standing or lying next to each other. Maybe after we got this round of sex out of our systems, she would let me bite one of the fleshy cheeks.

I'd let her do it back to me if she wanted.

I squeezed her there, the tips of my middle fingers teasing the divot in between. She had mentioned being open to ass play on our survey, but I wouldn't go there unless explicitly invited.

She pulled her lips from mine and looked me straight in the eyes. "You can." Her pink mouth was shiny.

"I can what?" I wanted full, enthusiastic instruction.

"You can, uh...use your fingers on me."

I quirked a brow. "On you where?"

"In my ass." I felt her pussy gush again. If just the thought of me filling her with my fingers had her this turned on, what would it be like when we played with a butt plug, or I took her there with my dick?

She reached back for one of my hands and brought it up to her mouth. She wrapped her tongue around my middle and pointer fingers before sucking them into the damp cavern of her mouth. My cock jumped like she was sucking on that too.

That infuriating tongue swirled down to the crease of my knuckles, wetting my finger from base to tip. When she pulled back, a string of saliva trailed from her mouth to my hand.

"You're a dream. You know that, right?"

She smiled, almost shyly, and I swore I caught a hint of a blush on the ridges of her cheekbones.

"Keep riding me," I said as I brought my hand back down to Jill's bottom.

She listened. I doubted she realized our roles had reversed yet again, this time with me telling her what to do. Surely there was some psychological explanation for why we liked what we liked, but so long as we both felt good, I wasn't questioning it.

I traced the tip of my wet finger back and forth around the tight ring of her asshole, delighting when her hips started jogging more and more, seeking me out.

I dipped the digit slowly inside her, letting her body adjust to the sensation.

"Feeling okay?" I asked, checking in.

"Uh-huh," she said with a vigorous nod and a downward stroke that had me groaning. "Feels so good."

"Yeah? You like me filling that pussy and ass at the same time?"

She smiled, looking like the cat that ate the canary. I was feeling pretty damn similar right now.

"Don't think this means you're the boss now, got it?" she said, her teeth a flash of wicked white.

"I wouldn't dream of taking over that job from you. I'm your favorite toy, remember?"

The hand I had clasped at her side guided her as she moved on top of me. I didn't need to do much, but despite my willingness to be...used...I wasn't a passive participant.

"Favorite is a bit strong, but..." She rose and fell, and I felt her legs quiver.

Yeah, *sure*, I wasn't her favorite.

She was close, but I wouldn't call attention to it. That would put too much pressure on this moment. Jill had proven several times over that she could achieve orgasm with me and get out of her head, but this was our first time having penetrative sex. If it didn't work this time, a small part of me worried she would make for the hills as soon as I fell asleep.

It wasn't a comforting thought. Not when all I wanted was to keep her forever.

Jill arched her back, pressing her breasts into my chest. Her pussy tightened around my cock, and she clamped around the finger I had in her ass.

"Kiss me, Ben," she said in my ear, the words all breathy and keening. Thank god we'd ripped through that no-kissing boundary.

I gave her what she wanted, capturing that pink lower lip between my own and giving it a firm suck. I swallowed her cries down my throat as I licked into her mouth, tasting what made her uniquely Jill.

Her hips jerked as her back bowed. The inner muscles of her pussy clenched around me. I couldn't stop my climax as her cries filled my ears, her face twisted in ecstasy.

She collapsed over top of me, spent. I ran a hand down her back, enjoying the way her skin pebbled under my fingertips. Her moonflower scent mixed with the smell of sweat and sex and my laundry detergent. If I pulled this off, I might have that scent in my nostrils every night for as long as I lived.

Jill pulled up abruptly, and my eyes flew open. Was she okay? Did I hurt her? Was she reliving an uncomfortable memory from her past?

But she was grinning, wide and hard.

"I came!" she cried before I could say a word.

I cupped her chin in my palm, rubbing my thumb along the smooth edge of her cheekbone. "Yeah, you did, Blossom."

"I—I wasn't sure I would be able to. Our first time having sex this way, you know?"

I gently brought her face down to mine and pressed a light kiss to her lips. "You were sexy, and beautiful, and incredible. And I can't wait to watch you come again." I was letting it all hang out now. The words *I love you* were hovering on the tip of my tongue.

"I think I finally got his voice out of my head," she said, dazed with wonder, like she almost couldn't believe it.

"If he comes back again, you tell me, okay? We'll figure it out together." I wasn't naïve enough to think that all of Jill's insecurities were gone for good. I doubted she thought that either. But I was in this with her for the long haul.

"Mm-hmm," she said, pressing the cold tip of her nose into my neck.

I shivered before giving her a tap on her ass. "Come on, let's get you cleaned up and under the covers. You're freezing."

And cum was leaking out of her, all over the bedspread.

T HE BED WAS A downright disaster as Jill scooped a handful of churro-flavored popcorn into her mouth, crumbs flying. She kicked her legs out in front of her, clad in a pair of my checked boxer briefs. She wore my white dress shirt, partially buttoned and hanging loose off one shoulder.

I'd never predicted that my dreams would be so messy, but I was okay with it.

"So, what do we think of them? Will they end up together at the finale, or do you think she breaks it off at the last second?" She motioned toward the small TV in my room where our favorite reality show of the summer flashed through a montage of generically happy couples.

"I'm predicting they stay together."

"Yeah, but what about Cate's aversion to love? She did say she's never been in a serious relationship before Monty."

I shrugged. We didn't know these people at all, but the speculation was fun. "He seems like a patient guy, willing to wait for her. I don't know, they seem like the real deal to me."

"Is he too nice for her, though? She's definitely got a bit of a snarky streak to her."

"Yeah, and? Some men like that. Maybe Monty's one of them." I was one of them. If I didn't think Jill would flip her lid about it, I'd rent a billboard and put it in right across the street. *Ben Till likes snarky women.*

Or maybe it would be more accurate for it to say: *Ben Till* loves *snarky women.* One in particular.

"Want some?" the object of my musings interrupted my thoughts. Her hand beneath my nose held out the popcorn bowl.

"No, thanks. Getting full."

She snickered as she stuffed more into her mouth. "I know something else that's still pretty full too."

I rolled into her, snatching the bowl away. "Is that a reference to what I think it is?"

She nodded proudly, her eyebrows dancing. "It is. Am I not allowed to be happy? I mean, cream pies *are* one of my top fantasies. Direct from the source this time. *Finally.*"

"Yeah, yeah, yeah. Try telling me it wasn't worth the wait."

I turned away and snatched the remote off the nightstand, powering off the TV as outtakes played over the show's end credits.

"Are you looking forward to the finale tomorrow night?" The final episodes were double-headers, airing back-to-back days this week. "You wanna watch it here? I'll get another bag of the churro popcorn, since you like it so much."

"Oh, could you get the chicken-and-waffles flavor too? I want those."

"I can do that. Or...if you're up to it, we could go to the grocery store together tomorrow. Pick out all the snacks and drinks we need."

Was I manipulating her into spending more time with me through snacks? Yes. Was I at all ashamed? Not a bit.

"That could be fun. I don't have to work at any of my jobs tomorrow."

"Planning to do any work at Velvet?"

"I'm expecting my liquor shipment to get delivered in the afternoon. The vendor said it could be anytime between two and five."

"Sounds like you don't have to be up early, then."

"Nope," she said, her salty lips tipping up.

"Wanna have a sleepover?"

She leaped onto my lap, sending the popcorn bowl careening off the bed and onto the floor.

"Absolutely, I do."

After that, I got lost in her smile, and her eyes, and her hips.

Tomorrow, we would talk.

CHAPTER FORTY-FOUR

Ben

MY MORNING ALARM BLARED far too early. I'd forgotten to turn it off, too used to my habitual early wake-ups. The Till Lawn and Landscape crew had a rare day off in honor of Dany's birthday party. I'd have to thank my boss later for the privilege of waking up with Jill's ankle crossed over mine and her hair tickling my nose. Oh wait, I was my boss. Maybe I'd give myself a raise too while I was at it. I definitely deserved it.

"Make it stop," my blonde bedmate said from under the rumpled sheets.

"Sorry, Blossom. Forgot to turn it off last night before we fell sleep."

"I'll forgive you if you come back to snuggle with me. I'm cold." Her grumpy morning pout was adorable.

"How are you cold? It's supposed to be almost ninety degrees today. I bet it's already in the eighties." Another reason I was happy to have the day off.

Jill pushed up on an elbow and narrowed her eyes at me. "Don't tell me you're one of *those* people."

"Who are those people?"

"People who are always hot. Because I'm always cold. We'll constantly be battling over the thermostat, and it won't do."

"Does everyone in the world fit into this dichotomy?"

She tipped her chin up. "It's an age-old debate, Benny Boy. And I will always win."

"Yeah, you will," I said, grinning as I tugged her back down into the blankets with me. She was welcome to think that, but I was the real winner so long as I had her.

"Thank you for staying the night."

"Mmm. Thank you for asking me." I could tell sleep was claiming her again.

"Always."

🌰🌰🌰🌰🌰🌰🌰🌰

WE WOKE UP FOR good when the light shining through my blinds became unbearable, and I could no longer ignore the growling in my stomach.

"Want breakfast?" I asked.

Jill glanced at me over her shoulder as she made her way to the bathroom. "Can we eat something greasy and super unhealthy? Jimbo is always offering egg-white omelets, and I'm just not sure I can tolerate it if you are equally as yolk-averse."

"I was thinking pancakes. Lots of syrup. Maybe some whipped cream too. Fresh fruit if that's not too offensively healthy for you."

She clapped her hands together. "I want all of that. Okay, I'm gonna pee and presume you have spare toothbrushes somewhere in this place?"

"Might be one under the sink. The bottom drawer."

"I'm shocked you're not better stocked."

"I used to get a bunch at the dentist, but I skipped my last cleaning. Too awkward to have an ex digging around in my mouth."

"Is that the only reason you don't have supplies for overnight guests?"

"Are you fishing for information?"

She giggled as she sidestepped into the bathroom and started sliding cabinets open. "When have I ever been subtle?" she asked.

"Never," I said, sidling up to her as she found a cellophane-wrapped toothbrush in the back of the drawer and held it aloft. "And, Jill? I like that you're not subtle. So, I'm gonna tell you that I haven't had anyone stay over in a long time. Long enough that I don't remember the last time. Feel free to leave that in the toothbrush holder because, Blossom? As soon as you're ready, you can claim me and my space as your own."

I spun on my heel and headed to the kitchen, too much of a coward to watch her reaction to what I'd just said. Although she'd stayed with me last night—and I knew that wasn't meaningless—we still needed to have a conversation.

No matter what, I would wait until she was ready. I wouldn't *like* it, but I would do it. For her.

I got to work mixing up pancake batter, thanking my past self who'd remembered to buy batter at the store last week.

I was enjoying the sound the whisk made as it dragged across the metal interior of the mixing bowl when Jill padded on bare feet into the kitchen.

"Warm enough?" I smirked at the sight of her bundled in my long flannel bathrobe. Ma had bought it for me a couple of birthdays ago.

It stayed on a hook in the back of my closet unless my parents were visiting.

Jill tugged the robe up so she could hop up onto the counter to watch me work.

"You never wear this, do you?" she asked around a strawberry she had snatched from the plastic container sitting out on the counter. I envied that strawberry in the worst way.

"Nope. Don't tell my mother."

Jill chewed for a moment. I could see her calculating an approach as I poured batter into a cast iron pan.

"Do you think your mom will like me?"

I didn't turn from the stovetop as I answered. There was the small issue of Ma's past with Jill's building, but I had enough trust in Ma that she would work that out.

"My mom already likes you." They'd met before.

"She doesn't know me—not as anything more than your best friend's sister or the girl who works at the library."

"Yeah, but what she does know, she likes."

"Ben, I think we need to talk about Velvet and what it means for us. I mean, I'm in the business of selling sex toys for a living. Is that going to be a problem for the mayor?"

I flipped the pancake and glanced at her over my shoulder. Was she saying what I thought she was saying? Here I'd been pussyfooting around having an important talk, while Jill was casually dropping *us* into the equation like it was nothing.

"I'm sorry, I got a little distracted by the word *us,* and I missed the question. Could you repeat that for me?" I made the shape of a funnel with my hand around my ear.

Her sassy eye roll was my reward. "I'm serious, Ben. Have you even thought about any of this?"

I scooped a pancake onto a plate and crossed the kitchen back toward her. Stepping between her spread legs, I gave a playful twist of the robe's waist tie at her belly button.

"I'm not worried, Blossom, and you shouldn't be either. Not when being together feels like this."

She sighed into me, her upper back curving slightly and her legs falling open a fraction more. "What does being with me feel like to you?" She brought her knuckles up to trail over the bit of stubble at my jaw that I hadn't had time to shave off yet—too caught up in Jill.

I smiled and turned my head to nip at her fingers. "Like staring directly at the sun."

"Sounds like a fast way to burn your retinas."

I dropped a kiss on her collarbone, the lone strip of skin I could see in a sea of flannel.

"The sun is the source of life for our planet. Without it, nothing new would grow. It's the most important thing out there."

"Mmm, I don't remember photosynthesis being this sexy."

I laughed. "You make me happy, okay? That's a sun thing too. Seasonal Affective Disorder is no joke."

"Did you know you can buy special lamps now that are supposed to help with that? Plop one right on your desk this winter. You won't even need me."

I shook my head and kissed her smiling lips and then moved back to the stovetop. "I'll take you over the light. You probably use more electricity than a lamp does, but the other benefits are better."

"Speaking of benefits..." Jill kicked one leg over the other, swinging a foot in a circle.

"Yes? What about them?"

"That was sort of mind-blowing last night, wasn't it? I mean, it was for me, at least."

I poured more batter into the pan before casting her an over-the-shoulder glance. "It was amazing."

She flashed me a cheeky grin. "I wouldn't be opposed to doing it some more—if you're interested."

"What would give you the impression I wouldn't be interested, Blossom? Didn't you feel my cock pressing against your ass when we woke up this morning? I would have thought that was a pretty big clue."

"The *biggest* clue I've ever encountered."

I threw my head back, laughing, as the pancake batter bubbled. I gave it a flip before turning back to Jill. "In all seriousness, we probably should talk—about you, and me, and what we're doing."

Jill nodded slowly, some of that confidence she'd woken up with eroding from her face. "Okay. Yes. We should talk—about us...and about other things too."

That didn't sound good. I abandoned our breakfast, walking over to step between her legs. "Is everything okay?"

"Um, what the fuck is going on here?" My best friend slammed his way into the kitchen, glaring daggers at the side of my head.

CHAPTER FORTY-FIVE

Jill

I STARED AT JIMBO. He stared at me, clearly confused about what I was doing sitting on his best friend's countertop with said best friend pressed between my legs.

Not only was he interrupting breakfast, but he was interrupting the moment where I was finally going to open up to Ben about overhearing his phone call last year. I'd been avoiding it all morning, too content to enjoy Ben's company to risk ruining things.

And there *was* something to ruin with me and Ben. I was done fighting it, and I was ready to take a chance. Ben was mine, and I was planning on keeping him. Turned out, commitment wasn't so terrifying when you were committing to your best friend. Now, I just needed to get my brother out of the way so Ben and I could air it all out.

"You have no right to be mad, Jimbo," I started. "Ben and I are grown adults. You and I may share DNA, but that does not mean you get a say about who I'm sleeping with."

My brother's face grew redder, if that were possible. He reminded me of the cherry tomatoes Ben had growing out in his garden.

"I can't believe I'm about to ask this question, because I truly do not want to know the answer, but...are you two..." He made a little motion with his pointer finger, back and forth between Ben and me.

"I mean, what do you think?" It seemed pretty obvious from where I was standing. Or sitting. With my inner thighs flushed tight to Ben's hips.

"You've been insisting you were friends for months! What was I supposed to think?!"

"Um, surprise?" I had the grace to grimace. This was far from the ideal way for James to find out. "I'm honestly a little shocked that you didn't put it together a while ago. I think half the town knows already." I looked at Ben appealingly, but he kept his face pointed toward the floor. His shoulders were shaking—in laughter or tears, I couldn't be sure.

"I've been busy." Jimbo crossed his arms over his chest, a petulant expression growing on his face.

"If by busy you mean with wedding planning, then maybe you're just unobservant. Emma is planning the wedding too, and she realized something was going on ages ago."

He looked ready to explode. "Wait, Emma knew, and she didn't tell me?"

I shrugged, and Ben's whole body started vibrating. "Don't take it personally. I did swear her to secrecy."

He threw his hands up. "How am I not supposed to take it personally when the two most important women in my life hide something from me?"

"Maybe it's not about you?"

My brother looked around the kitchen in exasperation, as if searching for an audience he could appeal to about this madness. "And what do you have to say for yourself?" James asked, finally directing his attention to Ben.

Ben buried his face in his hands for a moment, still shaking, before stepping back from me. He swiped both palms down his cheeks, as if re-setting his expression.

"Is it finally my turn to talk?" he asked, glancing back and forth between me and Jimbo while fighting a smile.

I rolled my eyes and looked over to find my brother doing the same.

Ben had the nerve to chuckle under his breath before looking his best friend straight in the eye, opening his mouth, and telling him, "I'm in love with Jill. And we weren't lying, by the way. We are friends. But we're not...just friends."

Oh. Ben loved me. Tiny bubbles formed in my belly, fluttering up like I'd taken a gulp of champagne. Was this a good feeling?

Ben looked at me head on. I traced my gaze over the lines of his face, the sharp edges of his jaw, the colorful swirls inked on his collarbone. When I hit his mouth, I watched his lips as they slowly, fractionally tilted upward in a smile. I met his eyes and gave him an answering grin, letting my feelings shine through.

Yeah, being loved by Ben was a good feeling. The *best* feeling. Because I loved him too.

But that still didn't mean we could avoid having a conversation. I looked back at Jimbo as a tiny divot formed between his brows. He adjusted his shoulders—a movement I recognized well. My brother was always uptight, but this was genuine tension.

That bubbly feeling in my stomach turned sour.

James tilted his head to the side, cracking his neck. "When did this start?"

Ben answered, "Not long after I started helping Jill with the flooding at Velvet. We hit it off, started hanging out, and one thing led to
another. You know how that goes."

He was sparing my pride by not mentioning our initial conversation after my disastrous date with John, making the whole thing sound
less sordid.

"Yeah, no need for details," James said with a terse laugh. "But,
uh…" He flicked his eyes to me and hesitated, as if he didn't want to
say whatever he wanted to say in front of me.

"James, I promise you, this is a good thing. Jill and I are happy,
and no one is taking advantage of anyone here. No one is going to get
hurt."

My brother shot his friend a sardonic look. "Yeah? You sure about
that?"

My heart dropped to my feet as I realized what he meant. Usually,
guys warned their best friends away from their sisters because they
were worried about those sisters getting hurt. With Ben and me, it was
the opposite. James thought I would be the one to hurt Ben, not the
other way around.

"I'm actually looking out for you, dude," Jimbo continued. "It's not
Jill I'm concerned about in this equation."

I'd known it was coming, but hearing him say it out loud still stung.

I slid down from the counter, wrapping Ben's flannel robe tightly
around my center as my brother continued to drone on.

"Don't get me wrong, I love Jill. She's my sister, and she's a cool
person. But there are some fundamental differences between the two
of you. I mean, you're Mr. Commitment. You've been talking about
settling down with someone for years. And Jill? Have you ever had a
relationship in your life?"

Both their heads snapped to look at me. I fought the temptation to
run away, lifting my chin defiantly. "Yes. I have. It was a long time ago,
but I've been in a committed relationship before."

Through it all, Ben said nothing. How could he stay silent when he *knew* what I had dealt with in that relationship? I may never have told him Oliver's name, or shared every one of his cruel words, but Ben knew the scars Oliver had left on me.

Maybe Ben loved me, but did he agree with James? Was he only willing to be with me in spite of his concerns that we weren't truly compatible?

I wanted to be loved, but not against someone's better judgment.

A well of tears began to build behind my eyes, and I struggled to blink it away.

James sighed. "Look, I'm sorry, Jilly Bean. I know I'm coming across like a dick. I'm just worried. If this thing doesn't work out, it impacts all of us."

"It will work out," Ben said, finally speaking. But his earlier hesitation offered me little confidence that he meant what he said. The damage was done.

"How do you know that for sure? Fuck, dude, do you remember that time Jill decided she was going to go backpacking in Europe for two months with her friends but had to bow out at the last second because when she got to the airport, she realized she needed a backpack and didn't have one? Who does that? Backpack is literally in the name of the activity!"

Then Ben snickered. He *laughed* at me, and suddenly, I was right back in that restaurant last winter, hearing his ugly words.

"Stop!" I stepped up, putting myself between the two men. "James, if you keep talking, you'll be lucky if I ever speak to you again. I get that you're worried about Ben, but you don't need to insult the whole of my character while you're trying to convince him what a poor bet I am. Now, take me home."

Ben rushed toward me, but I stopped him with a raised hand. His eyes were darting over me, as if trying to calculate where he had gone wrong.

"Jill, please don't leave," he said. "We have stuff to talk about, remember?"

I shook my head, feeling a tear trail down my jaw and onto my neck. "I don't think there's anything to talk about, Ben."

He looked stricken, blowing past the space between us and gathering my raised hand between his own. "I meant what I said earlier. I love you, Jill. And we have plenty to talk about."

I snatched my hand from him, backing away from him until I felt my brother at my back. "You say you love me, but you laughed at me just now."

"It was a gut response! The way James told the story was funny, that's all. I'm sorry, Jill. Now, can you please stay so we can have that conversation?"

"It wasn't only that! You don't respect me. You don't believe in me, Ben. Even if you do love me, it doesn't count for much if you don't have faith in me."

His brow furrowed. "What are you talking about? Because I didn't react perfectly in an emotional situation one time, you're giving up on us?"

"It was more than once! I *heard* you, Ben! I heard you on the phone when we met up last year to talk about my plans for Velvet. You were shit-talking me, saying it would never stick because *I* never stick with anything. So don't tell me it was just the one time."

I felt James stiffen behind me, and he rested a steady hand on my shoulder. My brother might be a complete idiot, and he might be overly critical, but he had my back.

I watched the emotions play across Ben's face, plain as day. First, confusion—like he didn't know what I was talking about—then realization and, finally, resignation.

"There is a good explanation for why I said what I did. It was wrong, and *I* was wrong when I said it. I'm going to guess you're not going to give me the chance to explain, though, right?"

"Give her some time, Ben, okay?" James cut in, his deep voice firm.

Ben nodded, devoid of expression. He looked like I felt. Numb and wrung out.

"Yeah, okay. Bring the robe back when you're ready, I guess."

I didn't have the strength to look back at him as my brother steered me out the front door.

CHAPTER FORTY-SIX

Jill

I SPUN IN A slow circle in the middle of the speakeasy floor, taking in the empty room. There were only minor tweaks left to be made before I planned to bring in the furniture.

I heard a swish and watched as my brother stepped through the secret doorway from the shop area. "Opens smoothly," he said, gesturing toward the door. "You sure you're good to wait for the delivery on your own?"

As much as I'd wanted to stay in bed all day after my confrontation with Ben, I still needed to get shit done. "I'm fine."

"You had quite the morning, Jilly Bean. I don't mind hanging out with you for a bit."

He was hovering. After we'd left Ben's, I'd had it out with my brother, letting my resentment loose after years of being underestimated.

James had taken it on the chin, not only apologizing but reflecting on how he could be better moving forward. I'd even shared my history with Oliver at long last, deciding that the shame and embarrassment of his abuse wasn't mine; it was Oliver's alone.

As cathartic as the experience had been, I was raw and exhausted. I needed a hug, but the only person I wanted a hug from was Ben.

"It's okay, Jimbo. I think it might be good for me to be alone for a little while."

James looked like leaving me on my own was the last thing he wanted to do, but he listened, saying goodbye with a press of his lips to my forehead.

"Take the time you need, but give him a chance to explain, okay?"

He left me no room to respond before walking out the door.

An hour ticked by while I waited for the delivery truck. It was just after four o'clock when I heard the heavy wheels crunching over the gravel lot. I opened the back door for the delivery driver as he hopped down from the cab, hitching up his stained jeans as they slid down his wide hips.

"Jill Klein?" he asked.

"That's me."

"This place looks great. Really different from that last time I was here. It used to be a pretty rough crowd, if you know what I mean."

I didn't know what he meant. My realtor had given me little history on the building before I'd put in the offer, and I'd had precious little time to do independent research during the remodel.

"Let me go get the dolly while you look this over. When you're done, you can sign right here," the man said, jabbing a finger down on a clipboard that he passed over to me.

My eyes bugged out as I took in the full order sheet. It was all wrong. Just what I needed after the morning I'd had.

"Hey! This isn't my order!" I called out, approaching the rear of the truck.

The man ignored me, hitching several large boxes onto the lip of his dolly before rolling it down the truck's ramp.

"Don't think so. The boxes all have your name on them, same as that order sheet," he said as he wheeled the boxes inside the building.

I followed at a clip, arguing, "No, no, it's not what I ordered, though." I shook the paper at him as he shifted his load onto the floor of the backbar. "I remember what I ordered. This is the most expensive package. I can't pay for it. It's way too much." I would be screwed if I had to foot the bill for all of this. This had to be an error on the distributor's end. I *knew* I hadn't messed this up.

He went back to the truck, and I watched in horror as he rolled back in with stack after stack of boxes. Top-of-the-line liquor. This was not happening.

"You really need to stop. I can't afford this. You got the order wrong. Here, I'll show you what I submitted to the distributor on-line," I said, frantically searching through my emails on my phone.

"Don't bother. I have it all up here," he replied, tapping his forefinger to his temple. "My mind's a steel trap. That order was changed—upgraded, rather—two weeks ago. Fully paid for, so you're not on the hook."

I looked helplessly at the floor. I was an island in a sea of booze boxes.

"Anyway," the strange delivery man continued, "I've gotta get out of here. Still got one more shipment to deliver. Have a nice night."

I closed my emails and opened up the contact list on my phone to make a call.

❧ ❧ ❧ ❧ ❧ ❧ ❧ ❧

I T HAD BEEN ROUGHLY seven hours since I had last seen Ben, and the only way to describe the way he looked was *wrecked*.

"You got the delivery," he said, his voice husky.

"I did. We'll circle back to that. First, I want you to tell me about the conversation I overheard you having on the phone." We were not going to get sidetracked again before we had this out.

"Okay, yes. Can I—" He stopped, taking a deep breath. "Can I sit down? Please?"

I nodded, using a foot to scoot over one of the plentiful boxes for him to use as a chair.

"Thanks," he whispered as he flopped down, as if all the strength to hold himself up had left his body.

"Careful, there are breakable things in there. *Expensive* things." I shot him a knowing look and sat down on my own box. Slowly and gracefully. Like a lady.

He disregarded my comment. "That call you heard when we met up last winter? I was on the phone with my mom."

I stiffened. I wasn't sure what I had been expecting him to say, but it hadn't been that.

"You probably don't know this—they always kept it pretty hush-hush—but my grandfather, my mother's father, used to own this place."

"I had no idea, Ben."

"That's what I figured." His lips twisted. "I doubt James even knows the story. It was a long time ago and Ma isn't too public about it. I've never even met my grandfather. From what I've heard, he was a pretty lousy excuse for a father. He owned this place for about five years, and used it for some shady things. Drugs, illegal gambling, you name it. I've even heard rumors of organized crime rings doing meetings."

I definitely should have done more research.

"It was a dark time for Ma growing up. He eventually lost the building—a foreclosure, I think—but it's a sore subject with my family. Ma happened to call me when we met up last year. I asked her if she knew the place was for sale and mentioned you were thinking about buying it. She freaked out a little. What you heard were my frantic attempts to reassure her that she didn't have anything to worry about. That the building would remain a falling-down dump forever, and she wouldn't have to hear it mentioned in town. And I guess, in my mind, the best way to convince her of that was to convince her that you weren't serious about Velvet. And I was wrong. So, so wrong, Jill. You have to believe that."

I stood, pacing as I tried to wrap my head around what he was saying. "But did you believe what you said to her?"

He grimaced. "A little. Then. But not now. Definitely not now. Jill, as much time as we've spent together over the years, I can't say that I really *knew* you until this summer. Not the way I do now. In my mind, you were still twenty-year-old Jill. The one I helped James bail out of one messy situation after another. There *was* some truth to what I said—at least from my perspective. But I was definitely exaggerating for my mother's sake. Other than my initial concern about the location, I've always thought you had a good idea for a business on your hands. And once I saw your drive and passion firsthand, every outdated notion I had fell away entirely. I'm sorry I hurt you, and I'll do everything in my power to never, ever do it again."

As far as explanations went, that one was pretty good. And the truth was, I'd already been most of the way to forgiving Ben before he'd even gotten here.

I stopped pacing and shuffled over to him, pressing his booted feet apart with my gold sandals.

He gazed up at me with tired eyes. I settled my hands on his shoulders. "I accept your apology. Now, we need to talk about you spending all this money on—"

He surged up, silencing me with his lips. It felt like joy and relief. When he pulled away, both our cheeks were damp.

"I won't apologize for upgrading the bar package. You're going to be in business for years to come, and you need the best."

I wrapped my legs around him, my ballerina skirt easily accommodating the movement. "Then I'll accept that too."

Ben sighed, hugging me tight to his torso. "I love you so much, Blossom. I have for a long, long time."

"I love you too, Ben," I said into the curve of his neck.

Ben groaned. "Thank fucking god. I thought I lost you, Jill. I can't lose you, okay?"

"You won't. I trust you. And I think I've loved you a lot longer than I realized too. It was the reason hearing that phone call hurt so much. Because for some reason, I've always felt like you were my person. The one who believed in me when nobody else did."

"And I'll spend the rest of our lives making sure you know how much I believe in you. You—and Velvet—are going to kick ass, and I can't wait to see it." He started walking us around the room, circling around aimlessly.

"What are you doing?" I asked as he stepped through the hidden door.

"Looking for that cushion thing you showed me. I want to tie you up. You're not going anywhere."

"It's behind the cash register. But Ben?"

"Yeah?"

"Only if I get to tie you up after."

"Done."

Epilogue

BEN

"Looks good, doesn't it?" James asked me as we looked around the bustling crowd at Velvet. Red velvet booths and curved sofas lined the walls of the speakeasy, and shiny brass light fixtures offered subtle illumination above each marble table-top. In the corner opposite the long bar, was a small stage shaped like a half-moon, one of Jill's last-minute ideas. Velvet would soon host burlesque shows, pole classes, and BDSM workshops.

All I could see was Jill, holding court near a shelf of dragon dildos, enthusiastically gesturing to a group of women who stood there listening, rapt, to her explanation. She was brilliant.

"It looks perfect."

"She really pulled it off, huh? Never a doubt in my mind."

That she had. Velvet's grand opening had kicked off with resounding success, with people streaming in and out the doors for the last several hours. The bartender, a special guest mixologist named Margot, that Jill had booked specially for the event, had been busy slinging one drink after another.

I wasn't sure how a mixologist differed from a regular bartender, but I knew the espresso martini in my hand was the best one I'd ever tasted.

I shot James a skeptical look. "Not a single doubt? Ever?"

He laughed. "Jill proved me wrong this summer—in more ways than one. She's lost some of that wild recklessness."

James and Jill were more open now, in a way they hadn't been before. They still bickered, of course, but the underlying edginess to their interactions had eased.

"Um, did you see this place during the bachelorette party? There was plenty of wild on full display that night."

The event two weeks ago—Jill's first at Velvet—had been rowdy, raucous, and the best reward for Jill after the long months of renovation.

James grinned. "Trust me, Emma and I had ample fun when I picked her up afterward."

I opened my mouth to share my own crazy story with Jill before censoring myself.

"Smart move there, Ben," James said, clocking my reaction.

"Sorry," I said, feeling the flush spreading up my face.

"All good. It might be a little weird sometimes, you dating my sister, but you know what? I'm glad it's her. For you, I mean. She deserves you, Ben. I'm just sorry I didn't realize it right away."

"I'm glad it's her too." It had always been Jill.

James clapped me on the shoulder as he headed to find his fiancée. The wedding was next weekend, and he and Emma had plans in the morning to finalize last minute details. Harry, who had turned out to be a shockingly good best man, would be joining them to take notes for the rest of the wedding party.

The air shimmered around me and I smelled it.

Moonflowers.

I turned my head to find Jill nestling into my side. Her dress was checkered white and pale yellow, with inch-wide straps and a neckline tied up in a pretty bow.

"Hey, Blossom."

"Hey, Benny Boy."

"You tired?"

"*So* tired. I can't wait to get out of these shoes."

"You want me to kick everyone out of this place so we can go home and go to bed?"

Jill wasn't officially living with me, but she spent more nights in my bed than not. Several of her sundresses and her favorite sets of lingerie had already found homes in my closet and dresser. It was only a matter of time before she and her treasure chest of toys moved in permanently.

"One more hour to go. Where did your parents sneak off to?"

Jill had been worried about my mom's reaction to our dating, especially considering the complex relationship Ma had with Velvet's building. Thankfully, her concerns had been in vain, and both my parents welcomed Jill, and all that came with her, into the family with open arms. Ma privately confessed to me that her initial reaction to Jill's purchase of Velvet originated in the traumas she was still processing. Over the year Jill had been avoiding me, Ma had been working with Dad and her own doctors on coming to terms with her past.

It had been her idea to attend Jill's grand opening tonight, and so far, things were going well. If Ma's face had shuttered slightly when she'd first walked in, Dad and I were the only ones to notice.

She had even been fascinated by the small, yet growing, collection of vintage 1920s era sex toys Jill had on display. Jill used the money she saved on the bar package to put in a bid at auction for the items. The small shelf had been a favorite attraction tonight, even more popular than the mannequin wearing a large purple strap-on.

"They snagged a booth over there." I tilted my chin toward the far corner where my parents were cuddled up in an oversized wingback chair.

"Let's go sit with them," she said, taking me by the hand.

I tugged back, wanting her to myself for just a moment more. She looked at me, smiling expectantly.

"I love you, Blossom."

"I love you too, Ben."

"I'm so proud of you."

She stretched up on her tiptoes to kiss me. Lingering at my ear, she whispered, "I'm proud of me too."

THE END

I F YOU ENJOYED THIS book, please consider leaving a review! Reviews are so helpful for indie authors, and are a key part in helping our books reach new readers.

If you'd like to stay up to date on new releases, events, and other fun things, sign up for my newsletter!

Also by Rachel Kaye

The Greyport Series
The Christmas Fake (Emma & James)

Curious about Merlin Heights? Read more in Jennifer Aline's The Ex Project and The Naked Book Club!

About the Author

Rachel writes small-town romantic comedies with plenty of steam and twice the heart. She is a reader first, writer second, and holds the principle of happily ever after as sacred. Rachel lives in Western New York with her bearded husband, two rambunctious children, snuggly cat, and a one-eyed Chihuahua.

If you loved hanging out in
Greyport, you'll love
visiting Merlin Heights!